PRAISE FOR *THE ECHOES OF US*

'Spellbinding ar
HOLLY

'Unputdownable, utterly
JENNY (

'*The Echoes of Us* has just broken me . . . if
you love *The Time Traveler's Wife* or
One Day then you'll love this'
EMMA COOPER

'Heartfelt, romantic and compelling'
PERNILLE HUGHES

'A glorious, epic love story'
EMILY STONE

'This warm, wise and weep-inducing
read will stay with you'
FABULOUS MAGAZINE

'A time-travel mystery and an enduring
romance . . . extremely enjoyable'
GUARDIAN

ALSO BY EMMA STEELE

The Echoes of Us

The Love of
Our Lives

First published in Germany in 2024 as *Während ich
hier bin* by Verlagsgruppe Droemer Knaur

This paperback published in Great Britain in 2025 by Mountain Leopard Press
An imprint of Headline Publishing Group Limited

1

Cataloguing in Publication Data is available from the British Library

Paperback ISBN 978 1 8027 9821 0

Offset in 10.68/16pt Sabon by Jouve (UK), Milton Keynes

Printed and bound in Great Britain by Clays Ltd, Elcograf S.p.A.

Headline's policy is to use papers that are natural, renewable and recyclable
products and made from wood grown in well-managed forests and other
controlled sources. The logging and manufacturing processes are expected
to conform to the environmental regulations of the country of origin.

Headline Publishing Group Limited
An Hachette UK Company
Carmelite House
50 Victoria Embankment
London EC4Y 0DZ

The authorised representative in the EEA is Hachette Ireland, 8 Castlecourt
Centre, Dublin 15, D15 XTP3, Ireland (email: info@hbgi.ie)

www.headline.co.uk
www.hachette.co.uk

The Love of Our Lives

EMMA STEELE

MLP

The Love of Our Lives

EMMA STEELE

PROLOGUE

Dear Recipient,

It's with great sadness, and some hope, that I'm writing you this letter. One I never thought I would have to write. One no mother should ever have to write.

My daughter, my life — my heart — died unexpectedly almost a year ago now, on a bright summer's day in July. She was just thirty years old, at the start of what should have been a long and beautiful life.

This past year has been worse than anything I could have imagined, and we are still trying to find a way forward without her. Because it is unfathomable that she's not alive; that she isn't somewhere in this world.

She was such a dreamer, my Stella. So full of ideas and colour, but very smart and determined too. She excelled at everything she did — her studies, sport and music — even as a child. And she was infinitely kind. I remember when she was about twelve, and found a stray kitten. She cared for it around school hours — until we made her give it up, that is. She called it Polly, because she used to call everything Polly when she was younger. I think she would have loved a little sister to look out for — to be close with — and I'm sorry we never gave her that.

She had many friends, though. Everyone who knew her loved her, because she had that kind of magnetic effect on others. She loved being around people, socialising, and parties too, but I'm afraid she didn't get to go to many. I regret restricting her; I regret so many things. I know I'm rambling on now, but I've written a hundred versions of this letter and I'm not sure I can do it again. There is an endless amount I want to say about her, but each time I bring pen to paper, it's an awful reminder that she is no longer here.

I do have something to ask of you though, so if you can, please read on.

After school she went on to study at the best university, attained a placement at a prominent firm thereafter, and rose quickly to the top. She did everything we hoped she would do, and more.

And then, something changed in her. Something I don't yet understand. Because the truth is, I hadn't seen her for six months before she died. We had an argument about some decisions she'd made, then she moved up north, to this little flat above a bakery of all places, and when I went to see her — convince her to come back — we had another argument. I was too stubborn to hear her out, and said some things I shouldn't have. For that I will be eternally sorry.

I still dream of her though, every single night. Then I'll wake up and realise once again she's not here, and never will be, my darling girl.

The reason I lived.

I just wish I knew more about her life before she went. I wish I knew what she was doing, and who she was with. I wish I could connect those final missing pieces of my only child's life. But more than anything, I wish I could hold my Stella one more time and tell her I love her — tell her how she was my whole world, and always will be.

There have been so many dark days since the moment I found out she'd died, so many times when I felt there was no point in going on; and there will be more to come, I'm sure.

It's all I deserve really, after what I did.

But then I realised something recently, something that gave me some shred of hope again — maybe she is still alive in the organs she wanted to donate, in the lives that she saved.

And most particularly in her heart, the heart that you now carry. Because she had such a big one, my Stella — the biggest you can possibly imagine. And so, I want to tell you about her. I want you to know how special her heart is, so that you can keep her alive in you too.

Would you do that for me?

Would you keep her alive for me?

CHAPTER ONE

Late morning light shines through the canopy of leaves above, dappling the pebbled pathway ahead of me. It should be beautiful, yet all I can think about is that letter in my pocket again.

Like a blow to the heart.

'You OK?' Jess says beside me as we walk along. I glance at her dark blonde hair and sunglasses, three yellow balloons bobbing up from her hand for today's celebrations.

'I'm doing absolutely fine,' I say cheerfully, even as I recall the moment the post came a week ago.

But there's no need to talk about it now, no need to get into it today.

I focus instead on my four-year-old nephews firing ahead in their matching navy shorts and white t-shirts, russet hair flapping as they go. All around us are thick, aged trees and secret passages leading to hidden patches of grass, and I can't help remembering how my sisters and I used to play here in the Botanics when we were kids too. Cat would be shouting loudly and leading the game, while I would be going along with whatever she said, even though I was only eleven months younger. And a three-years-younger Jess would be trailing somewhere behind, trying desperately to get involved.

'Hunter, Sebs, don't go where we can't see you,' Jess calls from beside me. 'Graham, go after them.'

Obediently, my brother-in-law jogs ahead in his chino shorts and blue shirt, his geek-chic hair waving in the breeze. He growls and the boys screech with delight, scattering like rabbits as they try to escape his outstretched claws.

I hear our parents' laughter from somewhere close behind and smile.

And then, in a rush of light, we come out from under the leafy awning again. I feel the sun on my face and immediately put on my wide-brimmed sun hat. On one side, the skyline of Edinburgh rolls majestically across the horizon, from the jut of Arthur's Seat on the left, all the way along to the castle on the right. On the other side, an apron of green is set in front of the sandstone Georgian house, the heart of the Botanics. Children turn cartwheels in the late July sun, and families wander around, coffees in hand. The air smells of warm pine and grass; rhododendrons from the bushes beyond.

'So,' I say mock-innocently, as we wander along, 'did you get those fabulous silver trainers in the end?'

Jess shoots a guilty smile at me. 'I'm sorry, but I had to. They matched with everything I had too well.'

I let out a laugh and point down at my feet. 'Of course, they bloody do, I picked them first.'

She grins, and I give her a gentle nudge.

'So,' Jess says, in the same light note as mine, 'are you excited about your big day?'

I glance up at the balloons in my favourite colour. 'Yes, of course.' I say brightly, even as my stomach contracts.

Because exactly one year ago today, I got a new heart. Due to a progressive genetic heart disorder.

'More to the point—' I say, pushing the anxiety away '— are *you* excited about your big adventure coming up?'

Jess pauses, her face unreadable behind her sunglasses.

'I guess so,' she says eventually, 'but I'd be much happier if I knew you were coming to visit. You could come help us get settled in even, see the sights while you're there?'

'Come on, Jess,' I try to say in an upbeat voice, 'you know I can't go anywhere yet. Maybe next year, though.'

She looks disappointed, her brow furrowed in that way she does, and I can't help feeling bad.

It's not like I'm not desperate to visit her when they move to Amsterdam in two weeks' time for her teaching job. Jess is my sister – my best friend too, these days – and I'd love to go away somewhere, anywhere, after not being able to for pretty much the whole of my life. But there are consequences to pushing myself.

And she knows that better than anyone.

'But how can you not come visit us in the house that *you* found us?' she continues. 'Which, by the way, is amazing. Did you see the open-plan space for the boys?'

I laugh as I catch a glimpse of them in the wooded area ahead. Hunter launches himself out of a tree he definitely shouldn't be on. 'I had them foremost in mind, if you can believe it.'

Jess puffs out air, looks ahead, and I get that weird sense again – the one I've had a lot recently – that she's not telling me something. At first, I put it down to the move, but more and more recently she's felt sort of distant. And we're never distant from each other – argumentative sometimes, yes, but that's different. It's not the same as it was with Cat, of course, where we finished each other's sentences and called at the exact same time – I could tell Cat needed a packet of her favourite peanut M&Ms just by looking at her, and she knew when I needed to put my head on her lap and just stop. But Jess and I are still close. We had to be, after everything.

Heading up on to the pathway next to the lawn, the green grass seems to glow in the sun. There's a steep slope ahead of us, and I find myself pausing.

I start walking up, but, just as fast, an image of Cat appears in my mind. My breathing quickens, heart pounds; I come to an abrupt stop.

'You all right, Maggie?' Jess says, appearing beside me. She grips my arm, gives me a determined look. 'Come on, I'll do it with you.'

'No, it's OK,' I say, smiling at her. 'I'm just going to walk around the side.'

A flash of worry crosses Jess's face, and I hate how pathetic I sound. But I don't want to strain myself.

Not today of all days.

Footsteps crunch over the gravel behind us, and I turn around to see Mum running across.

Shit.

'What's happened? Are you OK?' Mum's voice is tense and breathless, and I realise now how that must have looked – me stopping dead in my tracks like that.

'I'm absolutely fine,' I say quickly, and walk back down the hill. 'I was just saying I'm going to go around the other way, that's all.'

'All right,' Mum says, 'all right.' She takes a deep breath herself. 'I'll come with you.' Turning back, she yells, 'Iain, she's OK!'

With the picnic basket and chairs tossed somewhere behind him on the path, Dad nods, but I can see the strain and sweat on his face as he turns to go back for them.

Slightly deflated now, I head around the long way with Mum and Jess. We walk across the lawn, past picnic blankets and sunbathers, before Mum inevitably stops at a shady patch – I can't be in the direct sun for long with my immune system the way it is these days.

'Let's set up camp here,' she says, her voice that bit sharper now, and I feel bad for her – it's her day out too. She's even wearing her big straw hat and her favourite white dress with the poppies on it. She bought it for a holiday a few years back, which inevitably got cancelled.

'I'll go round up my brood if everything's OK now,' Jess says, bounding back off down the slope, and I watch her go wistfully. It's not that I'm not used to being left with Mum and Dad – I've always lived at home, after all – it's just I'd really like to be in her shoes for a moment.

In front of me now, Dad sorts the logistics as usual, laying out the tartan picnic blanket and a couple of deck chairs for 'the oldies', while Mum and I take out all the other stuff: I *yum* at the sandwiches and *ooh* at the nibbles from M&S – salami and cheese, fat olives and velvety hummus – before Mum takes a Tupperware box out and passes it to me.

'Thanks,' I say, smiling. Through the white plastic I can vaguely make out the shape of my brown bread sandwiches and I can't help sighing as I look back up.

Pop.

I look up to see Dad holding an open champagne bottle. Fizz bubbles over the glass lip, and I feel warm at the sight of him in his favourite checked shirt today. His white hair is almost transparent in the sunlight but the big silly grin on his face makes him look years younger today.

'Here you go, Small,' he says, passing me the glass, and I light up briefly at the pet name. But in a flash, Mum is there.

'Don't be silly, Iain,' she says, taking the glass from him. 'I don't even know why you brought this stuff anyway.'

Dad's face immediately falls, and I feel annoyed on his behalf.

'It was just a little sip,' I try, but she's not listening.

'Exactly,' Dad says, 'a little half glass isn't going to kill anyone.'

A horrible silence falls between the three of us, and I'm about to say something to ease the tension, when I see a couple strolling our way across the lawn. And there's something about the man that makes me stop. He's all shorts and t-shirt vibes, sunglasses on, but I would know that firm jawline anywhere, that sweep of dark hair. My stomach drops.

Nick.

CHAPTER TWO

A few moments later, I'm still mentally processing who I'm seeing. I try to look away but he's already clocked me sitting here and I know it's too late.

We're going to have to do this whether we want to or not, and panic floods me.

As he approaches, I can better see who he's with too – an equally attractive girl with long golden hair and long tanned legs in denim shorts. He whispers something to her, and she smiles curiously at me, which makes me burn up inside.

As quickly as I can, I stand up, suddenly conscious of how pale I look in my loose dark dress, my red hair pulled back out the way. It's only when they're almost in front of me, that I see – the hard curve of her stomach below her fitted vest, the sparkle of the ring on her left hand. I swallow.

'Maggie,' Nick says, coming to a stop. Propping his shades on top of his head, those sparkly blue eyes I used to adore focus in on me. 'I thought it was you. How have you been?'

'Oh, good,' I say immediately, heart racing, tongue thick with nerves. 'Great really, we're just here celebrating . . . a thing today.' I don't want to get into it.

'Nice,' he says, and turns to the girl. 'This is Sophie, by the way.'

'Hi, Sophie,' I say a bit too enthusiastically.

'Lovely to meet you, Maggie,' she replies genuinely, which makes it all even worse. I glance briefly at the bangles down her lean arms, the well-worn flip-flops on her feet.

'Nick,' a voice behind me says, and I die a bit inside as Mum appears smiling beside me. 'I thought it was you.'

'Hello, Sue,' Nick says, 'how have you been? Lovely weather for a picnic.'

'Oh yes,' she gushes, 'isn't it? And how are you, dear? Where are you based these days?'

'Geneva, actually. We're running our own ski company there now—' he and Sophie glance briefly at each other '—but we're back visiting my parents while we can.' He indicates at the bump, and even though I smile and immediately say *congratulations*, my chest is pulling so tight. Why is this happening today of all days? And why did I have to be having a bloody picnic with my parents?

'Oh, that all sounds lovely,' Mum says.

'And you, Maggie?' Nick says. He glances behind me at the blanket where my dad is rummaging about in the cool box. 'Are you still . . . here?'

'Yup, in Edinburgh, as always,' I say, trying for chirpy but it ends up landing flat.

'At the same agency too,' Mum quips, and my eyes start to burn.

Nick nods, as if he's not remotely surprised. 'Well, if you're ever in the Alps . . .' He trails off, something like regret crossing his features. 'Anyway, it's been great seeing you again.'

'You too,' I reply, and a second later they wander away across the lawn.

Once they're gone, Mum turns to me, a slightly sad expression on her face. 'Well, that must have been a little painful. He was quite a catch, that one . . . though I'm not sure it would have ever worked out.'

'Mum,' I say, throwing my hands up to my face in frustration, and I wish in that moment that I was anywhere but here.

'What? What is it?' she says, but I can't even answer.

A moment later, Jess appears beside us. 'Just in time for the champagne, I see,' she says, then looks between us. 'What happened?'

There's a strangled pause, as Mum goes to get a glass of bubbles for Jess. Before I can say anything, Hunter and Sebs rush over, no doubt to argue over who gets the blue cup. Two peas in a pod. Just like Cat and I were. She would have made this whole situation lighter somehow; a story to laugh about during the continuing celebrations later.

God, I miss her.

As my heart rate finally starts to slow again, we all settle down with a glass of something, at long last – Mum and I with our Pellegrino, the boys with lemonade and the others with their contraband bubbles. Awful moment with my ex forgotten, for everyone else at least.

'Well,' Dad says eventually, 'I think it's about time we toasted our darling Maggie. And what a perfect place we've picked for it. I can still remember when the three of you were just little things pelting around here,' he says, looking at me with watery eyes. 'Happy one-year heart anniversary, Maggie.'

Jess gives my hand a squeeze, and I take a breath in.

'Happy heart anniversary,' Graham chimes in from his lounging position on the blanket. He raises his glass.

'Happy heart anniversary,' they all say.

Jess smiles down at me, mouth trembling, as if to say, *you made it.*

Yet all I can think is: but Cat didn't.

Because of me.

CHAPTER THREE

Later, once everyone else is happily fed, I move to a bench across the lawn to keep an eye on the boys playing. But I've been distracted, scrolling through my phone since I saw Nick, finally allowing myself to look at his page again – at all his travel pictures after we broke up, then ones of meeting Sophie: the two of them trekking in jungles and hanging out on beaches, their glorious wedding in what looks like Bali – and I wish in that moment that I hadn't banned myself from looking at his account a few years back. If I'd just been a bit more prepared, then I wouldn't have been caught out like that. But I did it out of self-preservation.

I had to.

Seeing Nick has also made me think about when I still used to go into the office. I wouldn't now, of course – too much risk of infection, too much strain going in and out every day – but I work all the hours I can at home. And I like working as a tour organiser well enough; at least in one way I've already explored the grand hallways of the Rijksmuseum and wandered down the glittering canals of Amsterdam. I've jumped out of planes and swung across canyons in New Zealand; I've looked out across Mont Blanc and scaled the Dawn Wall. The people are nice too, albeit transient in the travel industry – everyone leaves except me. And the money's decent, not that I go out much anyway, so there's nothing to complain about. Not really.

But still, what might it be like to be one of my clients? To decide to go somewhere and then actually go; to surf a turquoise wave or jump into a crystal-clear lake; to climb a sun-soaked mountain or float up and away in a hot-air balloon. To do all these things in real life and not just on a screen.

Right now, I wonder what it might be like to be the one in Geneva with Nick.

I think about the letter again too; pat my pocket down for it before remembering I moved it to my bag for safekeeping earlier. It's not like I didn't know it was coming of course – the Donor Family Care Service team told me after all. It was all anonymous at this stage, and I had no obligation to read it, they said. The truth is, I've read it so many times this morning already, I could probably recite it off by heart.

Dear Recipient, it starts.

I'd considered writing first, of course; started a hundred letters and emails to them to say thank you. They've given the most amazing gift a person could possibly give, and gone through their own incredible hurt, just like ours.

It's just—

I have no idea what to say, no idea what they could possibly want to hear from the person who took their loved one's heart. I just feel so guilty about benefiting from someone else's death, about *wanting* them to die. Because that's effectively what happened, isn't it? When I dreamt about getting a new heart, I was dreaming about someone else's life ending. But when I spoke to the doctors about it, they told me that I shouldn't think of it like that; that the person whose heart I have was going to die anyway, and there was nothing I could do about it.

The best I can do, apparently, is make the most of the gift – keep her alive, like Stella's mum has asked me to do.

And I am, I think, by staying healthy, by looking after this heart in the best way I can.

Graham appears now with another glass of bubbles Jess must have snuck him, and I muster a smile for him. For all his digs, he's become like a brother to me. I've known him for most of my life and he loves Jess like nothing else, which makes him a hero in my books.

'So,' he says, 'survive the day OK?'

'It was a hummus-covered dream, Graham,' I say, placing my phone on the bench. 'Though I do feel a little bad for the boys; this can't be too exciting for them.'

'The boys are happy to be wherever you are, just like their mother,' Graham says. 'So, they had a great time.'

'Well, maybe you guys could do something more adventurous before you head off. Maybe you could go to the cottage or something? Mum and Dad didn't rent it out this month.'

'And you could come too?'

I pause.

'You know I'll only slow you guys down.' I try to sound light about it.

But when I look up, he's looking right back at me, an almost annoyed expression on his face. 'You need to stop worrying about what other people need, Maggie, and just go do. For everyone's sake.'

I don't respond immediately, because I'm slightly surprised by the tone, and I'm not even sure what he means – for everyone's sake? He can definitely get a bit loose-lipped with a drink, but although he was around when it happened, he just doesn't understand what it's like to actually be the one who got it wrong.

To cause that level of devastation for everyone.

And anyway – I haven't been able to go back to the cottage since it happened.

'The boys will be shattered later at least,' I say, in an attempt to move the conversation along.

'I should bloody well hope so,' he laughs. 'They've been running around for hours.'

'Well, you and Jess can sneak back home for some wine later?' I say. 'The boys could have a sleepover at Mum and Dad's.'

I feel a little bad about still being there too; taking over their dining room like I have. But I couldn't keep going up and down the stairs in the condition I was in before the transplant, and it's probably sensible to keep avoiding it now, I guess. Sometimes I like to imagine what my own place would be like; what my own *life* might look like – perhaps I'd live in a cabin on a far-off mountainside and teach yoga for a living, or take off around the world in a campervan and start a travel blog, or live in a penthouse in the city and have an exciting job and international travel – I'd go out for dinner every night and work my way through all the cuisines in the alphabet, I'd date anyone I pleased and do anything I want, knowing that no two days would ever be the same.

But that sort of life isn't something that I can have. What if something went wrong and I got sick? I couldn't do that to everyone again.

'That sounds good actually,' Graham says with a sigh. 'Maybe it's no bad thing if we don't end up moving.'

I stop; look at him.

He must read my expression, because all the blood seems to drain from his face.

'Oh god . . .' he says, glancing around. 'I thought Jess had spoken to you earlier.'

'Graham, what are you talking about?' I say, utterly confused. 'Why wouldn't you be going?'

And why wouldn't Jess have spoken to me about it?

He opens his mouth again to speak, when I suddenly realise I can't see Jess anymore.

And I have a strange feeling.

'Hang on,' I say, getting up and walking back across the lawn. Weaving between children running and adults smiling, I scan our blanket set-up. Mum and Dad are off somewhere, but Jess is there. She's staring at something white in her hand.

The letter.

'What the hell is this, Maggie?' she says, looking up as I approach.

'What are you doing?' I say, heart pounding. 'Why are you going through my stuff?'

'I wasn't going through your stuff, Maggie. It was laying out on the picnic blanket for anyone to see.'

Shit, it must have fallen out.

'But why didn't you tell us you'd got this? After everything we've been through together.'

Frustration courses through me. 'Because I only got it a week ago and I'm still processing it.'

Her eyes widen. 'But did you even read what it says?'

'Of course I did, Jess.'

'Do you agree with it?' She holds it up to my face.

20

'Yes,' I repeat, but more hesitantly this time.

Jess throws her hands up. 'Then I don't understand why you're not doing it all.'

'All what?'

'Everything, Maggie. You've got a new heart. You're healthy now. So why aren't you making the most of it?'

'You know why,' I say annoyed now. 'You know I can't do any of the stuff I really want to.'

Jess just stares at me, like I've said something crazy.

'But why not?' she says. 'You did when Cat was around, and—'

'And look what happened,' I finish.

A silence passes between us in the warm air, and I know we have the same images in our minds.

The hospital, everyone weeping.

A darkness like no other.

'Maggie,' she says, softer now, 'Cat died, and it was awful, for everyone, but that doesn't mean you stop doing anything.'

I'm about to repeat the fact that this new heart is only 70 per cent well, that I will always have to take far less risks than other people, or I could die, pulling down everyone else with me, when she starts up again.

'This heart was supposed to give you a second shot at it all, Maggie. Hell, it was supposed to give you a first shot,' she says, 'and you're doing nothing with it.'

It feels like I'm being punched in the stomach.

'Nothing?' I snap. 'I'm out today, aren't I?'

'Barely! This was a picnic for a few hours, before you go back to Mum and Dad's for some grilled chicken.'

Something hot rises in my belly now.

'What exactly do you want me to be doing? Necking alcohol and climbing mountains? Do you even understand what the doctors say? I'll have to be careful for the rest of my life if I don't want something to go wrong.'

'I'm not asking you to climb mountains, Maggie, far from it. But what about art school? What about fun and friends? What about love? Because I heard about Nick, by the way – I know you saw him earlier.'

I close my eyes briefly, the image stinging again. 'Don't talk to me about love, Jess. You will never understand what it was like for me after Cat.'

Immediately, I regret my words.

'So, what you're saying is her *sister* wouldn't understand?' Jess says, her voice strangely quiet. 'Because you guys were always closest, right?'

'Jess,' I say quickly, 'I'm sorry; that's not what I meant at all.'

'Then what the hell did you mean?'

I don't know what to say – how can you explain losing your other half the way I had?

Eventually Jess throws her hands up in the air when I don't reply. 'Jesus Christ, Maggie, how can I help you if you don't tell me anything?'

'Oh, you're one to talk,' I say without thinking. 'How come you never told me you were reconsidering Amsterdam?'

Jess stops; her face falls.

'Look, I'm sorry about that. I told Graham not to say anything,' she starts. 'It's just . . . it's just—'

'Just what?'

She says nothing, and I have to close my eyes as a heat starts to build behind them.

'Jess,' I say, opening them again, 'you don't have to worry about me anymore. I'm doing everything in my power to keep this heart healthy, so everyone can go live their lives and I'll live mine.'

'But that's the point, Maggie,' Jess cries now, 'you're not living.'

My breath catches, like I've been winded. But she doesn't stop.

'To be honest,' she says, a fire in her eyes now, 'I'm not even sure you deserved to get the heart.'

The words are like a slap in the face, and my whole body stiffens with the shock of it.

'I'm going for a walk,' I say, and before she can utter another word, I turn on my heel and head across the lawn.

As I go down the pathway again, I think I can hear Mum calling my name from somewhere, but the words muffle, then evaporate into the sky.

Blood rushes in my ears.

Heading along the gravelled walkway under the trees, the area is quieter here. I stride as quickly as I'll let myself, finding that my feet know where I'm going before I even do.

I keep going until I hit a crossways, the sycamore and the ash trees beckoning gently in the summer breeze above me. But then I stop.

I go no further.

And in this moment, I know I never will.

Because I was right – I can never have the life I truly want. I gave it a shot before, and my sister died.

Then a wonderful woman called Stella died too, so I could live. There's no way I'm risking this heart now.

Turning back on the path, I feel a pull at my chest, sudden and sharp. And in seconds it's tearing across the whole of me, and I'm slumping to the ground.

My head hits the sand with a silent thud.

Pain soars.

I grapple to say something, call out to anyone who might hear, but nothing comes. I stare up at that endless blue sky, one solitary yellow balloon rising up through it, and I cannot breathe.

CHAPTER FOUR

Light.

Soft material against my face.

I take a moment to open my eyes. Turning over, the scent of jasmine floods my nose; a washing powder I don't know.

Weird.

It doesn't smell like home, or the hospital.

Hospital.

Collapsing on the pathway.

My eyes snap open, body instantly rigid. I frantically scan my surroundings to find that I'm in a bedroom, but not one I've ever seen before. It's small and airy, with a large window raised open to the breeze. A dreamcatcher is hanging down the glass pane, its beaded tassels fluttering back and forth above. An old desk is crammed in below.

Where the hell am I?

I place a hand against my chest. Up, down, up, down. It's beating insanely fast. *Oh god, why am I not in a hospital? Or home?*

Think, Maggie.

Did a passer-by find me in the Botanics? Maybe they took me back to theirs and then called the ambulance.

But it shouldn't take this long.

It never takes this long.

I just need to stay here, stay calm. What time is it?

Turning to the white-washed bedside table beside me, I spot a radio alarm, one of the modern ones with the time and date on its face. I must still be groggy because the date in the corner of the radio alarm doesn't make any sense. It's saying it's the twenty-sixth of July, but that's tomorrow.

And the date is behind by two years.

Blinking away from it, confused, I turn my attention to the time now – 11 a.m.

Shit!

I must have spent the night here; Mum will be so worried.

'Hello?' I call out desperately, except my voice comes out half a step lower, smoother and in a different accent – as though I'm from the South of England or something. I reach for my throat.

What the hell is wrong with my voice?

With shaking hands, I shove back the flowery sheets to find I'm wearing a stranger's pyjamas – silky blue ones, with little fireflies on them.

26

But why did someone change me? What's going on?

Oh god, what if someone drugged me? But then, surely someone who did that wouldn't change me into nice pyjamas. No, that can't be it.

Sitting up in bed, I step out and on to the cool wooden floor. I keep waiting for those stabbing pains again, some sign that my body is failing me, but nothing comes, thankfully.

'Hello?' I try again, upright now. *Oh god, where am I?* Glancing back at the window, there are more flats opposite – old Edinburgh tenements. But I'm in a completely different part of town from the looks of it.

None of this is making any sense.

Walking out of the room now, I find myself in a narrow, whitewashed corridor. What looks like a small living room sits at the end and I stumble towards it.

I pass a main door on the right, with a row of coats hanging beside it. I'm in a flat then. I keep going blindly to the end, clasping on to the slightly uneven walls like I'm drunk, even though I never really have been. In the living room now, I take in the small tatty sofas, the worn wooden floor. Sample pots of paint sit beside one white wall, like someone's been trying to pick a colour, and a big bay window at the back casts shimmering light across an old circular dining room table. A warm breeze drifts in from outside and, though it's all sunny summer skies on the other side of the pane, a tingle goes through me.

This isn't right.

Just breathe, Maggie.

A small internal kitchen sits at the back of the living room and I head there next. It's a bit haphazard, with jars of pasta and spices all about the place; a box of pans on the floor like someone's just moved in. Looking back to the living room, I notice something on the mantlepiece. Walking over, I pick up what appears to be an invite. It's on stiff letterhead and across the top, in gold lettering, are the words *Toby and Fran*.

To Emily, it starts, followed by information about a wedding somewhere in London next year. OK, so an Emily must live here then. But who is she? And where has she gone? Why has this Emily person left me here?

All I know is I have to get to a hospital; I have to get checked out. Turning back out of the room, I head towards the coat rack. *Please let my stuff be there.*

Rifling through yellow rain jackets and colourful coats, my hand eventually hits something cold and hard, and I pull the clothes aside to find a mirror behind.

A reflection stares back out.

My throat catches.

And everything around me stops.

CHAPTER FIVE

When I was a child, I found a small window in the attic. I used to pretend my reflection was another child sitting on the other side of the glass, playing in a mirror house, in a mirror attic. That girl was called Tina, and after I got sick, I would go up there again sometimes, alone. I'd wish so hard that I could become that girl for a day, living in her healthy body and having exciting adventures, so I never had to worry about hospital appointments and surgeries and making everyone sad all the time.

Now, as I stare into this other mirror, I wonder if by some wild imaginings of my brain, I've finally taken myself to the other side of the glass. Because standing in front of me is someone I don't know – someone with long dark hair and golden tanned skin. She has bow-shaped lips, a small freckle above one arched eyebrow and ridiculously long lashes. The only thing that's the same is the eye colour: a warm hazel.

And that's how I know I'm in the hospital.

It's the only rational explanation for what's going on: I collapsed in the Botanics, someone called an ambulance and now I'm in an induced coma.

There's nothing I can do but sit it out.

Wait to wake.

Feeling numbly calmer now, I take a better look around the flat in my dreams. It's incredible how real it all feels, with the clear light shining in past the dreamcatcher and this citrus-sweet perfume permeating the air, like lemons and roses. Curious, I look inside the old wooden dresser. There's lots of colourful clothing in the drawers – pink vests and yellow t-shirts, chemical-blue leggings and ripped denim shorts. Crossing to the wardrobe now, I find an equal number of loud, fitted dresses, the type I would never have the confidence to wear; a range of trainers and boots and bags beneath them.

I feel a pretty realistic kick of hunger now, so I wander hazily back to the kitchen. Opening up a cupboard, I spy a packet of tortilla crisps. It's funny how, even in a dream, I can feel myself hesitating over them, wondering what I should do. I never eat crisps, obviously, but given this is a dream, it seems vaguely ridiculous to quibble over it, so I pull them down, start eating them hungrily and without restraint.

God, they're good. All salty and cheesy and crunchy in one.

With the packet still in my hand, I check in the fridge next and find it's bizarrely cool on my skin when I open it, like it would be normally. I'm delighted to find a large bottle of Coke, half a bottle of Prosecco and what appears to be a half-eaten bowl of ramen inside. With a slightly heady feeling now, I pull them all out too, already hoping I don't wake up before I can get through it all. Taking a glug of the Coke, I grab a fork from a nearby drawer and unclip the top of the plastic container. The scent released is incredible – garlic and chilli and pork rolled into one; the literal stuff of dreams. I eat standing up, wolfing it down so fast that a little broth ends up on the firefly pyjamas.

Should I change?

The clothes.

With a buzz of excitement, I head back to the bedroom. A moment later, I track back and pick up the Prosecco.

Standing in front of the wardrobe a minute later, I take a little drink of the bubbly liquid straight from the bottle, feel it slip into my system in the most realistic way. Then I gently run a hand through the clothes, across a pink sweater and a turquoise skirt, a yellow summer dress fluttering in the breeze from the window. One dress in particular catches my eye, a floaty one in splashes of red and blue and green, like a butterfly's wings. It has a low V at the front and the skirt flares out at the sides. Placing the Prosecco down with a clunk, I strip off the pyjamas, slip the dress over my bare shoulders. Turning to the long mirror in the corner, I can't help thinking how pretty I look, or rather my dream body looks, standing here in what appears to be a flat of my own. It's not exactly how I'd imagined my dream home, this small flat in Edinburgh. It's no penthouse in the city or cabin on a lake, it's more like a blank canvas to play with. But perhaps that's what I'm meant to be doing in this dream?

'The paint pots,' I whisper, and with another fizz of excitement, I head back along to the living room. It's flooded with a hazy morning light, and, for a moment, I imagine what it might be like to wake up here every day, and drink a cup of coffee, or five, all by myself, before doing whatever I like with the day.

Walking back over to where the pots are, I kneel down to check the colours. I'm delighted to see they're all bright and vibrant, sunshine yellow and ocean teal, fuchsia pinks and clementine orange. It's not that Mum ever stopped me making the dining room my own, of course, but it's hard to get overly excited about decorating one small corner of your parents' home.

Opening the teal pot first, I dip one of the brushes into the vivid paint, before applying it straight to the wall in one luxurious stroke. The colour immediately pops against the white and I marvel yet again at the realness of it all. I do the same with the next colour, then the next, dunking the brush in each time and dragging it across the clinical white expanse. Before I know it, the whole wall is covered in stripes and swirls, circles, and dots and rainbows of technicolour madness.

I'm splattered in paint, but there's something about it all that fills me with joy.

And I'm not done yet.

Because I'm not in my limited body, and the sun is shining, and right now I think I need to run free in it. Taking a final drink of the Prosecco, giddiness entering my mind, my body, I head across to the front door and look down at the array of shoes there – flip-flops, rainbow wellies and hiking boots. I opt for some neon-yellow trainers, and a second later, I'm out the door. It looks like an old tenement building out here, which makes sense since that's the sort of building I've always imagined myself in. I appear to be on the top level, opposite another flat with a freshly painted white door and large, muddy trainers outside. It's cool and dimly lit, the only light coming from a murky glass skylight above, and looking down through the dark centre, I calculate that there's maybe three floors below.

I bound down the circular stairwell now, two at a time, so fast I'm almost gliding down it, and as I reach the bottom, I have the most incredible fluttering in my heart. Opening up the flat door, sunlight floods down on a busy Edinburgh street – tenements, shops, cars – and I pause, as I try to process what's happening.

Because the problem is, it feels pretty bloody real.

And my dreams never make sense like this. I don't know what exactly I was expecting when I walked out that door, but it wasn't anything quite so . . . true to life.

Unnerved now, I head down the road, as the door swings firmly shut behind me.

As suspected, I'm across town, in Tollcross, it appears. I used to come to this area occasionally to get art supplies from the shop nearby, maybe have a green tea at Victor Hugo on the Meadows. I haven't been since the transplant, come to think of it. But then I haven't been anywhere really.

To the right of me, tall trees sway in the breeze above the green fields, and I walk towards them, drawn by a place I know at least. It's busy out here, realistically so, and a bubble of panic starts to rise up through me. When I arrive at the Meadows, I sense people glancing across at me and realise I'm still covered in paint.

I feel groggy and strange from the Prosecco, and eventually I sit down on the grass, uncertain what else to do. I lie back flat on the feathery blades now, stare up at the wide expanse of blue above, and with the sounds of kids playing and mowers going, I let my eyes fall shut.

* * *

I wake blearily sometime later to cool air on my face and the scent of trees. I'm still in the Meadows, except now the light has changed and the blue sky has drifted into pink. Most of the kids have left.

Pulling myself off the grass, I find myself covered in tufts of green, and it strikes me harder how very lifelike it is that

I would have grass stuck to me. Also, that I've woken up still in the dream. My heart starts to pound lightly, and all that gleeful joy I had earlier evaporates entirely.

Everything seems really strange.

Walking quickly back across the Meadows, the paint-splattered dress flutters about my legs, and I feel even more outside of myself than before. Passing a now darkened deli, I pause to stare at the reflection: same medium height I saw before, same kind of lightly curved body shape, but with dark hair flying around in the breeze, and a pretty heart-shaped face.

What's going on?

With more urgency now, I pick up my pace. By the time I get off the Meadows, I know where I'm headed, because it's the only place I can think to go now. I have to just get back to where this all started. I have to get back to bed, and when I wake up, all of this will be gone.

It has to be.

As I hit the street I came from, I start walking faster, back up to Tollcross where I started this morning. But what door was it? Which number?

Shit.

I left in such a spin this morning because I never thought I was coming back. Walking past the little restaurants and cafés, it all slides together loosely again – the tapas bar, the newsagent and the café with the purple front. That card shop with the jewellery display in the window. I came out of the door beside it – the dull red one with a rusted seven on the front.

But how the hell am I going to get back inside? I didn't take any keys.

Shit, shit, shit.

I just need to get back to that flat – if I could even get into the stairwell.

Staring at the row of flat buzzers down the side, I pick one at random and press it.

Nothing.

Tentatively, I press the next one, and a voice comes out angry and sharp, 'I'm not due a delivery, I don't want pamphlets, I'm not going to buy anything, so just bugger off.'

I stop short.

But I have to get in.

I press the next one, then the next, my heart rate rising with each responding silence.

Finally, I press the buzzer at the top right – for what must be the flat opposite with the muddy trainers.

A crackle.

'Hello?' a friendly male voice says.

Relief floods through me.

'Hello,' I start, 'I'm sorry, but I've forgotten my key and—'

To my surprise, the buzzer immediately goes, and I hesitate for a moment before pushing it open. Inside, the tenement is dark and cool, a welcome relief after the huge expanse of sky out there. I can't quite get over the sound of my voice sounding so . . . English. It's unsettling, even in a dream. Walking up the stone steps, I have no idea how I'll get inside the flat door, but at least I'm one step closer. Rounding the last set of stairs, I'm surprised to see a man on the top floor with messy dark hair and lightly tanned white skin. He's in khaki shorts and a scruffy black t-shirt, but his eyes are what get me – the most incredible forest green I've ever seen. With his large hands on the banister, he throws a lopsided smile down at me. When I get to the top, I pause in front of him, uncertain.

'So, locked out then,' he says easily.

Now that I'm standing right in front of him, I see the scuff marks of dust on his top, the dimple on one cheek, his lean but strong-looking arms. An unusual-looking tattoo trails down one, and despite the weirdness of the situation, I can't help feeling a twinge of attraction.

And something like recognition.

'Forgot my keys,' I say finally.

He thumbs back at the open flat across the hallway. 'Good thing I came back from the workshop early, or you might have had to do some late evening sunbathing.'

He grins, but I'm still too dazed to respond. I did catch the faint trace of an accent though – American? Canadian?

'You all right?' he says after a moment, his grin fading to something more like concern.

I start to nod. 'Yeah, I'm OK,' I say, like this is all totally fine, like I haven't been supplanted into another life somehow. 'Too much sun today, maybe.'

'One sec,' he says, and bounces back into the other flat.

Confused, I just stand there. I hear a tap running, footsteps, and a minute later he reappears with a big glass of water. He holds it out to me, our fingers brushing lightly as I take it from him. Glugging it down, I realise how thirsty I was.

When I look down again, I realise he's still watching me, with those incredible green eyes.

'You really were parched, weren't you?' he says. 'I can get you something to eat if you like? I make an excellent pastrami sandwich.'

My mouth opens in confusion.

Pastrami sandwiches. An insanely attractive guy I've never met before.

I need this to end now.

'That's OK,' I say, forcing a smile. 'I just really need to lie down.'

He smiles, but I'm sure a vague look of disappointment crosses his face. 'No problem at all, Emily.'

That name again.

I turn back to the white door I came out of this morning. *Shit, the key.*

There are pot plants all around the door, just like in my room at home, actually: pothos, peacock and fiddle leaf – I didn't notice them this morning, but then, I'm not sure I noticed anything this morning.

I bend down to lift the biggest one in case there's a spare underneath.

Nothing.

'Geranium,' a voice says, and I turn back. The guy is standing just inside his doorway now, pointing to the right of me. 'Sorry, I probably shouldn't know that,' he says, 'but I noticed you putting it under that one a couple of weeks ago.'

Looking over to where he's pointing, I lift the geranium up, and sure enough, there is a silver key, speckled in soil. I pick it up and brush it off before standing up to face him again.

'Thanks,' I say.

'No problem.' He claps the side of the door with one solid hand, his eyes resting on mine, and I get another undeniable twinge of attraction. It's odd, because if this really is all a big dream, I usually know the people I conjure up – from school, or work; people I lost touch with when I kept saying no to everything.

But this guy is entirely new.

Almost.

'I'll see you later,' he says.

'Sure,' I reply, and before I can say anything else, he's closed his door with a soft click.

Turning back to the flat, I push the key into the lock, and feel it open. Breathing a sigh of relief, I head inside, take in that alien scent of someone else's place; that lemon-rose perfume again. Then I head straight to the bedroom. Everything is exactly as I left it – bed covers tangled in the middle of it, the little clock face down on the floor. Going across to the window, I tug the window blinds down so it's as dark as I can get it, then collapse down on the bed. I pull the unfamiliar covers up again and press my face into the pillow.

Hope to wake.

CHAPTER SIX

Light again.

The metallic sound of something being unloaded somewhere outside. I'm warm and sleepy still, so I don't immediately open my eyes.

Images float to me, running around in someone else's body, trying on their clothes, wandering through the Meadows, a gorgeous guy across a hall. I roll on to my side and let out an audible sigh, as my eyes flutter slowly open.

Chipped wooden floor.

A clock lying on its face.

Hang on.

Eyes snapping open, I jolt bolt upright in the bed. The window, the blind I pulled down, this room.

It's all the same.

Shit.

My heart is pounding and blood rushes in my ears. But how can this still be happening? I went to bed, then I woke up. I'm supposed to be out of this now. I'm supposed to be at the hospital, or at home, or just anywhere but here.

Launching myself out of bed, I feel my feet hit the cool wooden floor. I pick the clock up from the floor, stare at its face once again.

27 July now.

But still two years ago.

I walk over to the chest of drawers and stare into the mirror, only to see that face again, those features. My fingers go up to touch them, the soft cheeks, the neck, the long dark hair.

It's all still there – this body, in this flat I've never seen before. And deep down, I know it's not a dream.

Which means, I must be very sick right now: the other face in the mirror, this whole flat actually, is a symptom of my illness, or perhaps a side effect of the anti-rejection heart meds I'm on. These are the only rational explanations now. But oh god, this is still awful. My heart is pounding and I feel sick; outside of myself completely. Dissociation – isn't that what they call it?

I just need to get back home, then we can go to the hospital and explain what's happening to me. The doctors will know what to do.

Pulling a blue raincoat off a peg, I grab the keys this time and stumble into the yellow trainers by the door. I feel vaguely guilty about stealing someone else's clothing, but then I'm not even sure any of this is really happening. I'm still wearing the paint splattered dress I put on yesterday.

Before I can descend into a proper panic attack though, I head out of the flat and back down the tenement steps, making sure to slow down this time. Because if this isn't a dream, then I was taking my life in my hands yesterday.

Outside on the street, I cast around for a taxi, throw my arm up high when I see one. The taxi driver glances at me briefly when I get in and I'm suddenly aware of how wired I must look. He probably thinks I'm crazy.

But then, maybe I am right now?

'Primrose Street please,' I say, before I've even sat down. A furrow of the driver's eyebrows in the rear-view mirror and the taxi speeds off. More tenements flash by, pedestrians, shops, like everything is normal, and that overwhelming sickness comes over me again, that unrelenting panic. I close my eyes, trying to stop the swirling feeling inside.

Make it stop.

Eventually I open my eyes again, the darkness is only making the nausea worse. I look down at my hands – still tanned. Still that lemony rose scent permeating everything.

I just don't understand how this can have happened. My annual check was totally fine; I did everything perfectly. I managed to get to a year post-transplant with nothing going wrong.

So why would this happen now?

A flickering of red ahead. The amount on the taxi metre is going steadily up.

Shit.

I pat down the coat I'm wearing until I feel something wallet-shaped in the pocket. *Thank god.* With fumbling hands, I pull it out and am relieved to see a few notes sticking out the top of the soft beige leather. At least I can pay, even if I still don't understand what's going on here. As the taxi zips down the road, I look inside. I still have that sense of guilt, messing around with someone's stuff like this. Because, clearly, I've somehow ended up in someone else's flat. That must be it.

There are a few cards in the side compartment, and I pull the top one out – a gym pass for somewhere in London. With my heart hammering, I stare at the picture.

My stomach falls out of me. Because it's the same image I saw in the mirror earlier: same eyes and hair and features. I quickly scan the details to the side.

Emily Perin, thirty years old.

'Like me,' I whisper.

Oh god, oh god.

It's one thing hallucinating another image in the mirror, but a driver's licence too? A whole identity, in the past?

Looking outside the window, I see we're out of the centre of town now. Almost there.

Just breathe, Maggie.

Eventually the taxi pulls on to my parents' street, and I let out a sigh of relief, but at the same time, regret floods me. This is going to absolutely ruin my family's day, their week, their month.

But I've got no other option right now.

'Just here,' I croak, as we approach the worn white gate. As soon as the man has stopped, I take a note out of the wallet and push it through the divider.

'Keep the change,' I say, before launching myself out the door and on to the pavement. Running up the gravel pathway to our old semi-detached house near the water, I realise what I'm doing and force myself to slow down: no point exerting myself and making everything worse. Walking up the steps, I only vaguely register that my wheelchair ramp has gone as I start fumbling for my house keys.

I stop.

Because I don't have them, of course – or any of my own possessions, for that matter.

Oh god, it's all too much.

I knock, but there's no answer. They're probably all out looking for me, probably checking every possible place I might have gone, which is nowhere really. I head around to the kitchen door instead, honeysuckle waving at me in the breeze as I go. Summer light floods towards me on the ramshackle path, and I imagine, on another day, Mum would be out the back weeding, or hanging up laundry to dry now the sun's out.

Desperation tears through me and I close my eyes briefly as I try to work out how to handle this. What am I going to say to her? I don't even know what's happening myself.

But, ultimately, I know Mum will take me straight up to the hospital, which is exactly where I need to be right now.

I'm about to walk out on to the freshly cut lawn, when I stop. Because Mum really is there, hanging out laundry like normal.

Energy punctuates the air, and my stomach curdles.

Something isn't right.

'Mum,' I start to say, and almost walk towards her, but a sound makes me stop. A voice.

And there's something about it that makes all the blood rush to my head and my body turn cold. Retreating back on to the shady pathway, I press myself against the wall as I try to process what it is I'm hearing. Who I'm hearing.

'Are you almost finished work?' Mum says.

'Getting there,' the other voice says, 'just finishing up a little tour of Italy for a honeymoon. Did you know that Michelangelo didn't even want to paint the Sistine Chapel? He actually saw himself more as a sculptor than a painter.'

'I didn't know that, dear,' Mum says, and I hear sheets being shaken out, as my mind scrambles to keep up. It's like I'm watching a car crash unfold, or rather hearing it – horrified but unable to move away.

'You went there once, to Italy, didn't you?' the other voice says.

'I did, a long time ago now with your dad.' A small laugh. 'That was a very fun trip now you mention it, before you girls were even born. I was playing with the orchestra there and your father came to meet me when we were done. We explored the city by day, stayed out dancing till dawn every night.'

'Seriously?'

'Oh yes, your father used to love dancing, just like Cat.'

Silence stretches out, and I remember how Mum would tail off like that whenever she mentioned her.

I also remember this day, come to think of it – right before I got put on oxygen. Right before the ramp got put in.

This day has already happened, except, somehow, I'm back in it. And I'm here, and not there. I'm someone called Emily, and over there is Maggie.

This isn't the meds.

'You actually look quite pale,' Mum is saying sharply now, all previous softness gone. 'I'll go and call Doctor Peterson, see if he'll examine you.'

'I'm fine, honestly,' the other voice wheezes. 'It was probably that walk earlier that got me. I'll go get some water.'

'No, I'll get it,' Mum says firmly, and a second later I hear the crunching of gravel.

My stomach drops, as I realise I'm beside the kitchen window. I know I need to move but something in the kitchen makes me stop.

Mum's calendar.

With a sick feeling in my stomach, I peer through the glass at it – the twenty-seventh of July, two years ago.

Same as the clock.

A movement inside makes me duck down, and then Mum's footsteps on the tiles come, quick and light. I start to breathe hard. After a few moments, I glance inside again to see the familiar form of her at the sink, her back to me now, and I want to look away, want to scream at the horror of this all, but I can't help staring.

'What's happening?' I whisper.

She looks up sharply and I dip down again. Because I can't cope with this; can't process any of it.

Keeping low to the ground, I crawl back along the pathway until the extension ends and I can stand up again. Then I get up and walk quickly away down the drive.

I have no idea where I'm going now, or what I'll do. All I do know is that I have to leave.

* * *

Feeling lost and confused a while later, I find myself drifting off down to my favourite spot on the beach, where I come to process things sometimes. It's the only other place I can think to go, because there's something about the beach, about the millions of grains of sand and the crashing waves, that's timeless and soothing.

I sit on my rock, watching people come and go, dogs running, parents chasing kids, and I think about what Mum said – about Cat loving to dance.

I think about the last summer she did.

* * *

It was a few months after my nineteenth birthday, and for one small moment, I was stable. I was still living at home, but I'd been accepted into art school up in Aberdeen for the forthcoming autumn. It had taken a little longer after several missed years of school, but with an extra year at college, and a lot of encouragement from Cat, I'd done it – and I was going.

My artist sister, she liked to call me proudly.

Mum tried to stop me, of course. Told me it was fine to want to go to art school, but it should be here in Edinburgh, where she could keep an eye on me, where I'd be close to doctors who knew me. And I felt bad about it, I did. Because as my prognosis reduced what I could do, it made Cat determined to do as much as possible – for both of us, she always said – climbing, diving off bridges, raves, you name it, she did it. The more extreme the better. The arguments between Mum and Cat naturally increased, so they were always at each other's throats, with Mum repeatedly telling her she was being reckless, and Cat repeatedly refusing to listen. There just wasn't the space for another daughter to act out. So, each time she stepped forward, I took a step back. For everyone's sake. But she would always make sure to introduce me to new friends passing through Edinburgh and bring me back little tokens from her adventures – ticket stubs from festivals and postcards from sunny Greek islands.

But art school was different – this time it was about something very important to me. I'd be learning to do what I loved.

Cat, on the other hand, had no further education plans and left home as soon as humanly possible, despite how much Mum tried to reason with her. She moved into a shared flat with two girls she knew from the bar she worked in, and even though I missed her around the house terribly, I could see how happy it made her – living however she wanted. Plus, I visited all the time, and so in a way, it felt like we were both moving on.

Life was happening, and it felt good.

I suppose I knew somewhere inside me that it couldn't last like this, that my health would slowly, inevitably, go downhill. The signs were there already, the shortness of breath, the paleness, the dizzy spells. But there was just something about having Cat as my sister that made me feel stronger. Nothing would get me because she wouldn't let it.

Or so I thought.

Cat met Fraser at the bar a few days into that hot and hazy June, and from the first time she told me about him on the phone, I knew she was gone. He was a musician from Edinburgh, gigging his way through the summer at various bars, including hers. He was the same age as her, and just incredible, she said. He loved animals and the great outdoors, and when the two of them weren't on shift, they would disappear for camping trips in the Pentlands, or up to the cottage.

And I liked him too – it was hard not to really, despite the creeping jealousy that would sometimes surface. Because Cat was my other half, my person, and yet here she was spending all her time with someone else. I can still remember the first time I met him – the long sandy hair pulled back in a ponytail, the glittering blue eyes that barely left my sister. 'You're Maggie then,' he said easily, pulling me into a hug. 'I've heard a fairly insane amount about you – it's good to put a face to the name. Shall we all go get some drinks together at Malones?'

Over the course of that hazy summer, I'd get all these messages and pictures from Cat, of her and Fraser out on bikes together, or off up hills under skies of neon pink and parma violet, him playing his guitar beside a fire they'd built together. They would head out to his gigs until late, and Cat would get to dance the night away to her new favourite music.

I wanted to go too, of course; was desperate to just let go like Cat did, but my condition always stopped me, even then.

'Maybe next time,' I would say each time she asked.

Then, as the summer started to draw to a close, the news came that she and Fraser were moving in together, after only a few short months. I was happy for her, of course, but I couldn't help feeling a little jealous too, and it spurred me on with my own packing for art school – the halls of residence was all booked, the future was imminent and, with Cat trail-blazing the way, I had the feeling maybe anything was possible.

It's funny how life does that, shines light all over you one minute, then takes it away the next.

* * *

Now, as the sun sinks down in a final burst of orange and blue ahead of me on the beach, the memories fade back, and I think about the date on the clock in the bedroom again.

'The twenty-seventh of July,' I whisper into the salty air.

Two days short of a year before my transplant.

I just wish I could make sense of this all somehow. I wish I knew what the hell was going on. Because right now all I know is that I'm in someone else's body, in someone else's flat, two years in the past. And somewhere across town is another version of me; a sicker version of me, before I got my new heart.

I am there, and yet I am also here, in the life of someone called Emily.

How can that be happening?

And, more importantly, *why* is it happening? Why now?

CHAPTER SEVEN

The next day begins largely the same: wake up in Emily's room, check my hands, see they're still not mine, check the clock, see we're still two years in the past, just a day on now. Time is running normally here.

It's just me that's different.

Desperately, I start searching around the flat. There isn't much other than some clothes and bags in her bedroom, including a Mulberry. There are some boxes of papers in the hall cupboard and odd trinket about the place too. But where is her phone? Or her laptop? Something that might actually give me some concrete information.

I shower next, mainly to see if it might calm me down, but also because I really have no idea when the last time this body was washed – and it's started to show. As I step in the shower and hot water rushes over this new body, a thought dawns on me; I look down at the centre of my chest.

Nothing.

No scar splitting my chest in two, just beautiful skin for miles. The stomach is taut too, as though this body has been at that gym in London a lot, and looking down at the arms, I can see the same effect – lean, lightly muscled limbs. So very different to my scarred, softer physique, and I can't help thinking how different this Emily person's life must be to mine.

Hypertrophic cardiomyopathy. That's what they diagnosed me with, when I was twelve: *a genetic condition,* I read online, *which causes the heart muscle to be thickened, and can eventually lead to sudden death.* All cases differ, and some barely impact on a person, but, for whatever reason, my condition was severe, and as with all cases, progressive.

I guess I wasn't too affected by it in the early years – I went to school, went to parties and played sports; had a full life. If it wasn't for a great-aunt on Dad's side dying of it a few years back, we might not have known what my fainting spells were. But we did know, and Mum took me to the doctors immediately. I think they screened Cat and Jess as a precaution more than anything else, and their results thankfully came up normal.

And Cat and I were no longer two peas in a pod.

I remember being completely floored. With only eleven months between us and matching red hair, we were more like twins than sisters really, and we already did everything together: same year at school, same sports, same friends. We even chose to share the same room. How could this be any different? I just wanted to be well again, like her; live exactly like her.

But as the doctor's concerns grew bigger, so did Mum's attempts to ensure my life got smaller – sports rapidly decreased, parties were frequently cancelled and going anywhere even vaguely far away from a known hospital was an absolute no-no for our family. I suppose, looking back, it's a wonder Cat didn't rebel even more. My prognosis became grim, and the doctors couldn't say if I would drop down dead in two years' time or two months' time.

Tomorrow.

But it didn't change the dreams I had – it didn't change the fact that I wanted it all, just as much as her. But the one time I tried to live like Cat, I ruined everything.

After washing, I get dressed in the one grey t-shirt I find in all the colour, and a pair of slightly too-short denim shorts. Then I pull the covers back up on the bed and place the little clock back on the side table. If there's one thing I'm not going to do, it's mess another person's life up: because the more I think about it, the more I'm convinced that this is all surely going to stop soon, and I can chalk it all down to some glitch in the universe's fabric. I just have to wait it out, so that when this person – this Emily – does come back to her life and I go back to mine, everything will be exactly as she left it.

I can't help wondering, though, if the Maggie I saw in the garden could have been Emily – as if, somehow, we've done some sort of *Freaky Friday* body switch. But at the same time, I heard her speaking just like me. Those were my words about the Sistine Chapel, and no one else's. There wasn't even a hint of someone else being there.

So where has Emily gone?

I go to find food next – more out of basic necessity given I can't recall the last time I ate properly – at the little purple café with the gold outline of a pineapple on the front. And after chatting with the friendly girl with bright-purple hair and red glasses called Zoe, I establish that Emily even has a regular order here: double shot latte and a pain au chocolat. I'm surprised, given Emily's physique seems to suggest a slightly different diet, and I opt for a more familiar porridge in the end anyway. I know I had all that ramen and Prosecco two days ago when I thought it was a dream, and nothing bad happened, but still, I just feel too weird eating it.

Too guilty.

I also manage to glean from Zoe (after a faintly awkward exchange due to me not actually being who I appear to be) that Emily has been coming here for two weeks and I find a mystery card in Emily's wallet. But when I try to tug it out, it won't budge.

Walking back out on to the street a little later, I look across to the Meadows. Just the sight of the familiar green trees and the rolling grass soothes my frazzled mind; grounds me to this moment.

I have no explanation for anything, but all I know is that some way, somehow, this is all actually happening.

This is real.

I wander down the street for a while, simply taking in the sun, the sky, because I have nothing to do and nowhere to go.

Or do I?

I stop.

Feel my eyes widening in panic.

CHAPTER EIGHT

With my heart pounding against my chest, I run back to the flat, weaving in and out of people on the street as I go. I can't believe I was so stupid, just sauntering about for days, without a care in the world. I have no idea what Emily does with her time – what if she's a carer or a doctor or something? What if I'm supposed to be somewhere right now, looking after an invalid, and I don't even know because I'm wandering around eating porridge?

When I eventually arrive back outside Emily's building, I stop for a moment to catch my breath. I wait for the laboured sound to start, that feeling like everything in my body might just fall apart.

But it doesn't come. I'm barely sweating. Before I can process it fully, a figure appears across the road and my stomach flips.

Adam, as I discovered from some mail outside his door.

He's wearing the same khaki shorts and a black t-shirt again, and he's got shopping bags at his side, a head of celery sticking out the top of one. His eyes light up when he clocks me, and he raises a hand in greeting, smiles that lopsided smile again.

God, he's attractive.

But it's not the time or the place to get chatting to some guy, no matter how good-looking he is.

Giving him a small wave back, I let myself in and head to the top floor. The door downstairs opens, closes, and I quickly slip back into my flat.

Heading into the bedroom, I cast back around the space. First things first, find Emily's phone. And I have a feeling about where it might be.

Hauling the Mulberry bag out of the cupboard now, I open it up, see something dark at the bottom.

'Bingo.'

Pulling an old-looking handset out, I try to turn it on. Nothing. I plug it into the charger beside the bed and dash back to the hall cupboard to check the box with the papers. It looks heavy when I pull it out, but when I actually lift it, I find myself carrying it into the living room like it weighs nothing. It's unsettling and freeing in equal measures.

There's a lot more inside than I realised, and I can't help wondering what the paper trail's about. Isn't everything online these days? Maybe she decided to go off-grid for some reason.

I can't think why but I guess there would be something freeing about cutting yourself off from it all. I'm just so dependent on technology to live that it's never been an option.

At any rate, I start rifling through all the paper, find various utility bills addressed to Emily Perin at an address in Highgate.

She did move up from London then.

Concentrate, Maggie.

Rooting further down, I finally find what I think I'm looking for – an employment letter for some financial company. So, not a carer, thankfully.

Phew.

With my heart rate a little lower now, I settle down to go through this stuff properly. I probably should have checked this earlier, but I was so hungry and freaked out by everything – still am, really.

Some of the papers I find are around pension contributions, a rental agreement with a landlord called William Johnson. Another about a promotion; *congratulations on the move to Director*, it says. The pay rise printed below makes my eyes water – Emily has done really well for herself – and as I look around the room again, at the frayed rug and shabby sofa, I find myself frowning.

None of it quite adds up, though the next letter from her company explains it in part – they are formally agreeing to a one-year sabbatical, following her 'sudden' exit. There will be no pay given during that time, but they welcome her to come back at the end of a year.

Placing the papers gently back in the box, I pull out her passport next. Emily Isabella Perin, born in London. The pages are absolutely littered with stamps – America, India, Japan, the list goes on, and I can't help but feel a little jealous, even if I don't know this person. But then I spot a driver's licence application form – *she didn't drive either?*

I pull out a stack of photos next and take my time sifting through them all. The ones at the bottom are in black and white, of a thin little blonde girl mainly. There are tightly packed terraces, washing strung up across the front, lots of kids everywhere. The next ones are colour photos of what looks like a baby Emily in the nineties. She's in a paddling pool in an expansive, English-looking garden, with what must be her parents behind her. Her dad has olive skin, the same thick chestnut hair and hazel eyes as Emily, which look kind, if a little distant. Her mum, on the other hand, stands slim and pale beside him, a stiff-looking cream dress on, and I realise she must be the little girl in the older photos. The next photo I pull out is one of her and her parents in some grand hall, except Emily's a bit older – perhaps early teens. She's stood neatly between them wearing a smart white dress, her smile set in a tight line, and she's holding up some sort of certificate. Another photo of her working at a desk in her late teens, one long strand of hair hanging down her still childish cheek as she concentrates, another of her graduating from a fancy-looking school with her parents on either side, her mum's hand firmly around her waist. Then a final shot of Emily standing in a cap and gown in some sort of archaic quad (is that Oxford?) on a sunny day.

But close to the bottom is a different kind of photo, a loose one of Emily and a pretty girl with a dark, shiny bob. She has deep brown eyes, bronzed skin, and the two of them have their cheeks pressed up right against each other. They look like they're mid laugh, out on a busy street somewhere with high buildings and electric lights behind them, London, from the looks of it. And they look vaguely similar too; could be sisters. I turn it over to see the words – *E and Fran's summer of Elton. Love from your favourite cousin (Fran!).*

That it explains who she is. But who is Elton?

At any rate, this must be the Fran on the mantlepiece, the one getting married to Toby next year.

There's something else at the bottom of the box too – one of those old disposable cameras. I pick it up, turn it over. It's clearly been used to the end. What's on it?

It's only then that I look up and see what I didn't before, because I was too panicked, too tired and hungry and utterly lost – but now with a little food in me, I do see it: a DSLR camera hanging from one of the chairs around the dining room table. Forgetting about the disposable now, I go and pick the camera up, feel the familiar weight of it in my hands. Turning it carefully over, words come back to me – *Digital Single Lens Reflex, interchangeable lenses.* I used one of these when I did a course on photography at college once.

I can't help thinking about the sketches I did at home just before all of this happened – how there was something more urgent about the pace of them, something odd about the content too – blurry shapes and profiles, patterns and colours, which had no resemblance to what I'd seen or done that day.

I shiver.

A phone beeping cuts through my thoughts, and, turning away from the camera, I head back to the bedroom. I get a dull niggle again that perhaps I'm doing something wrong; after all, I would never usually look through someone else's phone, but I'm starting to realise that I have no choice. This is my reality right now, and more than anything, I need to know why I'm here in this body. In this time.

Sitting down on the edge of the bed, I pick up the phone and look at the screen. No password to get in, and no apps, social media or emails. Not on an old-school model like this.

But there is one message waiting, from Fran. Tentatively, I open it up.

Is everything OK, E? Xxx

I look through the rest of the messages, but there's only one other to 'Mum' with the address of this flat in Edinburgh – no response back – and I wonder if Emily switched her phone from something fancier. No other contacts saved either.

But why all the changes? Why the big move?

And why hasn't her mum replied?

For the hundredth time today, I find myself trying to solve an unsolvable riddle and I place my head in my hands, attempting to quell the rising panic. I just wish I could talk to someone.

I wish I could talk to Jess.

Pausing for a moment, I key in the number I've called so many times in my life that I know it by heart.

I listen to it ring once, twice.

'Hello?'

I immediately freeze at the sound of my sister's voice.

She won't know who I am.

'Hello?' Jess says again, wearily this time. A baby-ish shout from the background, one of the boys – two years ago.

My stomach lurches.

'Who is it, honey?' Graham's voice.

'Dunno,' Jess says, 'no one's there.'

And with my head on my knees now, all I want to say is, 'I'm here, Jess.'

I'm here, somewhere.

CHAPTER NINE

For the next few days, I stay close to the flat, trying to figure out what to do. I feel anxious and outside of myself, so I don't go back to the Purple Pineapple again or put myself in any other strange situations where people think I'm someone else. But I do take short walks around the sunny Meadows, and I do keep the flat tidy. I find some other stuff as I go: a few flyers on the side table Emily must have picked up – for wall climbing, cooking lessons and a dance class in Edinburgh, for skiing in the Cairngorms, and even for a few nightclubs I've heard of in town. There's a guitar at the back of the hall cupboard too and I give it a nervous, unmelodic strum before placing it back where I found it. A few books lie around the place, including an atlas, and some quirky little diving figurines. But nothing really tells me anything about what's going on. Or why I'm here.

Eventually I venture to the little supermarket along the street to get provisions. There's not a lot of money left in the wallet, but I manage to pick up some fruit, milk and whole-meal bread. I go to pick up porridge oats then stop myself.

Will I actually be here to eat it all?

Surely this has all got to end soon. Grabbing the box anyway, I add it to the basket. Just in case. But as each morning drifts to afternoon and then evening, and right back around again, I find myself realising that none of this is going anywhere.

Eventually I head to the local library, find a computer I can browse the internet on. I search the terms 'woken in someone else's body', and 'woke up in the past', but most of the stuff that comes back is metaphorical – people talking about how they *don't know how they got here* in life generally. Some people talk about it more literally, in fairness, this feeling of waking up in someone else's life, but it's all just on chat sites, and I can't deny they sound a little bit crazy. I think about going to see a doctor, but then stop myself. What the hell would they say about any of this? What could I possibly say that sounds even vaguely sane? I don't want to get sectioned.

And so it all drifts on, my panic steadily humming throughout.

* * *

On the sixth evening here, I'm sitting at the big bay window, looking out across the city. The sky has started to take on the pearly hue of evening, and I can't help feeling a deep sense of dread – and something like restlessness. Here am I again, all alone in this flat, with no one to talk to and no idea what to do with myself. I'm just so used to being in a house where Mum and Dad are somewhere close by, or I'm on the phone to Jess, or seeing her. I have none of my art stuff here. No laptop either.

Wandering around the dining table now, I pick up the camera and go back through the images on it again. I had a look at them all eventually, hoping to find something that would give more of a clue to Emily's life, but they're all of scenery mainly, images from around the city. And all of them seem to have been taken in the last two weeks. It's as though there's this invisible line in Emily's life, and before that line, it's all blurry and grey. All I know is she lived down in London, had an amazing job and at least one great friend, and then for some unknown reason, gave it all up.

For what?

I look back at the one selfie of Emily I found before, right at the end of the reel, like she'd taken it the day before I got here. She's sitting in the Meadows alone, ice cream in hand, and she just looks so relaxed compared to some of the older photos; so very happy.

And for the briefest of moments, I imagine myself out tomorrow with this camera doing exactly the same thing as she did: taking in the city, alone, with no faulty heart to worry about, and no other people to worry about – no concerned mother breathing down my neck.

Could I?

A whisper of a thrill goes through me unexpectedly, as a knock sounds on the door.

I turn to it sharply and pad, barefoot, across the cool wooden floor. In front of the door now, I peer through the small eyehole.

It's him again.

Adam.

I step back quickly, heart racing.

Why is he here?

For a moment, I think about not answering, when I realise just how pathetic I'm being. He seemed friendly enough, and he helped me when I needed it. What if he needs help now? Opening the door, I look out to see him standing there in jeans and a plaid shirt, which exposes his muscular forearms, the end of that tattoo.

A kick of attraction again.

Then he smiles, that dimple appearing in one cheek. 'Hey.'

'Hello.'

'So, this might be a strange one,' he says, 'but I saw your light was on tonight, a Friday night, and I was just heading out for something to eat, so I thought I might see if you fancied coming with me? I have a great place in mind.'

I open my mouth in surprise.

'I don't know,' I start automatically, because I can't actually remember the last time I went on a date. Let alone in someone else's life.

'No pressure at all,' he says, 'but I thought you might not know anyone here and fancy some company.'

His eyes are soft on mine, and I feel that unexpected pull to him; that wave of attraction, and something else like longing – to go outside and take in the city like Emily did, to stop trying to figure this all out for a moment and let my brain rest. I look down at the grey t-shirt I'm wearing, the shorts. I could stay here in the flat and do absolutely nothing. Completely alone.

Or—

'If you give me a minute,' I say, pointing back inside, 'I can change quickly and come with you.'

'All right,' he says, eyes alight.

'Just give me ten minutes, OK?' I say, ushering him in. As he passes me, I can smell toothpaste and a woody natural scent.

'Have a seat,' I say, leading him into the living room. My heart is beating very fast now. 'Sorry, I'd offer you a drink, if I had anything in,' I say, unsure what to do.

'I'm OK,' he says easily. 'Thanks, though.'

Heading back away into the bedroom, I strip the t-shirt off as I go. I hear the creak of him walking across the living room as I pull down the shorts.

'Can I take a look?' he calls through.

I pause, thrown by this question, before realising he must be meaning the camera.

'Um, sure,' I say, even as I frown at the dresses hanging in the wardrobe. I would never have the courage to wear any of these normally, but I have to admit, that dress I had on the other day looked pretty good.

Which one tonight?

I find myself touching the buttercup-yellow one, then before I can overthink it, I've taken it off its hanger.

'Wow, these are really good,' Adam calls through.

I'm not quite sure how to reply for something I didn't do, so I find myself replying for Emily instead. 'Thank you.'

Pulling the dress down over my head, it slips on effortlessly, hugging my sides in all the right places, and kicking out at the waist. Stepping in front of the long mirror in the corner, I can't deny I look nice in it, the yellow bringing out the gold in Emily's big hazel eyes. And there's something about speaking with her English voice and not my Scottish one that gives me an added boost of confidence too.

I'm someone else entirely tonight.

With a slight skip in my heart now, I step into some white trainers by the bed and throw a silver bag across my shoulder.

Should I apply some make-up? I barely apply it to my own face normally, let alone someone else's, but I suppose I should try. Tentatively, I peek into the little pink case on the windowsill, look through the impressive eyeshadow palettes and striking lipsticks. I keep finding these little glimpses of another kind of life – an expensive one, which feels different from this flat.

I eventually apply a little mascara and blush, but after a quick internal debate, I decide it's probably safer not to try anything else with so little time. The natural look will have to do.

Walking back through to the living room, Adam turns quickly from the mantlepiece.

'Wow,' he says, a soft smile appearing on his face, 'you look amazing.'

My body is pumping with nerves, with anxiety, with this overwhelming feeling that this is a bad idea, and I should just tell him I can't go anywhere. But then, I hear Jess's words ringing in my ears.

You're not living.

And maybe I should live a little.

While I'm here anyway.

'Well,' Adam says, smiling at me, 'shall we get going?'

After a moment's pause, I nod.

'OK.'

CHAPTER TEN

The evening sky is a hazy blue above us, streaked with whipped-cream clouds and dotted with soaring birds. The air has that warm stillness about it, the scent of hot pavements and grass rising up around us. Adam and I are walking side by side down the street, and I can practically hear my heart thudding in my chest.

'Did you manage to get away from him?' he says.

I turn. 'Who?'

'The psychopath who was running after you across the street this morning.'

I can't help smiling as I think of him at the lights, that wave he gave me.

'Sorry about that, I've been having a bit of a . . . weird time recently.'

I feel him glance at me, a curious look on his face.

'Yeah, I was wondering if I should check on you after yesterday. You didn't seem quite yourself.'

Yourself.

What even is that right now?

'So, what do you make at your workshop?' I say, more because I don't know what else to say and it seems like something people would ask on a date.

I just really hope Emily hasn't asked this before.

'Furniture . . . well, I upholster it really, upcycle too. It's not as technical as actually making the furniture itself, I realise, but I'm more into taking something old and making it new.'

'Giving it a new lease of life,' I offer.

'Exactly.'

He smiles at me, and heat rises up my neck.

'What about you?' he says. 'Have you looked into that course yet?'

Course? I can't remember seeing anything about a course.

'Not yet,' I say carefully.

'Well, no time like the present,' he says, as we wander along a walkway.

I'm still trying to work out what he's talking about, when glittering lights appear ahead of us, tents rising up into the sky, and the hum of people. The Edinburgh Fringe. I haven't been in years, not since that one time Cat dragged me along in our teens. But I've always dreamed of going back; read about all the shows online and wished I could see every last one of them. Now I find myself following Adam through one of the entrances to a beer garden. Wooden benches are already filling up across fake grass, while multi-coloured Chinese lanterns bob lightly in the breeze above. Leafy garlands are strung up around the sides, little lights already twinkling out at us, and the most incredible smell rushes towards me, rich and wood-smoked.

'What is that?' I say, gazing around in wonder.

Adam turns, his eyes lit up. 'Didn't I say I had a great place in mind for dinner?'

I look around at the empty picnic tables in confusion. 'Where?'

'There.' He points across at a food van sitting to one side. 'I give you the world's best pizza and pint van. Hey Sven.' Adam walks up to the guy working inside it.

A very tall man with dark-brown skin and a closely cropped afro immediately looks up and grins. He stops chopping something and comes out the back of the van. He's wearing a white t-shirt and a red apron with 'The Scandi Pizza Man' on the front, and with his smiley eyes and slightly sticky out ears, he's an endearingly good-looking guy. He walks straight up to Adam and gives him a hug, before stepping back.

'I didn't know you were coming down tonight,' Sven says, before glancing at me, one eyebrow arched. 'Who's your friend?'

'Emily, this is Sven; Sven, meet Emily.'

'Ah, the pretty girl across the hall,' Sven says, his face lighting up. 'So, he finally plucked up the courage to ask you out.'

Adam glances at me, a smile playing on his lips. Heat rushes up my neck again.

God, this is awkward.

'Charlie not about tonight?' Adam says now to Sven.

'Oh, she is,' Sven says, 'but she's actually performing this evening.'

'I forgot she's actually *in* the festival this year.' Adam turns to me. 'Charlie, Sven's partner, is an amazing dancer. She's got her own dance school and everything.' He turns back to Sven. 'She must be really chuffed.'

'She is indeed.' Sven beams proudly. A second later, he claps his hands.

'Right, pizza. What can I get you guys tonight?'

I stare up at the menu on the blackboard: it all looks amazing, with every pizza topping coming from a different country: olives on the Italian, chorizo on the Spanish, and buffalo chicken on the American. My stomach rumbles aggressively again, but that feeling of guilt is still there, sitting at the bottom of it.

Though, should I feel guilty? As far as I can tell, Emily is healthy – more than healthy from what I've found out about her. So surely, I can just keep eating the same things that she did.

It's not like I'm dealing with heart transplant stats here: *only 50 per cent of people make it past the ten-year mark*, I can still hear the doctor saying as I recovered in the hospital.

Hell, only about 50 per cent make it past the one-year mark.

As it all starts to sink in, that I'm dealing with an entirely different body to my limited one, I find myself saying, 'I'll go with the plain cheese, if that's all right.'

'Always a classic,' Adam grins back. 'I'll have the same – thanks, Sven – though how many times have I told you to put a Canadian on that list?'

Sven laughs. 'And how many times did I tell you I'm not putting poutine on a pizza?'

I guessed right on the accent then.

Adam turns to me. 'Drink?'

'A water would be great,' I say and he nods.

'One water and a pint of lager with those slices please, Sven.'

I reach for my wallet. I should just about be able to stretch to this.

'No, no, no,' Adam says, shaking his head. 'This is all working out better than I thought; you'll only ruin the vibe if you pay now.'

'Well, OK, but the next time's on me.'

He grins and my heart skips. Shit, I don't know why I said that, given I might not actually be here, and also given I have absolutely no desire to get involved with anyone generally. But it seems to have made Adam smile, and he has a great smile.

After Sven has passed our pizzas and drinks through the hatch, we head over to an empty bench. Under the garland-strung coverings, with the now blushing sky above, we could almost be abroad. Or what I'd always imagined it might be like.

I take a bite of the pizza. It's all gooey cheese and juicy tomatoes and it explodes on my tongue. 'Oh shit,' I say through a mouthful of food. I look at the pizza, look at Adam. 'That's insane.'

He swallows his mouthful, the amber flecks in his green eyes sparking. 'I told you, right?'

I take another bite, the combination of great food and easy company relaxing me slightly; making me momentarily forget how wild this whole situation is.

'So,' I say, 'how long have you and Sven known each other?'

'Well, I met him when I was twenty and travelling in Sweden, and I'm now thirty-two,' Adam says, like he's thinking it over. 'So over ten years. He suggested I move here to set up the furniture thing. He'd recently moved over and didn't have any friends here so . . .'

'So you became that friend.' I smile. I get the sense he's friendly to everyone he meets.

'Exactly. Plus, I was working through some stuff of my own,' he says, as a shadow passes across his face, 'so it was good to meet someone new.'

I'm about to ask what he means when an older couple walk over to us. 'Mind if we sit here?' The woman asks.

'No problem at all,' Adam replies, and shifts up the bench to give them room. Doing the same on my side, I manage to briefly look at his tattoo a little better – a spiky tree weaved into a river, then a horse and a hand above that, and something else random above that. It still makes no sense, and I want to ask him about it, but I don't know this guy at all, really.

He turns back to me a moment later, the darkness all gone. 'Why did you decide to move up here?'

What to say? I have no idea why Emily came up here, and for some reason I really don't want to lie to this guy. I may have only known him for twenty minutes but he seems so very open and kind and, sometimes, you just get a feeling.

I take a sip of my water. 'I don't totally know, if I'm being honest.' I pause. 'I guess I'm still figuring things out.'

He smiles in a way that starts that fluttering in my chest again. 'Well, I'm glad you chose to figure things out in the flat opposite mine.'

I take a quick sip of my water. 'And how long have you lived there?'

'Oh, I don't really *live* there exactly; I don't really stay anywhere for long. It's more a base for when I'm back. And I always try and catch the Fringe, you see.'

For some reason my stomach sinks just slightly.

'And on that note.' He pulls two white tickets from his pocket, sliding them apart with his thumb and forefinger.

I stare down at them.

'Show tickets,' he says before I ask. 'A comedy act in a couple of hours. I got them on the off-chance that you would come out tonight. A little presumptuous, I know, but failing that, there was always Sven.' He laughs.

I feel myself hesitating. A show? I've just got my head around having a slice of pizza with this guy.

'Not keen?' Adam says quickly, and holds up his hands. 'No pressure, honestly. If you're bored by my chat before then, I will gladly walk you back home.'

The way he's so open and friendly about the whole thing makes me like him even more, and I have the strongest sense that I should at least try.

'Well,' I say eventually, smiling across at him, 'let's see how the rest of the evening goes, OK?'

He nods. 'Good plan.'

We finish off our pizza slices and, for the next while, I find myself talking easily to him. It's soothing after everything that's happened in the last week, as though somehow he's managing to ground me to this time, this life, and I stop thinking about the hows and the whys of it all. He tells me about his upholstering business, how he started it a few years back, and despite some initial setbacks, he's done all right. His bespoke stuff is even in some of the fancy hotels around town apparently, and he travels around the country to deliver his orders personally, partly because he likes meeting new people, and partly because he just likes exploring. He's incredibly easy to talk with, warm too, and I have the strangest sense that maybe I met him before in my own life.

'Well, enough about me,' he says eventually, 'I want to know about you. What's your family like?'

I pause.

What can I possibly tell him? Dad, Jess and the boys, Mum – they all feel so far away right now, like they're in another life.

'Let's just say I needed a fresh start,' I say eventually. And with a jolt, I realise that perhaps that's true.

'Well, I hope you find it, Emily,' he says, his startling green eyes on mine. 'And would you look at that?' he says suddenly, turning an old brown-strap watch on his wrist to me. 'Looks like we made it to showtime. You game?'

I'm not sure if it's the full-belly feeling I have or the smudges of happy pink in the sky above, but I find myself nodding at him.

'All right,' I say, 'I'm game.'

* * *

All around us, the venue continues to fill up, and my breathing quickens. When we first got in, there were very few people here, and I still felt light-headed with the evening, drifting along in a pleasant, dream-like state.

But now, as I walk through the darkened theatre, the haze of the evening is starting to wear off and that fresh openness of sky above has vanished.

Everything seems so very solid and dark in here.

'This is us,' Adam says, pointing to the middle of a row, in the middle of the theatre.

My heart quickens.

What am I doing here with this guy?

Did I just think I could pretend all of this was normal? That I could go on a date and pretend I was someone else entirely?

This isn't my life to mess with.

Adam has walked along the row to the seats now, and glances back at me.

He smiles. 'You coming?'

I can't think what else to do but nod; follow Adam along the row to the seat beside him.

I sit in the hard chair as people continue to stream into the theatre around us, and the murmur of voices grows steadily louder. It's filling up fast and Adam seems delighted; he's looking around at the stage, at the people coming in the door. If I didn't feel so panicked right now, I would find it sweet how excited he gets about small things.

But my whole body is riddled with anxiety now.

I can't breathe.

Instinctively, I touch my chest, the place where my scar usually lies, and it's as though I can still feel that same limited heart there, under the skin somewhere.

People are all around us now and music blares from speakers at all points of the venue, smashing through my skull, firing through my body. A vaguely familiar guy from the TV walks on to the stage and now everyone is applauding, whooping. Adam is clapping beside me, clearly very relaxed, but all I can do is sit rigidly against the seat, hands gripping the warm plastic arms.

I feel his hand on the back of mine now. He leans towards me. 'Emily,' he says, concern in his voice, 'are you OK?'

I'm struggling to breathe, a feeling I know only too well. Except this time it's got nothing to do with any medical condition.

'I need to get out of here,' I mutter.

'What did you say?' he asks above the noise.

The man on the stage is talking now – something about a house party he went to, an incident with whisky and a washing machine.

Barks of laughter all around me.

I need to get out of here.

And then I'm up on my feet, squeezing along the row to tuts and sighs. 'Sorry,' I'm saying, 'sorry, sorry.' I don't look behind me, just keep going until I'm at the end of the row, and then I'm running up to the back of the venue. I faintly hear the name 'Emily' being called behind me, but all I can think is, *I can't do this.*

Out in the beer garden again, I walk swiftly towards the exit, past the wooden table and red umbrella we were sitting laughing at only a short time before, past Sven's pizza truck, which is still in full swing. I eventually turn and look behind me, towards the venue I came out of. Adam's not there, of course, and he'll probably never want to see me again. But maybe that's the way it's supposed to be.

All this could be gone tomorrow.

I start walking away along the cobbles, under the now star-speckled navy sky, and head back home. Alone, as always.

* * *

I can't exactly recall what I felt about relationships before Cat died, but I like to think I was optimistic. I didn't think too much about how, or when; only that if Cat could find love, I probably could too – even with my condition.

And after? After I'd lost the other half of myself the way I had – after I'd caused that level of pain for everyone, well, it all changed after that. I started to worry about everything and nothing, what happened when I left the house, what happened if I walked too quickly, or strayed too far from home. Because the one thing I knew was that me taking risks could end in disaster for everyone. And I'd caused quite enough grief already. I tried to pretend that everything was fine – after all, my parents' lives were falling apart as well; Jess's too. But like with everything else, I kept all those worries pressed right down, hidden where no one could see them.

Aside from stolen kisses at the odd high school party before Cat died, my first relationship was a few years into working at the tour operator because my place at art school was one of the first things to go after Cat: the job was based in Edinburgh, and it just seemed like a more realistic thing to do in the circumstances. My health was better, and for that short moment at least, I could breathe; take a stab at a normal life. His name was Theo, and he was sweet and funny, and easy to hang out with. He didn't seem overly bothered by my health issues, but then I'm not entirely sure we spent enough time together for him to be properly bothered about anything. We had the kind of relationship where you only see each other for a couple of evenings a week, hanging out at his flat, of course, because I was still living at home.

I think I liked how easy it was; that I didn't have to worry too much about whether he really loved me or not, because the truth I realised about four months in was that I didn't really love him either. And maybe it was wrong of me, taking up his time like that. But I'm pretty sure it suited him well at the time too.

We started to bicker eventually, that novelty of easy sex and companionship wearing off, until one day I asked him if he saw us going anywhere.

He said no, and I was relieved.

It only lasted for about six months in the end, until we sort of mutually faded out on each other, like a star that had never really gotten up in the sky to begin with. And then he moved on from the tour operator, to have more adventures himself, as most of the other people in there tended to do. I got out unscathed, undamaged, and that suited me fine.

There was nothing for a few years after that. I had a string of heart issues again, and when I wasn't in the hospital, I was working or hanging out at home.

The years came and went, and I would see all the photos online of people I knew leaving to study or work in other countries or go trekking in far off places, sunbursts of colour all around them. And I would cry quietly into my pillow at the unfairness of it all. Did they know how good they had it?

Eventually, I met Nick. At work too, of course, given I never really went anywhere else. If the feelings with Theo were lukewarm, then the ones with Nick were everything I had imagined love would actually be like. He was kind and funny and loved travelling and high-adrenalin sports, and he wanted to do more; experience as much of the world as he could. And I would wish him luck before he did a marathon or before he'd go climb some Munros, and I'd sit in the Nepalese or Japanese or Greek restaurants and watch as he tried everything they had to offer, while I'd stick to my usual plain meals. I'd grin happily as he'd tell me about all the places he wanted to see, and the experiences he wanted to have – scuba diving and swimming with the sharks in

Australia, climbing Table Mountain in South Africa and trekking unaided across Antarctica. I loved him, and I think he might have loved me too – for a moment, at least. Not that we ever actually got to the point of saying it.

We did dreamily talk, though, about going away together after six months, something that I'd never even considered with Theo, but with Nick it felt possible. I guess I rushed in, hoping for the best, still clinging to that more optimistic version of me before Cat died, while also pushing down every fear that threatened to overwhelm me – that I might not be able to do what he wanted.

That I shouldn't cause any more stress for my family.

It was maybe eight months into the relationship when I found it – an article on his laptop about whether people with my condition could travel to remote places or do any high-risk activities.

Not recommended was the result I already knew it would show.

I didn't ask him about it in the end; couldn't face hearing it out loud. But I'd seen his strained expressions sometimes when he thought I wasn't looking, that pain I was causing him, just by being me. He was with someone who could die any day, after all – just disappear off the face of the planet. And the honest truth was, I was worried that he would up and leave one day, when it all got too hard. So eventually, I was the one who suggested we call it off – for both our sakes – and I figured if he really loved me, he'd stay. But even though he seemed hurt at first, he didn't fight it.

The next day, I packed up my stuff as he watched sadly from the door. We said our goodbyes, promised to stay in touch, and that was it. I moved back home, and he went away travelling.

As it happened, a couple of months later I contracted a virus, which compromised my condition in a way we'd not seen before. And if I'm honest with myself, I was relieved I wasn't with Nick then. At least he wouldn't have to pretend to be OK with it all.

That's when I knew that that part of my life was over.

And I would never risk my heart again.

CHAPTER ELEVEN

With each sunrise, I try to get to grips with this new reality, but it still feels so strange, being in this other body. My heart rate keeps anxiously flying up, to the point that I've actually wondered if Emily has a condition too – I've spent so many years being careful all the time, I'm not entirely sure I know how to do anything else. Plus, I still get this feeling that Emily hasn't totally gone – as though at any moment, she'll come back, and pick up where I left off. And until then, I want to make sure I keep everything going as it should be. Don't cause any problems.

I take the disposable camera to a kiosk along the street, telling myself that it's a necessary invasion of privacy in order to figure out what's actually going on. But my lack of funds means I won't be able to pay for them on collection, and I finally realise that I might have to think a little longer term. So, I go to the bank with paperwork to figure out what's actually available. I need to know how I'm going to look after

Emily's life while I'm here; how I'm even going to pay her rent. I'm pretty amazed to see what's in the account too – Emily has clearly been saving up for a while. It's nothing mind-boggling, but certainly enough to last her a good year without working and, given what I know about her quitting her London job, I have to assume that that was her plan all along.

A cat starts showing up, and I'm glad to have some sort of company again, at least. He's got no collar or tag, and I can't help wondering if Emily named him something. But, for now, I call him Ferris, something I think Cat would once have found amusing.

I don't run into Adam again, and he doesn't come to see me. I hear him coming and going though, the soft click of his door, his footsteps on the stone steps, but he leaves me be, understandably. I just can't decide if I'm glad or not. I feel bad for how it went, but there's not much I can do about it, I suppose. I could disappear any day, after all, and so could he. Just like at home – because as soon as they find out the prognosis for people like me, I see the shadow passing over their face; hear the death knell of the relationship.

So, it's easier this way, not putting either of us through the pain of it.

Not getting involved at all.

I take a few random pictures around the city like Emily did, start finding myself homing in on specific angles and objects, just like I would do with my drawings. And it feels good trying something completely different for a change.

Something new.

I find myself walking by my home most days also, uncertain what I'm doing exactly, but just keen to be close to the familiar. Occasionally I'll catch sight of Mum in the garden or Dad coming back from work, and there's something soothing about those routines and patterns.

But sometimes I'll see myself at a window or heading out for a walk and I'll walk away very quickly – it just feels too painful, witnessing myself getting increasingly more sick, knowing how bad it gets. I call Jess twice more to hear her voice, much to her obvious chagrin. *Graham, it's those prank callers again!* she cried, in a way that made me want to laugh and cry at the same time. God, I miss her a ridiculous amount. Luckily, it doesn't take me long to figure out how I can still see her because her life was full of small routines and outings at this point; ways to get her through each week with two high-energy toddlers in tow. So, on Wednesday, I walk to their favourite playpark on the Meadows. I don't go up to them; don't know what I'd say to them given they'd view me as a complete stranger. But just seeing them there together makes me feel better, and perhaps right now that has to be enough.

I struggle to sleep at night, rising at various points to much confusion, then, after about five days, I start to feel this physical itch in my body, an energy thrumming through my limbs. By the time it gets to the Thursday morning, I know I have to do something about it. I rummage through the bedroom drawers until I find expensive-looking sports leggings and a running top. It feels odd initially with all the nylon against my skin, but pretty quickly, it settles. Sticking on the bright-blue running trainers at the door, which fit like a glove, I can't help smiling into the mirror. I look like any other runner, going out for a normal morning jog in the sun.

The air outside is slightly cooler than the rest of the week, the sky bustling with soft white clouds. I start with a brisk walk first, until my heart beats faster, getting excited almost – like a muscle flexing instinctively. When I hit the Meadows again, other joggers are already out doing laps. One passes me, and the woosh of air tickles my skin. As though mirroring the woman, I suddenly find my legs going into a bound, and then my arms are going too, and then I'm running. I smell the sweetness of the grass, the trees all around me, and almost instantly I'm flooded with the greatest physical relief. That itch, which was building in me for days – those random heart elevations I was worried about – all start to dissipate, and in a rush of unexpected joy, I find myself running even faster, speeding past the first woman I'd begun to follow at the start. I turn down the path, utterly amazed by the power in this body.

This absolute feeling of freedom.

I lap the Meadows four times, before that itch inside me finally begins to fade, and as a new sense of peace enters my body, I begin to jog back in the direction of the flat.

Just as I'm sticking the key into the door, I feel a drop of water on my skin. Then another. Then suddenly what feels like a waterfall is coming down all around me, soothing my hot skin, my dry mouth. I stop where I am on the pavement, the thick scent of rain hitting concrete all around me. I close my eyes, tilt my head up to the sky, and I don't move a muscle, as I just let myself get steadily wetter – not caring at all if it makes me cold or sick or any of the things Mum would have shouted at me about before.

When I finally open my eyes again, I look up at the top window to see Adam standing there looking right back down at me, a curious smile playing on his lips. Blood rushes to my face, and I duck inside the building, before jogging up the stairs two at a time to the top.

How long was he watching me for?

I stare at his door, heart still pounding, but I'm not definite on why this time. As I head back into the flat, I have the most amazing feeling running through me, like the world is brighter and lighter and I'm capable of anything.

Almost skipping through to the bathroom now, I strip off the wet clothes, discarding them in a puddle on the floor. Summer rain beats against the thin glass window, and as I step into the hot shower, I allow myself to actually look down properly, to take in this body which is giving me the strength to run like that. I linger in the water a while, enjoying the feel of being cleansed all the way through. As the whole of me warms up, I let myself feel one pure moment of peace.

With the towel wrapped around me, I pick out a pair of denim shorts and a berry-pink vest top. Surveying myself in the long mirror, I trace my hand across the exposed skin on my chest, down the sleek lines the clothes create. Next, I brush all the knots out of my hair, until it's smooth yet wavy, like I suspect Emily usually has it. I have no make-up on, no creams or potions on this skin at all, but the way it's glowing from that run . . . it's amazing to see.

I'm about to make a cup of tea when I find myself pausing, then walking towards the front door instead. I open it and cross the landing. My heart is thumping in my chest, but I can't just keep ignoring Adam, given he lives right opposite me. And anyway, maybe I should apologise for how I left like that the other night, and if he never wants to speak to me again, well, that's OK too.

I'm reaching up to knock, when the door swings open and Adam appears on the other side with his backpack on, like he's going somewhere.

'Oh, hello again,' he says, his expression a mixture of surprise, and something possibly bordering on pleasure.

'Hello,' I say, trying to hold my breath steady.

A silence passes between us as he looks at me expectantly.

'I just wanted to say,' I start finally, 'that I'm really sorry about the other night, leaving the show like I did. It wasn't cool of me, but I think I got a bit panicked. I'm just . . . dealing with a lot right now.'

For a moment, I think he might shut the door in my face but then he gives me that easy lopsided smile again and my stomach somersaults.

'Apology accepted,' he says, 'and in fairness to you, you did say you were still working some stuff out. So, take all the time you need, Emily, and if you do ever need to talk to anyone, then I'm right here. Literally,' he says, thumbing back behind him into the warm-looking flat.

'Thank you,' I say, relieved, then add, 'for not thinking I'm a total arse.'

He looks at me softly. 'That's the last thing I think, Emily. I just like getting to know you is all. I'd like to get to know you more, even if it's as friends.'

'Friends,' I repeat after a moment. 'I think that could work.'

'Well, that's great to hear,' he says, a genuine smile on his face. 'Oh, I got this out of my cupboard for you, in case we happened to run into each other again.'

Pulling something orange from his pocket, he passes it to me, our fingers grazing as he does. It's a headband of some sort. 'I saw you running out there in the rain,' he says, 'and I have this, which I've never worn, so I thought maybe you could use it on your next run. Or if you ever need to bolt out of a show again . . .'

I let out a laugh, even as I raise my eyebrows in mock annoyance.

'I'm not sure whether to say thank you,' I say, 'or throw it back at you.'

He grins, those green eyes dancing. 'It's good to see you smiling again.'

A pause.

'Well, I'd better get off to the workshop,' he says. 'I'll see you around, Emily.'

Locking the door behind him, he heads down the stairs, and I can feel something rising up in me; words burbling at the surface. I walk across to the banister.

'Adam,' I call over the top, and he looks up sharply from the landing below.

I take a breath in. 'I don't suppose you fancy a walk with me later?'

He doesn't answer for a moment and my breath catches. Maybe he didn't really mean any of that.

Maybe it was all just hot air?

But then he smiles up at me. 'Yeah,' he says, 'I think that might work. Early evening OK?'

'Early evening is great.'

He grins and a moment later he's gone, leaving me standing on the landing with a tingling down my back and a feeling that perhaps I don't want to leave this life quite yet.

* * *

Later that afternoon, I head into the little express shop where I left the disposable camera. I'm curious about what might be on it and why it hasn't been developed yet. With Emily's one luxury item being a camera in the flat, I just don't quite understand why she would have a disposable. Still, it's the only stone left unturned as far as I can see.

Once I've paid for the photos, I walk quickly out the door and open the packet on the street outside. Taking out the first one, sunlight bounces off the filmy material, but I still see him – a sandy-haired man. He's handsome in that kind of chiselled jawline, film-star way, and he's smiling at the camera from across the table in some hot-looking piazza. The next one is a selfie of him and Emily kissing somewhere, her hair tangled into his jacket, his hand holding her cheek, and all of the ones after are similar, just photo after photo of him, or her, or the two of them together, clearly besotted.

Looking at the last one of them in an elevator, the strangest feeling runs through me.

Have I met him before?

I'm still staring down at the photo when I hear a ringing sound. I look around at the other pedestrians, initially thinking it must be one of them, before realising the sound is actually coming from me.

The phone.

Pulling it out of my handbag hurriedly, I look down at the name flashing across the front with panic.

Fran.

For a moment, I think about not picking up – after all, if Emily and Fran are cousins, then she'll know it isn't her Emily she's speaking to. It was different with Adam, because Emily had only recently moved in, but this is someone she's clearly close to.

No, I can't talk to her.

But then again, I don't want to cause Emily any friendship grief either and I can't just deliberately ignore all the people in her life while I'm here, cause even worse problems. I need to play along for the time being.

'Hello?' I say, picking up finally.

'Jesus Christ,' I hear a voice say. 'You are alive then.'

I can't help smiling. It's the sort of direct thing Jess might say.

'Hi Fran,' I try.

'Hi Fran?' she says. 'That's all I get? After a lifetime of friendship, then you move to Bonnie fucking Scotland and go radio silent. I know you said you wanted a bit of time to get settled, E, but still.'

Even though I don't know this girl, I can still hear the trace of hurt under the jokey words.

And a touch of panic too? Her and Emily must be very close.

'I'm sorry,' I start to say, 'it's just all been quite . . . strange, coming somewhere new.'

'So, tell me all about it then?'

I try to think what I should say, what would be normal for Emily, but before I can answer she says, 'Oh, and in case you're wondering, the wedding admin is going quite well, thank you.'

'Oh, yes . . . the wedding,' I say, feeling myself almost light up that I know something about Fran already. I can work with this. I think of all the prep I did for Jess and Graham's big day a few years back; she was already pregnant at the time, so I pretty much took most of it over for her and, in a way, it was nice – bonding like that after Cat.

'How are you coping with it all then?' I say to Fran now.

'Pretty good after you gave us that checklist of yours. It's only the seating chart we've got left to do. Speaking of which . . .' Fran continues, 'have you spoken to Simon?'

Simon. The man in the photos.

I don't know how I know that exactly but I just do, like a memory floating back to me. Despite this odd feeling, it dawns on me that Fran might actually have a lot of the answers I'm looking for.

'Not yet,' I say slowly, and at least that much is true. 'Have you?' I ask cautiously.

'No,' she says, 'although I can't say I really *want* to see him, after what he did.'

I pause, as those feelings come to me again, but stronger this time.

'He was cheating on me . . . when we were engaged,' I say slowly.

'Well, you don't *strictly* know that,' Fran says, 'it was a receipt for a dinner.'

'For two,' I whisper.

'I know . . .' she says slowly, 'it doesn't look great.'

Oh god.

So that's why Emily moved up here.

It's all starting to make sense suddenly – the big changes, the expensive stuff around the more humble flat, the man I seem to recognise from the photos. And looking down at it now, I see what I didn't before – a pale line running around my wedding finger.

But how the hell did I know they were engaged? How did I know he was cheating?

And who with anyway?

As though reading my mind, Fran says tentatively, 'Did you ever find out who it was? The person he met that night? I can't believe he left the receipt out like that.'

I find myself shaking my head, and in that moment, I know that also to be true.

'No, I didn't.'

'You sure you're OK?' Fran says, worry etched in her voice now. 'I could come up to see you if you like?'

'That's OK,' I say eventually. 'Maybe in a bit, I'm still getting used to everything I guess.'

A pause.

'All right,' Fran says. 'You just let me know when.'

I'm about to say goodbye when I hear her take a breath in.

'I really do miss you, E,' she says, and I stop. She sounds upset.

'I miss you too,' I find myself saying, more because it would be really harsh not to.

'But I suppose I get why you've made the move,' she continues, like she's trying to work it out, 'what with your work hours and the gym every morning and the grilled fish every night . . . though most people would have killed for your life with that rooftop apartment of yours. Not that you ever got to see it much. You were the same at university, looking back; work work work, remember? Then I guess it just didn't stop – we barely saw you in the last year.'

I'm wondering who she means by *we* exactly. And why did Emily come to Edinburgh, for that matter? When she could have gone anywhere?

'That doesn't mean I don't want you to come back,' Fran adds quickly. 'Just . . . what I'm trying to say, badly, is maybe you do need some time to chill. Process everything.'

'Well, thanks for clearing that up.' I smile.

'Anytime, E.'

'And if you need any more help planning your wedding,' I find myself adding, 'I'm only a phone call away. I have some experience.'

'I know,' she adds with a laugh, 'and I will hold you to that.'

We finally say our goodbyes and, putting the photos of Simon away in my handbag, I head back to the flat.

CHAPTER TWELVE

Later that evening, I wait for Adam on the street outside our building. He called me in the afternoon while I was buying a few things for dinner, told me he'd catch me after work around seven. He also told me to wear something warm on the top, which confused me – it turned into quite a warm day after I spoke to Fran, the air practically balmy. But I forced myself to find an internet café first so I could do a little digging on Fran and Emily, just so I know what I'm talking about next time. It turned out Fran's family was based in Kent while Emily was raised in London, but the wider family is all Italian and living in Rome. They went to the same elite school together, then Oxford, before ending up at the same company back in London. The best of friends as well as cousins it appears.

Once I'd ticked that off, I took a blanket from the cupboard to the Meadows and whiled away the rest of the afternoon simply soaking up the sunshine.

Now, as I stand on the pavement outside the building, I think about where we'll walk. Maybe around the area? Into town?

A white van drives along the road and I'm surprised when it pulls up right beside me. Adam grins out of the open window at me.

'Jump in.'

I frown. 'I thought we were going on a walk.'

'We are,' he says, arching one eyebrow at me and I shake my head lightly in amusement.

As I walk around to the passenger seat, I think about how he keeps surprising me and yet I have this remarkably safe feeling around him at the same time.

The van smells of wood and old leather seats, and him. He's wearing a scraggly charcoal sweater, the sleeves rolled up to his elbows, revealing those strong forearms and that tattoo again. Something twinges in my stomach, and I turn sharply to put my seatbelt on.

We're just friends.

For a moment though, I wonder about Emily. Did she speak to Adam too? Or would she have been out that Friday night he came by?

'So, where are we headed?' I say, as he pulls out on to the road.

'Out of the city I thought,' he says, looking ahead at the road, 'The Pentlands.'

'Sounds good, though I haven't been up a hill in years.'

He glances across at me. 'How is that possible?'

I think about all the things I stopped doing, all the places I ruled out across my life; too many to count really.

'Well, my parents weren't really "hill walking" people,' I say finally.

He just laughs. 'OK, well, I'm glad we're doing this then.'

We breeze up through Bruntsfield, through Morningside, the sky a burnished coral above us. The streetlamps are starting to come on below, like tiny suns trying to keep the day going. People are still wandering around, dipping in and out of bars and restaurants, laughing, talking, calling to each other.

'Hey, I noticed you don't have a car,' he says, 'so feel free to use this if you need it.'

I pause, and he glances at me again.

'What is it?' he says.

'Oh, just that I don't drive.'

'How come?'

I don't say anything immediately. How can I explain that I never drove – despite the doctors saying it was fine. Because what if I had a heart attack at the wheel? Or blacked out? Or hurt someone else.

'I suppose there probably wasn't much need to in London with the underground,' Adam says absently, 'but if you ever want me to teach you then just say the word, though of course I'm always happy to take you anywhere you want to go.'

The enthusiasm behind his words makes me smile, even though I think it's unlikely I'll try. Any time I've got behind the wheel I've frozen up and got straight back out again.

'Do you miss your old life?' he asks now. I know he's speaking about London, but the words still ring inside me somewhere.

My old life.

'Sometimes,' I say, thinking of the wanders outside my parents' house, the calls I make to Jess, this feeling of being completely cut off from the people I love.

They're all I've ever known.

'Must be hard,' Adam says, 'leaving everything you know like that . . .'

I pause at his words.

'It's not all bad.' I recall the run this morning, that energy coursing through me. 'And I certainly don't miss working around the clock at a desk.'

He grins. 'Too right, and for what it's worth, I think you're doing really well. Just give it a bit of time, and soon you'll feel like this life is all completely normal. Change is only jarring right before you do it.'

I let the thought settle as I stare out the window, and I wonder if this is how Emily felt at this stage – a little bit wobbly, a little bit good, just a few weeks after a big move. Alone and far from everything she'd ever known.

Adam sticks the radio on, and a Vance Joy song trickles out into the van around us, soothing my anxious thoughts.

We eventually settle back in a comfortable silence as we cruise out of the city, and after about ten minutes, the rolling hills of the Pentlands rise up ahead of us. The sky is lit up like a fire tonight, all reds and pinks threaded through each other like joint hands in the vastness above. Eventually Adam turns off down a track, towards a gravelly car park with tall trees at the end.

We're not the only people here for a walk; couples and families and lone walkers all seem to be milling around, and there's something lovely about that, knowing that other people had the same urge to seize this beautiful evening.

Adam turns to me as we jump out. 'I'll grab you a sweater from the car before we go. The weather can get pretty hairy at the top.'

I smile but really I'm nervous, uncertain what he means by *hairy*.

After I've pulled on the soft green sweater, we head on to the same dirt pathway as another few people, which cuts into the grass and stretches off into the rising hills. It smells of summer grass and bonfire smoke, and I think of how autumn is actually just around the corner.

What if I'm still stuck here?

'Penny for your ponies,' Adam says, and I turn, confused.

'Sorry, it's something Lilly says to me sometimes.'

'Who's Lilly?'

'My mum.'

'You call your mum Lilly?'

'Well, that's her name.' He raises one eyebrow, then grins. 'Don't worry, I know it's a bit weird, but my mum's always been a bit like that.'

I can't help noticing the slight stiffness in his jaw as he says it.

'She's probably what you would call a hippy,' he goes on after a moment, 'but I tend to think of her more as a woman with alternative views.'

'What do you mean?' I ask carefully.

He shrugs. 'Well, I was raised pretty much everywhere and anywhere. I was born in Canada, but Mum had a bucket list, you see, and she didn't really think that having a child should get in the way of it,' his jaw stiffening again, 'so, in between getting dumped at my grandparents' cabin from time to time, I had my third birthday in Nepal, my fifth in Papa New Guinea, my eighth in Kenya . . . I could go on.'

'It sounds amazing,' I say, thinking of how much I would have loved to have had those experiences and seen those places too.

'Amazing in some ways, yes,' Adam says with a half-smile, 'but a little disruptive for a child too. She had some mental health problems, you see, and never really addressed it, so I never quite knew if I was going to get happy Lilly, who would take me places, or the Lilly who would leave me. But it was fun too, I guess, getting to see the world like that. There were no rules, really. She even let me start this tattoo when I was fourteen.' He laughs, indicating at his arm.

'Yes, I was wondering,' I say, glad to look more closely now, and he pulls his sweater sleeve up a bit higher. 'It's really different.'

'Well, it's basically a big old mess of some places I've been, and stuff I've done.' He points to his forearm. 'That little river right there's from this beautiful little spot I was in in Venezuela, and that spiky tree twisted into it is from when I was in New Zealand, that horse was from when I was fifteen and went bareback riding in Belize. There is zero design to it, as you can see,' he says with a laugh. 'Just stuff I've enjoyed, or things that have stuck with me.'

'And what about this one?' I say, touching the badly drawn moose above his elbow. He flinches slightly.

'That,' he says, his eyes twinkling at me, 'was one of the mistakes. A drunken decision when I was eighteen and I was missing Canada.'

'It sort of looks like a small child drew it,' I say, looking at the mismatched antlers and large saucer eyes. I can't help laughing.

He examines it afresh and starts laughing too.

'Yeah, OK, it really does,' he says eventually, wiping a tear from his eye, 'but I promise my furniture is better than my animal drawings.'

I smile. 'I believe you.'

He grins back at me, and finally pulls down his sleeve.

'And what about school?' I ask after a moment, curious how it all worked.

'There were lots,' he says. 'But we'd stay on in a place a little longer sometimes, enough to keep my grandparents from flying out to get me anyway. And I'd usually make some friends, only to be dragged away again. I've kept in touch with a few around the globe though.'

I try to imagine it all, that level of uncertainty – that level of freedom too. It's all just so very different from my own cosseted life with Mum. She would *never* have let me ride horses bareback in Belize and miss school, and she certainly wouldn't leave me. I feel guilty to admit that I sort of wish she would have. Just sometimes.

'And do you still see your grandparents then?'

Adam pauses, looks straight ahead. 'No, they died a few years back now.'

'I'm sorry,' I say softly. 'What about your dad?' I query before I can help myself, because he just seems very alone in the world suddenly, and it makes me sad to think of.

'My dad has never been in the picture,' Adam says steadily as he walks on in his well-trodden boots. 'All I know is that he took off before I was even born. Lilly has always been a bit unlucky in love. There was always some guy who would hang around with us for a bit, then disappear again.'

I can't help thinking it's not the most stable situation for a child, but then he did get to see all those places and do all those things that I didn't.

'And where is she now?' I ask. 'Your mum, I mean?'

Adam looks up to the sky, as though considering it. 'Fiji, I think. I don't hear from her all that much, but when she does call, it's usually at some god-awful time for me,' he says with a half laugh. 'Occasionally I've managed to run into her on my own travels but the world is a big place. We've met up the odd time back at my grandparents' cabin, but it's probably more me that uses it when I'm passing through.'

I pause. 'So . . .'

'So why am I in Edinburgh now?'

'Yeah.'

He pauses. 'I went off the rails a bit, when I was nineteen or so. My grandparents both died within months of each other around then, which for some teenagers wouldn't be a big thing, I guess, but for me, well, it was hard. Suddenly I had no stable people in my life, no job, no . . .' He glances at me.

'I'm sorry,' I say softly.

He shakes his head. 'Don't be, it was a long time ago.'

'But it must have been difficult,' I say, 'coping with that at such a young age.'

He smiles, the setting sun throwing gold across his ridiculously handsome face, but there's a dark shadow there too, and his expression falters slightly.

'Truthfully, I didn't really cope with it at all,' he says. 'I sort of shut down, pushed everyone away – Mum, friends. I drank too much . . . did everything too much. I was a real dick, quite honestly.'

Now I understand what that pause was in the beer garden that night, when he spoke about the time before he met Sven.

'I think losing someone important to you can do strange things like that,' I say as we walk, and he looks at me almost hopefully. 'Perhaps some people get a bit scared . . . and others get angry at the world, for taking it all away.'

He nods quietly at that, some relief on his face, and I realise that perhaps he's not quite as done with it all as he thinks.

'And you seem to be doing pretty well now,' I say, nudging him lightly.

He nudges me back. 'I guess it did make me open my eyes to everything, made me think about what I actually wanted from life after they passed. I'd always lived in this really chaotic way, like Mum did.'

'And that wasn't what you wanted?'

'Well, I wanted to keep seeing the world, of course,' he says, 'but I also realised I needed an actual job – a way to make money, or at least enough of it to allow me to travel. My grandfather was a carpenter, so it made sense to do something with furniture. I knew Sven was enjoying Edinburgh so I thought – why not set up camp here? I had a British passport through my grandmother, so I decided to do a course in Scotland, keep travelling from there.'

I find myself hesitating. 'Have you got another trip lined up soon?'

'Well,' he says, 'I usually plan something last minute, see where the wind takes me.'

I can't help it but my stomach sort of sinks at the idea of him just taking off like that, like Nick did. Maybe it's a good thing nothing happened between us after all. As well as the fact this isn't even my life, I remind myself.

'But enough about me,' he says, 'I'd much rather hear about you.'

My stomach skips. I know he's not prying for answers but after how open he's been with me, I find I want to share something with him too.

'The thing I was thinking about earlier,' I say, 'was that I was worried about me coming here in the first place; whether it's the right thing. I might be needed at home.'

We round in the grass now, and the incline really begins.

Oh god, my heart, I can't help thinking, even though it's a ridiculous thought and clearly doesn't apply in Emily's body. But I'm starting to see that some habits are hard to change when you've been a certain way for so long.

'I just think you've come here for a reason, Emily,' Adam says eventually, 'and you owe it to yourself to make the most of it, surely?'

We catch each other's eyes and start smiling.

'Shit,' Adam says, 'that chat got intense pretty quickly, didn't it?'

I laugh. 'Just a bit.'

But I let what he's said roll quietly around my mind. Because for the first time in a long while, I've actually got a healthy body and money in the bank, and I don't have to worry about being careful or think about how I might affect everyone around me.

Not like before.

We're walking up the hill now, becoming more out of breath by the second, but in that good way again; little bolts of electricity are shooting through my body and my legs work harder. Wind whips past me suddenly, almost knocking me over with its force, and I take a moment to right myself. Then suddenly we're there, at the highest point. I stop and look out all around us, at the soft sloping greens and browns and the steadily reddening sky, and I can't help thinking how stunning it is from this angle. I'm so used to looking up at everything.

I feel this healthy new heart pumping inside this strong body, and an unexpected wave of something close to joy comes over me.

A second later, and another huge gust of wind hurtles at us, pushing me into Adam. We both start laughing as it howls in our ears and gallops across our faces. It blows so hard, I can barely take a breath, but this time, it doesn't feel scary.

It feels sort of good.

The wind drops again and the two of us grin at each other, our faces so close I can see the amber around his irises, feel the energy that comes from just being near him.

'Well, that was quite something, wasn't it?' he says, still holding on to me.

My skin is tingling from his touch, even through the woolly sweater.

We stand there for a moment, his eyes trained on mine, my stomach flipping like crazy.

'We should get back,' he murmurs after a moment, letting his hands drop.

My hands spark where he touched them. 'OK.'

He smiles at me and, together, we head back down the hill. The light fades on the horizon, turning the world shades of never-ending gold, chilling the balmy air.

But all I feel right now is warm, from the inside out.

CHAPTER THIRTEEN

I start running every morning after that, and as the trees turn a chestnut brown, I get into something close to a stride. I jog all the way back up to the Pentlands where Adam took me before, down beneath the city and along the wooded foot paths. I head back to the Botanics and stare out across that panoramic expanse of the city, from the jagged Old Town all the way to Arthur's Seat, and as October winds whip around me, I feel the softness of the orange headband on my skin. I stop walking by my parents' house because it all gets too much, watching myself decline. And not just that, I have no idea when I'll ever get back to my old life. So to try and be close to my family like I am is only going to end up freaking them out; no good can come from hovering near my actual home. But every Wednesday I make sure to run past Jess and the boys in the park, and although it's something, I can't help thinking about my parents too – Mum in particular. After all, I've never been far from her in my whole life. But I feel confused, because as much as I miss her, there's a strange sort of freedom to not being around her – all of them – which I'm recognising now.

Because my condition didn't only affect me, it affected everyone I loved too: Cat who was hampered by what I could and couldn't do until she left home, my dad who had to stay as a professor in Edinburgh instead of going abroad like I know he wanted to, my mum who had to stop being a flutist in an orchestra to care for me. And then there was Jess, my baby sister, whose birthdays were overshadowed by hospital stints and cancelled holidays and school dances forgotten.

And then after it happened, after we lost Cat so shockingly, well, there was nothing which could compel me to make the situation even worse for everybody.

I'd done enough already.

I start hanging out with Adam more and more, just as friends, of course. Sometimes we go to the Purple Pineapple for coffee and a carrot cake the size of our heads when he's back from the workshop, and sometimes we just while away a couple of hours talking about rubbish. He introduces me to a few of the eateries in the area too – Greek, Turkish and Italian, food from countries he's actually been to but I never have. The places are entirely new to me and yet, occasionally, I find myself recognising a waitress or the order of things on the menu. I think of that box of leftover ramen the first day, the way Fran said Emily ate nothing but grilled fish in a place like London.

Did Emily come to these places too?

In any event, I'm trying more and more new foods, and getting a little more adventurous each time. I even start to have the odd glass of wine with my meals, something I'd never have dared to do before, but I find that in small amounts, it really does relax me.

Turns out Adam and I have the same penchant for old John Hughes films and we quickly form a little routine of nipping across the hall to each other's and watching one on his laptop with a bowl of popcorn between us. I haven't felt so comfortable with anyone in a long time, where we can just sit in silence together or chat about nothing for three hours in a row. Of course, I had a couple of close friends from school and at the travel agency, but as with every relationship after Cat, they became harder and harder to maintain as I got sicker, until eventually they disappeared.

I speak to Fran over the phone from time to time too, and I can't help laughing at her directness, the way she simply says, 'Well, have you snogged him yet?'

So very like Jess.

I sometimes wonder why Emily's parents never call me – as much as I would be terrified to answer – and not for the first time, I question whether they're even still alive. Otherwise, why would they not be in touch?

But it's just not something I think I should delve into. It's not something I *want* to delve into, because quite honestly, I'm starting to enjoy myself.

I did get a text from an unknown number the other day though, and my heart started to pound oddly as I opened up the message.

But it just said three words:

I miss you xx

I couldn't say for certain who it was, of course, but if I had to guess then I'd say it was probably Simon. And I immediately felt nervous because from everything I saw in those photos of Emily and him, he definitely meant a lot to her, no matter what happened with that receipt. But I just had no idea what to say or what to do; he wasn't asking for any sort of response after all, and I knew Emily had made the decision to walk away from him, so, quite guiltily, I left it.

I'm still not sure if it's such a great idea though, hanging out with Adam like I am. I can't deny I'm attracted to him, those amazing eyes, those strong shoulders, oh god, he sets my heart racing when I see him. But it's not just about how he looks, it's the rest of him too – how he's always up for trying new things, how he got me a second helping of that cannelloni I went crazy about in the Italian along the road, how we always fall about laughing on what has quickly become our regular hill walks (he's tried to get me up an actual Munro, though I'm not sure I'm ready for that yet).

But just the idea of it going further gives me absolute panic too. How could I deceive him like that? It's one thing living Emily's life while I have no choice, but starting something up with someone? What if I suddenly go back to my old life and Emily comes back to this one and everyone is left utterly confused? No, it's not fair to anyone. Anyway, I get the impression he's not one to stick around for very long. And I'm just not willing to put myself through that sort of pain again.

I'm taking more photos though, and I'm quietly surprised by how much I'm enjoying something else – like a simple creative switch has got me looking at everything from a slightly different angle.

* * *

I'm coming back from a little afternoon photography session on the seafront about a week later, checking back on the photos I took – of the blue of the water under still-clear skies, of a solo paddleboarder floating out on the gentle waves – when I find myself going past the charity shop where Mum works sometimes. And thinking about it now, Tuesday is one of those days. My heart quickens and I pause outside the shop for a moment, uncertain what I'm doing exactly. Then I see her in the window, dressing one of the mannequins. I can't help smiling at the top she's put on it, in a burnt orange – her favourite colour – plus a cream scarf, which she's tying neatly in a bow. As though sensing something, she looks out at me and I freeze. But after a moment's hesitation, I head inside.

I've been here before, of course; helped Mum sort some of the stock out once or twice. There's something lovely and familiar about the slightly musty scent of second-hand books and clothes, bric-a-brac and random lampshades, and most importantly, my mother's light floral perfume. I'm still windswept from all that time on the beach and I'm aware I must look a little dishevelled, but Mum just smiles at me in that slightly stressed way she does, as she unpacks a box at the counter.

'Can I help you with anything?' she says distractedly. 'Or are you just here for a browse?'

'Oh, the latter,' I say and pretend to look around. My heart is pounding even as I'm sifting through clothes rails, and I can feel her glancing at me from time to time as my mind whirs with questions. Should I talk to her? What should I talk about? Can she sense I'm here at all? The real me.

Eventually my eyes light on a sea-blue colour, and I pluck a pretty blouse off the rail. I can't help wondering if this is what Emily started doing sometimes, away from London and her usual designer shops. Did she sell most of it? All the stuff in her wardrobe is a bit random, the labels slightly dated or unknown, and I've already found makeshift tags on a few items. So maybe this is something I could start doing too.

'That would look very pretty on you,' Mum says behind me and I snap around to see her standing there, all formal and business-like now. 'Would you like to try it on?'

I pause, uncertain. 'All right,' I say, and she takes it from me in that efficient way she has, hangs it up in the little cubicle at the back. Walking inside, I smile at her briefly, before pulling the curtain shut. Standing in front of the mirror, I let myself breathe out.

What the hell am I doing?

After a moment, I realise I have to actually try it on and finally change into the blue blouse. I have to admit I really like the colour. I turn to the side to admire it.

'Everything OK in there?' Mum says, and I look up. Walking out on to the shop floor a second later, Mum assesses me.

'Well,' she says, 'isn't that pretty on you? It really brings out your eyes.'

I realise Mum has more sales skills than I knew, though I know she's being genuine too – she may be blunt, but with that bluntness comes real truth.

'Do you like it?' she says.

'Yes, I do actually; I love the colour.'

'Me too,' she says a little more softly. 'Will you be taking it then?'

'Yes.' I nod. 'I think I will.'

'Great.' Mum smiles, walking smartly back around to the till. 'Feel free to wear it out of here. I always say that's the best sign, if you want to wear something immediately.'

'All right,' I say, happy to hear the familiar words. Picking up my sweater from the changing room floor, I put Emily's red coat straight back on over my new top and head over to the till – I've never owned a red coat before and I felt genuine excitement when it got cold enough to finally put it on.

'Any nice plans for the evening?' she says after I've paid.

'Not sure yet. I might grab an early dinner somewhere then just see what happens, I guess.'

She smiles, though it's sadder than before for some reason, and I wonder what I've said.

'Are you OK?' I find myself asking, and her eyes immediately brighten again. 'Oh yes, of course,' she waves me off quickly, 'nothing for you to worry about, go out there and enjoy yourself in your new top.'

'I will.' I still feel mildly confused by this whole exchange but say nothing as I head back over to the door.

'And drop in again soon,' Mum says. 'We get lots of lovely stock in regularly.'

'All right,' I say and my chest fills with warmth at the prospect of seeing her again, and without my heart – and everything it comes with – hanging over us too. As I open the door with a little tinkle from the bell, I look at her and say, 'See you soon.'

Mum.

* * *

Just like I said, I head off afterwards, not quite knowing where the night will take me. I feel this hum of happiness in my chest from seeing Mum; from simply engaging with her in that easy, normal way. For as long as I can remember, the dynamic between us has always been set in stone – she tells me what to do (or what not to do, rather) and I just go along with it for everyone's sake. There's so little play, so little fun, so little of us actually *enjoying* each other as equals, I'm realising now.

It felt good to speak to her on fresh terms.

I think about Mum's sad look as I go though, wondering what that was all about. She always kept such a front around me; always scarily organised and tough, unless we spoke about Cat, that is. I'm tempted to go and see her again soon to find out.

I walk all the way back to the flat, enjoying the cool evening air. The lights are coming up around the dusky city like fire-flies, and I find myself thinking about Adam again, wondering if he might be around when I get back, if I might get to see him this evening. Just daydreaming about him gives me butter-flies but I know it's a dangerous thing to feel. Something that can only end in upset. But as I arrive at the building, I see Adam already standing in front of it, smiling as I approach. He's in jeans, a white t-shirt and black puffer jacket. My stomach flips.

'I was just about to message you,' he says, and a ripple of warmth goes through me.

'I'm heading out to meet Charlie and Sven for drinks tonight,' he adds. 'You game?'

I think again of Mum in the shop; how different things felt with her, in a good way. And that perhaps in the strangest of twists, I've been given a second chance here.

Before I can overthink it, I say, 'I'm game.'

CHAPTER FOURTEEN

After dropping my camera back in the flat, we head to town.
The air has that crisp winter chill about it, which would usually
make me burrow down at home in the evening in my old life,
but out here with Adam, I'm energised by it.

While we walk, I ask about his work and he fills me in on
what he's upholstering at the moment, a whole suite of quirky
furniture for a wealthy client up in Aberdeen. He asks about
my day and I tell him about some of the pictures I took.

'You really have an eye for it,' he says. 'You're going to
walk on to that course.'

'Thanks,' I say, an anxious feeling coming over me.

I'd worked out what course Adam had meant that time at
the Fringe. I'd found an application form for a photography
degree, which made total sense with the camera, and I realised that this is what Emily had intended to do when she
came up here, and that I should probably be applying too,

if I don't want to mess stuff up for her in the time I'm here. But what if I don't get in? What if I ruin Emily's one shot?

If I'm being totally honest, I'm scared to apply for my sake too. What if I'm not good enough? I've spent so many years not taking any chances, not doing what I really wanted to do. What if it's all just too late?

'Well, I definitely think you should give it some thought,' Adam says, as though he's read my mind. 'There's never going to be a perfect time to try, and don't worry about whether you'll get in or not, because your photos are brilliant.'

A few moments later, and Adam comes to a stop in front of a strange-looking entrance. Across the door, I see the words Pharmacy written in gold lettering.

'Here we are,' Adam says.

I pause, confused.

'Here?'

'Yup,' he says, a smile playing on his lips. He opens the door, and I see a steep staircase going down behind it.

'It's a speakeasy,' he grins.

'Ah,' I say, as it finally makes sense, 'and here was me thinking bars were legal these days.'

He laughs, starts to walk down, and I follow. Glancing back, he says, 'You must have been to one of these in London, surely, when you were there?'

I shake my head lightly. 'I didn't really manage to get out all that much.'

'Well, you'll like this place,' he says. 'There's just something about a bar pretending to be a pharmacy that I kind of love. You wouldn't know the fun until you peel back the top layer.'

I smile, thinking I sort of feel the same way.

The inside is pretty plush in comparison to the rather sterile walk down – all dark floorboards and leather backs, red velvet seats and a bar filled with bottles of all shapes and sizes.

As soon as we walk in, one long arm shoots up in the corner, and we head towards Sven and who I assume is Charlie. She'd be pretty hard to miss anyway – with her head of blonde curls, scarlet-red lipstick and a retro polka dot dress. She looks more like someone from the fifties than this era. She beams widely and stands as we approach, but then something else passes over her face. Some trace of surprise and something which definitely looks like recognition.

Shit.

'Emily, isn't it?' She smiles, and pulls me into a hug.

My mind goes crazy as she holds me – how does she know Emily? And how much does she know about her? And then an image hits me: Charlie's smiling face in some sort of hall, her mouth talking as she passes me a yellow flyer – the one I found in the flat.

'I was so jealous when Sven said he'd met you already,' Charlie says, stepping back now, grinning, 'but turns out, I already have. I haven't seen you at my classes yet though, I don't think?'

'Oh, well, I've been really busy with some stuff,' I say, feeling a bit odd suddenly, dizzy, because it was like a memory

I've never had just came back to me. Just like with that photo of Simon and the receipt Fran mentioned.

'Hello again,' Sven says to me now, 'good to see you,' and he embraces me before clapping Adam on the back.

'Right, what can I get you guys to drink?' Adam says, rubbing his hands from the cold.

'I'll take a beer, thanks,' Sven says.

'The fizziest water you've got,' Charlie beams.

Adam touches my arm, and I blink up at him. 'Emily, you?'

'Um, I'll take a small red, please.'

'Great, I'll see if they've got any of that Malbec we enjoyed the other night,' he says and heads off.

As I sit down, I can feel Sven and Charlie both looking at me expectedly. I still feel confused about the strange memories and then renewed panic takes over as I remember Charlie knows at least something I don't know about Emily. I just need to figure out what.

'So,' Charlie says, 'this is certainly a very small world. Are you settling in OK? Did you ever find the Close you were looking for?'

I pause, my heart thumping. 'The Close?'

She smiles encouragingly but looks vaguely confused too. 'Yeah, the little alleyways on the Royal Mile? You said you were looking for one in particular. God, what was it called again?'

As she wracks her brain, I try to pull the conversation back to Charlie's first question. 'I'm settling in OK,' I say, 'and

I'm sorry I've not been to the classes yet . . . I've just had a lot on recently.'

'All good things, I hope?' Sven says.

'Oh, yes,' I reply, 'a bit of photography and running and stuff. I'll need to come back for one of your pizzas sometime.'

'Absolutely do.'

Charlie's eyes widen. 'Dunbar, that's it!'

'I'm sorry?' I say, my heart thumping.

'Dunbar.' She grins, and claps her hands together. 'That was the name of the Close you were looking for. God, that was killing me.'

'Oh yes, right,' I play along. 'So it was.'

Charlie leans in now. 'So tell me, what exactly is the deal with you and Adam?'

'Oh, nothing at all,' I say quickly, relieved to be changing the topic of conversation. 'We're just good friends.'

Charlie smiles mischievously at me. 'OK.'

Sven rolls his eyes fondly. 'You'll have to excuse my Charlie here; she gets a little excited about stuff like this.'

'And why not?' Charlie says. 'I can't remember the last time Adam was with someone, not since Claire anyway.'

'That's true,' Sven says.

I can't help but feel a stab of curiosity and confusion. I thought Adam never stuck in one place, so was Claire a long-term thing? Was it recent? But if I ask any questions, then they'll definitely think something is going on between us.

And there's nothing – obviously.

'It's nice still having him here at any rate,' Charlie says, and Sven shoots her a look.

'Oh yes, he did mention he likes to go away a lot,' I say, as nonchalantly as I can, but I can't help feeling vaguely unsettled.

'He's still in Edinburgh now,' Charlie raises one arched eyebrow, 'so maybe there's something keeping him here.'

My chest flutters.

'Here, try this,' Charlie says now, passing the cocktail she had previously been drinking across to me. 'I shouldn't really be drinking right now anyway.'

I don't ask her why because I've only just met her, but I take a small sip of the fruity concoction. The flavours are all kinds of wonderful and I feel myself warming up. 'Go on,' she says, 'you finish it.'

'Not unless you want me drunk by nine,' I smile, and Charlie just laughs before pushing it towards Sven.

'What kind of dancing is it you do anyway?' I ask.

'Can't you tell?' Charlie indicates at her dress. 'Swing.'

'Charlie here likes to do everything full hog, so that includes your everyday outfits.' Sven grins and I know instinctively I'm going to love these guys.

'I've got to admit,' I say, 'I haven't danced since I was about twelve.'

Charlie looks at me, her big blue eyes aghast. 'What do you mean?'

Beside her, Sven's eyes widen in mock-fear. 'Oh, you've done it now,' he mutters. I look at him confused.

'Explain again,' Charlie says, clutching my hand now. 'You never told me that the first time. What do you mean, you haven't danced since you were twelve? Because everyone should dance, honey. It's our God-given right, if I believed in that stuff, I mean.'

'You just believe in the dance gods,' Sven says, taking a sip of his pint.

I smile at Charlie's still vaguely traumatised face. 'I just . . . never got the chance, I guess.'

'What about school, or at festivals or parties?'

'What about disco dancing?' Sven says, making little pointy actions with his finger.

I shake my head. 'Not really, no. My older sister was the dancing queen in the family.'

Charlie looks genuinely troubled and I'm worried for a moment if my revelation has actually caused her some damage.

But then she squeezes my hand tighter, looks at me dead on. 'We can resolve this,' she says, and before I can say anything, she's pulled me up to the empty dance floor. Nerves surge through me and people glance over, as Charlie runs off to speak to the DJ in the corner. I look over at Sven, bewildered, but he just grins, gives me two thumbs up. Adam is over at the bar sorting the drinks and clearly hasn't noticed yet.

'What's she doing?' I try to say to Sven, but my words are immediately swallowed by the music. A sound I've definitely heard before.

Swing music.

Oh god.

'All right,' Charlie says, rushing back to me. She looks me up and down, repositions me slightly.

'All right, what?' I say, and she grins at me.

'We're going to start by taking our left leg, and then move it back like this.'

After a moment, I find myself hesitantly doing as she says. Heat flushes up my neck but I can't deny that the music is pretty fun. And no one is properly looking, I guess. Not *really*.

'That's it,' she beams, 'now forwards, like this.'

I copy what she does, leg back, leg forwards.

'Now the hands.' She raises them both up with a flick. I try to follow in time, end up pretty quickly in a tangle, but the funny thing is, I'm not sure I really care if I get it right. People are staring now but the way Charlie is so enthusiastic, so very determined about us dancing like this, makes me want to follow her; makes me want to have the fun she's having.

We keep going like that for a lot of the evening, in between drinks and chatting with Adam and Sven, and some of the other clientele even get up for a bit; bob around too. And it feels so damn good to just hang out with a group of friends like this, to actually let my hair down for a moment and not think about when I need to get home or if I'll 'overdo' it. Adam pulls me up for a dance too, and as he takes my hands and spins me about, I feel a rush of blood to my head. It feels good to hang out with another female again too, not just over the phone with Fran, and by some point later in the evening, with my mind hazy from alcohol, it hits me again how much I miss Jess. And Cat too.

I stop moving.

The music is still going giddily above us, but after a moment Charlie sees me and stops too.

'You OK?' she says, putting a hand on my arm.

'Yup,' I say, trying to sound upbeat, but suddenly all I can see now is Cat dancing around at one of Fraser's gigs, Cat with her long red hair flicking up everywhere and this look of utter joy on her face.

'I've . . . just got a stitch,' I say, and walk quickly back over to the table.

Adam is chatting away with Sven when we arrive, but when he sees my face, he says, 'Are you OK?'

'Yes, just a little stitch,' I repeat, as though on auto mode. 'All good.'

But even though Adam is smiling back, I can tell he knows it's more than that.

* * *

We walk back up the road a little later, past the elegant town houses of Charlotte Square and the grand West End buildings, up towards the grey hardness of Lothian Road. The air feels even chillier now but it's refreshing all the same.

Adam's walking so close to me, we could be holding hands, and I can feel that faint trace of electricity between our fingers; that sense that we could connect again at any second.

Or maybe it's the two wines I had, I'm not sure.

I do still feel a little woozy if I'm being honest, but in an easy, hazy way.

'So, what happened earlier when you were dancing?' he says eventually.

I tense. 'I don't know,' I say then sigh, 'I was reminded of something difficult in the past,' I finish truthfully.

A pause.

'You'll work through it,' he says. 'If that's what you want.'

And just the way he says it makes me feel like there's a chance I actually will.

'Charlie's great,' I say, after a few moments.

'Yes, she is,' Adam says, almost proudly, and I can tell how much he thinks of her – of Sven too. It's evident they're like family to him and I feel sort of honoured that he's invited me into his life like this.

'She's so warm,' I say.

'And wild?' Adam's eyebrows raise in humour.

'Yes, and wild, but I sort of love that.'

'Me too.'

We pass under some office buildings, their tall domes rising up in the sky on corners of a junction and I find myself uncertain as to whether to ask about Charlie and what she said about the cocktail. It seems a bit nosy when I've only just met her, but then again, she seemed very open about everything else.

'So . . . Charlie was saying she shouldn't really be drinking,' I say. 'Is she pregnant?'

He looks across at me. 'Trying, for quite a while now.'

'Oh, I'm sorry; is she OK?'

'She's all right, I think. You can see how incredibly upbeat they are about everything.'

'I know but still, it must be hard.'

It's not really something I'd ever considered for myself given my condition, having children. It just didn't seem fair to anyone, as much as I secretly would have loved it – creating a unit of my own. So, I can imagine if it was something I actually tried for, it would be awful not to get it.

I have this overwhelming urge to ask him about something else Charlie said now, about Claire, and I realise in this moment that I'm jealous. Pure, senseless jealousy for this woman I've never even met. Who was she? Were they really in love? How long were they together?

And I have a horrible feeling that I like Adam more than I know.

'Do you think you'll head to one of Charlie's classes?' he says, and I'm jolted away from my thoughts.

I give him a wry smile. 'Did you actually see me? Totally crap at dancing.'

'Oh, come on,' he says, his eyes glittering at me, 'you were not crap. And you definitely looked like you were enjoying it, which is the main thing. I'd go with you, if you wanted?'

My stomach flutters at the suggestion, at the way he glances at me.

'Perhaps,' I say, uncertain if I mean it or not. I do realise I should probably make the most of this healthy body while I have it, but I was telling the truth earlier – dancing was always more Cat's thing, even though I thought it looked like brilliant fun.

'I'm pretty sure I have two left feet,' I add, because I don't want him to feel like I'm blowing him off or I don't want to hang out with him. Because I really do.

I was just so badly burned before.

'Well, you'll never know unless you try,' Adam says, and I have to wonder if he has a point.

Maybe it wouldn't be a total disaster.

Once we've arrived back at our building, Adam unlocks the door and I'm walking in when I notice something outside the card shop next to it, and my heart stops. A second later and my foot catches on something and I go flying forwards into the dark.

'Shit!' I cry, just as Adam catches me deftly by the back of my coat; pulls me to standing.

I turn to look up at him, heart absolutely pounding in my chest, when an unexpected bubble of laughter comes out of me. 'Two left feet,' I say and start laughing again, and then he's laughing too in the dark, this rumble growing between us until we are howling in the echoey stairwell.

The sound of a lock clicking open; light suddenly floods on to us.

'What the hell is going on out here?' a sharp, yet vaguely familiar voice says. We both turn sharply to see an elderly man standing in the ground floor doorway. He's in pyjamas, a blue robe, a shock of white hair sticking up on his head. Despite the fragility of the situation for him, his pale-blue eyes laser in on us.

'So sorry, William,' Adam says quickly, apologetically. 'We just came in.'

'I can see that,' says William, 'but I've had enough of all this racket, people coming in later and later at night. Why can't everyone just shut up?'

The second buzzer I pressed that day.

Adam says nothing further, but I can't help feeling bad for William. It probably is a bit terrifying getting disturbed like that late at night, and looking down by my feet, I see what I tripped over finally – a box, with the name William Johnson across the front. *So, this is who I rent my flat from*, I think, before picking it up and carrying it across.

'Here you go,' I say, passing it to him. 'I fell over it coming in – that's why we were laughing, but I'm really sorry about waking you.'

William takes it from me cagily, like I'm giving him a bomb, until he looks at the label.

'Ah, yes,' he says, clearing his throat. 'My funeral pamphlets. Though I'll probably be dead by morning anyway after tonight . . .'

His words are jarring, but I'm sure I hear the trace of something lighter there too, some inkling of humour.

A shadow crosses his face again.

'Now, he says, 'would you kindly bugger off and let an old man sleep, or die – either one will do.'

And with that, he takes the box inside, and slams the door in my face.

* * *

'Don't take it personally,' Adam says a couple of minutes later, as he drops me at my door. 'I've tried with William before, but he was having none of it. Maybe it's too hard to change sometimes, after a certain point.'

But as we say our goodbyes, our eyes lingering briefly on each other as we do, I can't help wondering if that's really true. And I also can't help thinking about what I saw as we came in.

A *To Let* sign hanging outside the card shop beneath us.

CHAPTER FIFTEEN

'Happy Birthday, E!'

I'm just taking a sip of my post-run coffee a week later when I hear the words blasting down the phone. I'd answered Fran's call immediately before I saw it was still only seven in the morning.

'Sorry?' I say. 'Happy what?'

'Oh, for god's sake,' Fran says, 'have you actually forgotten your own birthday now?'

My heart thuds lightly in my chest. It's not like I feel I have to pretend to Fran really; there's something oddly natural about the flow of us, regardless of the situation. But forgetting my birthday? Well, that is just plain weird.

'No,' I say slowly, 'it's just, I wasn't really planning to make a big deal of it this year.'

'No change from any other year then,' Fran says. 'How can you be so good at celebrating other people's stuff but so absolutely crap at celebrating your own?'

I think back to my last birthday, how incredibly pressurised I found the whole thing, just the notion of everyone having to focus on me for the day, hoping I would make it to the next one. Mum fussed over me at every moment and I had to pretend to love the sugarless cake she'd made me.

'Well, anyway,' Fran continues, 'I knew you'd try and avoid it, which is why something is arriving for you this morning to help it along.'

'Oh?'

'You can *Oh* all you like, but you'll have to wait and see.'

I smile. 'Well, thank you in advance, that's ridiculously nice of you and I'll look out for it. And on the note of celebrations,' I continue, 'are you and Toby happy to confirm the honeymoon itinerary I put together for you?'

'Yes, I'll confirm the luxury resort tour,' she says in a mocking tone, and I frown. Doesn't she want to go? A trilling noise comes down the phone. 'Hang on, door,' she says.

While she's away, I think about how Fran's wedding prep had not got past the actual day itself, and suddenly I found myself in a place I was always so comfortable with – brainstorming ideas for where other people could go together. I'd been using Adam's laptop for anything I needed before, but as I became more involved in helping Fran, I finally gave in and got a cheap one of my own. At least I know I'm not just going to sit behind it anymore, and as I got to work on the sofa, I realised how long it's been since I actually sat down to create adventures for other people. I've just been so busy doing my own stuff recently, running, taking photos, hanging out with Adam, cooking, eating and exploring – having my own little adventures. I paused for a moment on the Royal Mile the other day though, when I saw the sign for Dunbar's Close. And even though my heart started beating a little faster at the sight of it, none of those strange feelings I'd had in the speakeasy came back again. I decided I'd maybe never need to know why Emily was looking for it, and carried on my way through the city. Because I have to assume that these strange memories are fragments from Emily's life. Nothing to do with Stella, or that *To Let* sign below.

I don't know why I'm thinking about my heart donor again – there are places to let all around the city after all – it's just in all the chaos of what's happened, I sort of forgot about the letter I'd received, and her. But that sign has got her back into my mind again. And I even wondered for an earth-shattering moment if I might be back in *her* life, which set my pulse racing – given that I know she dies. But my name is Emily, not Stella, and she lived above a bakery, not a card shop.

Pushing the troubling thoughts away again, I hear Fran faintly in the background speaking to someone, and I think again about her upcoming trip – how envious I secretly am. Her and Toby's budget was pretty punchy, so I booked them into a couple of impressive resorts in the Maldives, which Toby had apparently always wanted to try. I felt a little bad for Fran though, given I knew what she really wanted to do was go seafaring in the Galápagos Islands; search for some of the world's rarest creatures. Though if she jokes about finding the blue-footed booby one more time, I'll kill her. Her and Toby seem to have quite different tastes, I've sometimes noticed – what type of holidays they like, what they want to do with their weekends (he likes reading the newspaper in bed, she likes to get up and go on adventures) – which is fine if it works, I guess. But I just hope she's not putting her own dreams on hold for him too often.

Dear Fran – because that's how I've started thinking about her – this warm, reassuring voice I can call at any moment, whenever I'm homesick for Jess or Mum or Dad.

And, not for the first time, I get this genuine sense that I've known her a lot longer, that we've had hundreds of drinks and dinners and drunken one-in-the-morning conversations.

'Sorry, sorry,' she says, coming back on the line, sounding slightly flustered. 'It was the postie,' she explains, 'and on that note, I just got a text from the delivery company there. He's asking if you can let him in.'

'Oh,' I say, looking towards the door with a frown, 'my buzzer must be broken.'

'Well, go and let him in, and then go and actually enjoy yourself for once.'

I smile. 'All right, I will.'

Once I've hung up, I head across to the door, and I'm about to press the release catch on the intercom, when there's a knock. I open it up to find the most enormous bunch of Happy Birthday balloons on the other side, and behind them, Adam in his wool sweater, smiling at me.

'I took the liberty of taking these up for the poor guy who was trying to access the building,' he says. 'Oh, and there were these too,' he says, passing me a fancy bouquet of flowers. There's no card on it, oddly, though maybe they're from Fran too. All the same, my heart is fluttering.

'But my main question is,' Adam continues, 'how did I not know it was your birthday?'

He's smiling, but there's confusion too.

'Oh,' I say, batting it off, 'I'm just not huge on celebrating it.'

He tips his head up like I've said something mental, then looks back down at me. 'We need to do something for it. Dinner at my place tonight? And I promise I won't do that raw chicken thing again.'

I laugh, recalling how a failed dinner had ended up with us in the little pub along the road for a live music night with Sven and Charlie instead, staying with them until close. And I remember feeling in that moment that somehow, despite the setbacks, I was kind of getting in the sway of this life thing.

I smile across at him, still clutching the mystery flowers in my hand. 'I'd love that.'

* * *

Later that evening, I stand in front of the mirror and survey the outfit I chose for this evening from Mum's charity shop – a fitted blue dress with little sparkles across the front. I keep dropping in every now and then; keep running past Jess and the boys in the park on Wednesdays too, but there's just something particularly special about actually chatting to Mum, about letting her know everything that I'm up to, without her telling me it might be unsafe or running to call the doctor. I get to see what a normal relationship between us might look like, and I pick out clothes while I'm there too. She set this particular dress aside for me when it came in, and it hugs my body in all the right places, stopping just above my knees. My mane of dark hair is held back gently with a glittery head band, and I've lightly applied make-up below.

A burst of nerves shoots through me, because there's just something about tonight, about Adam's suggestion of dinner, and the soft look in his eyes, that gives me a thrill in my chest. And even though I know we're only supposed to be friends, and I don't want to hurt anyone here, I can feel something insistent pulling at me, begging me to let go.

Just for a little while.

Could I?

Before I can answer my own question, there's a knock on the door and my heart skips as I open it. Adam is on the other side, wearing his plaid shirt, a tweed jacket on top, which I suspect hasn't been out in a while from how stiffly he's holding himself.

But that awed expression on his face when he sees me.

My stomach somersaults.

'You look incredible,' he says, in this nervous way I've never seen on him before.

'Thank you, I'll just put on the shoes,' I say, stepping nervously into a pair of silver heels. I feel giddy suddenly, like pure serotonin is running through me and it might make me topple over at any second.

'Take your camera, and a warm coat too,' he adds. 'It might be a little nippy where we're going.'

'Why are you always trying to take me up high?' I joke, but I'm intrigued. Darting back to the bedroom, I pick up my camera with excitement, and head back to the door. Pulling a cream wool coat on, I catch him watching me again, and take a breath in.

A clicking noise across the hall makes us both jump. Someone coming out of Adam's apartment. 'Who is . . .' I start, just as Sven comes into sight. He gives Adam a double thumbs up, then both of us a mischievous smile. 'Bye, guys; enjoy.'

Before I can say anything, he disappears away down the steps, and I look to Adam, who gives nothing away. 'Come with me,' he says, and takes my hand as we walk back across the hall to his. It feels odd, because I've never actually held his hand before, warm and rough against my own. A twinge of something starts low in my belly; seeps up through me like hot cocoa.

At the door, he drops my hand again to open it (much to my disappointment), but inside, I'm surprised to see that his usually plain hallway is lined with candles all the way to the cupboard at the back.

'This isn't it, by the way,' he says, a hint of a smile in his voice. 'I didn't just take you for dinner in my hallway, I promise.'

I find myself grinning as he takes my hand again, and this time he pauses for a moment, his eyes lingering on mine in the darkness. My breath quickens and the energy between us is palpable.

'Just over here,' he says, and to my confusion, he walks towards the cupboard. Opening the door, a rush of air hits me as I see what appears to be a stone staircase leading up to the pitch-black sky above.

'What the—' I breathe.

'Just a little perk of living on my side of the top floor,' he says, and leads me up the steps. My heels ring out into the late October air, my breath coming out in soft wisps.

At the top, we step out on to what feels like the top of the world. The tumbling rooftops of Edinburgh lie below, while the castle above is lit up blue against the cold, night sky. But right in front of me is the warmest sight I've ever seen. A small table has been set with covered plates, a vase of evergreens and a chilled bottle of champagne at its centre.

Two chairs sit on either side, a plump velvet cushion and soft blankets on each one, and beside the table, an outdoor heater glows warm. Around it all, ropes of fairy lights have been strung through the iron railings, which enclose the area.

'But how on earth did you do this?' I say, still amazed.

'Sven and Charlie,' he says, then turns to me. 'I know it's not a fancy restaurant, so if you'd prefer to do that then we can—'

'It's perfect,' I say, cutting through his words. 'I just can't believe you've done all this for me.'

'Well, it's your birthday,' Adam says, 'another year on this planet, and I think that's worth celebrating, Emily.'

I take a breath, unsure what to say, but a second later he pulls one of the chairs out from the table, ushers for me to sit. After he's sat down himself, he pulls the champagne bottle from the bucket with a shuffling of ice.

'Not entirely sure we needed the ice out here tonight,' he says, pouring me a glass. 'Are you warm enough?'

'I'm very warm right now,' I say, truly meaning it. With the heater on beside me and the blanket across my lap now, I feel perfectly cocooned.

'To you, Emily, and your new life,' Adam says, and lifts his glass to mine.

I kiss my glass gently against his, the bubbles leaping to the top as I do so.

'Thank you, Adam,' I say, and think how handsome he looks, how insanely attracted to him I am. My heart is racing.

I take a quick sip, before nodding at the closed plates. 'Please tell me Sven's made his pizza.'

'Not tonight, I'm afraid,' he admits. 'I got him to do something a little fancier for the occasion. Take a look.'

Shaking my head in mock disappointment, I lift the top, and immediately grin. Because there on the plate is the most delicious-looking cannelloni, still piping hot, steam rising off it. It's coated in some sort of rich, red sauce, a shimmer of Parmesan on the top.

'Oh wow,' I say softly, recalling the little Italian we went to, how much I loved the food.

And he remembered it all.

'I'd suggest eating it pretty fast, given the climate in our restaurant,' Adam says pointing at the sky. 'And on that note, I should probably also have worn a warmer coat than this number,' he says, nodding at his jacket.

'It's very smart.' I smile, touched at the effort.

'And vaguely ridiculous?' he says, raising one eyebrow, and we both start laughing.

Relaxing a little, we set the napkins Charlie clearly crafted for us to the side, and tuck into the food, immediately getting lost in conversation about our days: I tell him I tried knocking at William's door, just to say hello, but he told me to bugger off again. Adam suggests leaving a cake at the door next time, and I think I just might. Then I fill him in about the photos I took at Calton Hill, and he talks about the finished suite of furniture for the client up north, which he's dropping off in his van tomorrow.

'You're welcome to come along with me if you like?' he says, his eyes flicking to mine, 'make a day of it. You could even take some photos on the way.'

I find myself pausing. God, I'd love to go with him, but I just don't know. That definitely feels like an acceleration of whatever is happening here tonight. Because I can't deny that this isn't about us being friends anymore, up here, in the most romantic setting of my life. I can't deny what I feel about him either, despite my fears about hurting him. Or me for that matter.

'You don't fool me,' I say eventually, 'you just want someone to chat to you on the way up.'

He laughs at that, that deep, genuine sound I love. He always makes me feel like the most interesting person in the world.

'Well, maybe it's also selfishly because I have a feeling you'd get on well with the client Magnus's wife, Daphne,' he says mysteriously. 'She'd love to throw some scones at you too, I'm sure. Together sixty years, the two of them, if you can believe it.'

'Is that . . .' I start, 'I mean, have you ever come close to being serious like that with anyone before?'

I'm not sure exactly why I'm asking the question – perhaps it's the champagne or the night sky above or the candles – but he doesn't miss a beat, as I should have known he wouldn't.

'Once,' he says steadily. 'Her name was Claire, and we were together for about two years, my longest relationship to date, but we broke up last summer.'

A twinge of jealousy jabs at me, though it's ridiculous, really – of course he had a relationship before; he's the most attractive guy I've met, in every sense.

I clear my throat. 'So, why did you break up then?'

His eyes darken slightly in the candlelight. 'It was good while it lasted,' he says, swallowing. 'But I'm not sure we were quite right for each other, and it wasn't fair to either of us to keep it going. I'm not sure what we had was what it should feel like.'

'And what should it feel like?' I say without thinking.

But he just looks across at me softly, and my whole body tingles.

'And you?' he says, taking a sip of his champagne.

'I guess I thought I'd come close to it once . . . but maybe not.'

'Why not?'

I pause, unsure how much to reveal. The truth is so complicated. 'We were just in very different places of our lives,' I say eventually. 'And in the end, he didn't want the relationship quite enough to stay with me, so I let him go.'

Adam looks thoughtful for a moment, and I think he's about to tell me something, when a gust of wind crosses us and he seems to stop himself.

'I have something for you,' he says, and reaches down under the table. A second later he places a white cardboard box in front of me and the moment is cut short.

'I'm sorry it's not wrapped,' he says.

I smile quizzically at him. 'What is it?'

He raises his eyebrows. 'You'll just have to open it.'

Taking the lid off, I peer through bubble wrap to see something black inside. Pulling it out, I look at him, amazed.

'I think it's the right one,' he says quickly, leaning over. 'I had a chat with the guy in the shop and he said that it was good.'

I look at the lens again, look at him. After the dinner set-up, it's probably the most thoughtful thing anyone has ever done for me, though it's not the lens exactly; it's the sense that he understands that I'm wanting to grow and to change, and he's 100 per cent behind me on it, no matter the outcome.

'Thank you,' I say finally.

For a moment, I don't know what else to say, so I take the camera from the side of the chair, twist the lens into place with a satisfying click. I walk across to the twinkling railing and stare out across the city. The wind canters across my face as I raise the camera to my eye, zoom in on all the old spires and puffing chimneys and little squares of yellow on the buildings below – snapshots of life: a man washing up dishes in one; a woman laughing to someone in the background;

two kids jumping up and down on a bed; a couple collapsing back on the sofa together.

I can see it all so clearly from up here.

What it could be like.

A scuffing noise. Lowering the camera again, I turn to find Adam right beside me, and he's looking at me in this way that makes my heart beat faster than ever before. And this feeling, which started in my chest earlier, slowly spreads out around my body.

Is he about to kiss me?

Oh god, I don't know if this is a good idea.

Then he turns and looks out towards the castle, and my stomach plummets. Maybe I've got this all wrong. Maybe that's what he was talking about earlier, when he said he didn't feel like how he should have about Claire. Maybe he also meant like us?

'Told you it would be good for photos up here,' he says, leaning forwards on the railing. I do the same, our arms just touching, and I can't help but feel desperately sad for a moment.

'Have you had a good evening?' he asks, turning to face me. I feel his warm breath close to mine. My stomach does that flip again but I try to still myself.

'I have,' I say softly, then add, 'You're a really good guy, Adam.'

He smiles at me. 'I just like being around you, Emily. Even if friends is as far as this ever goes.'

And in this moment, I know he doesn't see me as he saw Claire at all, and I know this was that other feeling he was alluding to, because I'm pretty sure I feel it too. It's been growing there for months now and, suddenly, it's like a flame has been ignited in my chest.

He's about to turn back to the castle again, when I reach for his hand and then our mouths are pressed against each other, and I have no idea who initiated it, him, me, both of us together, but it doesn't matter. We kiss in the night air, the taste of him new and familiar all at once, and I fall into it completely, pressing my body up against his, while his arms wrap tightly around me.

And with the fairy lights surrounding us and the starry sky above, everything else fades away to nothing.

CHAPTER SIXTEEN

In the morning, it takes me a little longer to come to and, for a moment, I feel something like terror.

Has it all stopped?

Has Adam gone?

Then I roll to the side and I see the clock and the dream-catcher, and I heave a sigh of relief. Because if I'm honest with myself, I'd be devastated if I was back in my old life right now with my quiet existence and Mum checking in on me every two seconds. I'm not ready to go yet.

Then last night all comes back to me and I press my eyes tightly shut at the awful way we'd parted in the end.

But how had that happened? It had all been going so well, with the perfect evening up on the terrace and the lens he'd given me for my camera. That magic kiss under the night sky.

We'd kept kissing later, I remember, back down on his bed. It was like once the tap had opened between us, it wouldn't stop, and it had felt like the most natural thing in the world, his mouth on my mouth, my neck, the perfect weight of him on top of me, for a time. But although everything in me had screamed for more, there was something still stopping me, and I'd found myself pulling back sharply.

'Are you OK?' he'd asked hoarsely, pulling back too.

I'd nodded in the darkness, but internally I had felt the anxiety rushing up again.

'It's all right,' he'd said softly. 'We have all the time in the world to get to that.'

And I'd wished to God that were true.

'Are you still coming up to Aberdeen with me tomorrow? I leave at nine,' he'd said at the door just before I'd left. He'd been standing in the dim light, bare-chested, his hair tousled from where my hands had been in it, and it had taken all my willpower just to take a step away.

'I'm not sure,' I'd said finally. 'I told Fran I'd help her finalise some honeymoon stuff. I can't let her down.'

I had felt Adam pausing and my heart had bled for him – for me too. But all I could think of was the pain I'd gone through after Nick left, of that feeling of being left behind like that.

'Are you sure that's it?' he'd said, frowning slightly now, and I'd known he'd seen right through my lie.

'Well,' I'd started, 'the thing is, I just don't want to get into something here, if one of us is only going to leave at the end of it. I don't want anyone to get hurt.'

His eyes had sparkled. 'And were you planning on leaving tonight?'

'No,' I'd said slowly, 'but who knows what could happen; I might go back to ... London, or you might decide to disappear off somewhere.'

A cloud had crossed his features then. 'And who said anything about me disappearing off?'

I'd paused. 'Well, Sven said you would usually be away travelling by now.'

'Just because I usually do something, doesn't mean I always do, Emily,' he'd said, but there had been a distance in his words, something I hadn't been able to quite read. 'Can't we just take things as they come? Enjoy it.'

I'd raised my eyebrows. 'See, you don't even know what you want. How do you know you won't change your mind? You said yourself you go where the wind takes you.'

Adam had pulled one hand through his hair. 'Look, of course I can't promise anything; I mean, who can? But all I know was that tonight was amazing, and I'd like to keep seeing you.'

A silence had settled between us, and I'd seen his chest lifting up and down. All I'd wanted to do was go to him again, disappear under his covers and stay there. But even he couldn't give me any assurance.

'Tonight was great,' I'd said slowly, steadily, 'but I just don't know if I can do this again, if it might all end tomorrow.'

And as his hands slipped from mine, I'd had the oddest feeling of déjà vu. Like I'd had these exact same concerns, in this same place, once before. But when I'd looked up, Adam had been shaking his head, and I'd known something had shifted in him.

'Clearly you've decided what's going to happen here already, Emily, so if that's the case, then maybe we should just leave it.'

'Fine,' I'd said, even as my chest exploded with pain at his words.

'Fine,' he'd said, and a moment later he'd turned to go back inside, his shoulder blades stiff as he'd moved. At the last second, he'd stared back out at me, and I'd allowed myself to look at his face again, at those startling eyes and the worried tension across his strong jawline.

Then he'd shut the door, and after briefly closing my eyes, I'd turned and disappeared back across the hall.

Now, as the clock ticks over to 7 a.m. beside me, I try to decide what to do about the trip up north.

Only two hours until he leaves.

*　　*　　*

Outside on the freezing pavement a little later, I run quickly away down the quiet, lamp-lit road, the dawn light only just starting to rise over the shivering buildings. I let the cold air hit my skin, hoping that it somehow blows away the intense pull I'm feeling towards Adam. I keep to the busy, safe part of the city, and as I stamp forwards alone, I wish with all my heart that I could just stop being so afraid all the time.

Just let go, like other people do.

But the deeper I get into this with Adam, the harder it will be for everyone to get out painlessly.

I loop the Meadows a few times, head down against the cold, before stopping at Victor Hugo for a coffee. Sitting completely alone at the little tables outside, the light rising higher in the sky, I watch it all go by again – the couples, the friends, runners.

I'm just getting up to head home when I see her, sitting down at a table across from me.

A woman.

She's dressed all in grey, her red hair tied back, face pale and drawn under her black woollen hat. And she's all alone. Her movements are slow, her breathing clearly laboured.

My heart is beating so fast right now. And that's when she looks up, clocks me too, and it's like I'm caught on a line.

Frozen in a moment.

She looks at me curiously, almost sadly, before glancing back down at her menu, and I watch as she gives her order to the waitress, almost murmuring it under my breath in time with her – *green tea and a water.*

I calculate when exactly this is. November, almost eight months before the heart transplant.

From here on in, she's going to go downhill, struggling, shuffling, towards an operation, which will ultimately save her but still leave her in a very limited position.

This was the last time she came up this way to get some art supplies.

Then I look down at the neon running gear I'm wearing, the thick croissant on my plate and the milky coffee to the side. I think of the flat I'm living in and the photos I've been taking. I think of the friends I've made and these moments of absolute joy I've experienced. I think of the rooftop with Adam last night. Those incredible kisses under the night sky, then later in his bedroom.

And I know I can't go back to it, won't go back to it, that life where I have to be scared all the time. Where I can't actually do anything or go anywhere without worrying about my impact on everyone. Where I can't fall in love in case I hurt them.

Or myself.

And maybe Emily didn't even want it, this life? Maybe that's actually the reason I'm here, and I can keep it a bit longer?

Maybe I can keep it forever.

And with that, I get up quickly and run away as fast as I possibly can.

* * *

When I get to the top of the steps, almost breathless from sprinting up, I knock hard on his door.

Please don't be gone yet, please don't be gone.

But I'm met with silence.

With a heavy heart, I sit down on the floor in the space between our doors. Why did I have to start on at him about his travelling? Why did I have to push him away like that, like I didn't really care?

I care about him more than I have about any man before. And maybe he's right, maybe we don't need to know exactly what's going to happen tomorrow. Maybe we can enjoy this space right now and simply take things as they come.

I just wish I could tell him all of this. But he'll be well on the road up north by now, probably regretting the whole of last night now. I just need to speak to him when he gets back, explain myself. I sit like that for a while, trying to figure out what to do, when I hear a noise beside me and I turn sharply to see Adam leaving his flat. He's wearing a black fleece, jeans, his hair darkly wet like he's just out the shower.

The two of us look at each other for a moment, before I get up and walk over to him.

'Emily,' he starts, like he's about to launch into something, but before he does, I go up and kiss him square on the lips. He hesitates for only a moment, before I feel him sinking into it, his arms surrounding me. And there is no explaining, and no getting into all the past trauma and scars of our lives, because time is short and right here right now is all that matters.

When I finally pull back in my nylons, he looks down at me, his green eyes on mine.

'Good run then?'

'The best,' I say, and he grins.

* * *

We head on to the road to Aberdeen soon after, and as we cross over the Forth Road Bridge, its incredibly tall spokes whizzing by above, I find myself exhaling as we leave the city, and my old self, behind.

'You OK?' Adam says softly, glancing across at me.

And in that moment, I know that I am. Because I'm still with him, and we can go wherever we want to go and do whatever we want to do. I'm not focusing on what happens if he leaves, or I leave, or who could get hurt. Because the point is, we're here together now, and that's enough.

'Yes,' I say, and put my hand on his leg firmly. We spend the rest of the drive like that. My hand on his knee, with his hand on top, his eyes flicking across to me from time to time.

We sing along to songs on the radio (Christmas already!) and chat about nothing much and everything at once. When we get hungry, we stop at a roadside garage and pick up coffees and greasy cheese pasties, and when I see somewhere that looks great for photos – purple hills, or five-hundred-year-old castles stamped against the white skyline – we pull over and I take a few along the way.

We sweep up through it all and then, eventually, the sky ahead seems to loom higher and I see it – the huge expanse of North Sea to the right. It seems to go on and on forever, a million waves chopping white into the steel water. The enormity of it takes my breath away.

Eventually we hit the city of granite with its centuries-old grey buildings and stern spires against the sky. But despite the initial hardness of the place, I can't help smiling at the way the sun glitters on the stone when pools of sunlight cascade through the clouds.

'I love the way you do that,' Adam murmurs.

I turn. 'What?'

'Act like everything is new to you, like it's all fascinating.'

'Well, maybe it sort of is.' I say happily, before turning back to the window, and realise in that moment, how true those words are. Even though I thought I'd experienced life before, lived in it every day even, I'd never actually witnessed the light changing on an unfamiliar hill, or smelt woodsmoke from a house in the middle of nowhere, or felt the subtle change in energy of a new town or city. Even my holidays before Cat died were identical. Everything was always the same, every rhythm, every scent, every feel. And changing any of that is more fascinating – more invigorating – than I can say.

Arriving at the client's enormous house in the West End, it's all gothic windows and turrets. We move the pieces out of the van together with some hilarity – it turns out I'm probably never going to be a removal worker, despite my new strength – and every time I catch Adam's eye, I feel that charge from this morning still between us. True to form, Daphne has us all sitting down for tea and scones in the Victorian orangerie soon after. Turns out she was once a famous photographer, travelling all around the world to take pictures, and as we sit down to talk about all things art, I can see Adam glancing across, a contented smile on his face.

With a strange sort of giddiness, we head into town next, barely able to keep our hands off each other, as though we both know how close it was this morning to none of this happening; to everything ending between us. Heading to the old part of the city, we wander hand in hand around the icy cobbled streets towards the university buildings. We stand in the cold afternoon light and, as students mill around us, coffee cups in hand, I think about what it might have been like to leave home for art school after all, if I'd done things differently after Cat.

For lunch, we pop into a little bistro Magnus and Daphne said was good; linger over local oysters and fresh hake. Then, as we walk around town, I spy a leaflet. Turning it to him, I say, 'Are you game?'

And he says, 'Absolutely.'

Twenty minutes later and we're walking into the fun fair on the seafront. Rollercoasters loom high in the sky and lights flash all around us, but even though my heart is beating fast, I'm excited too. It's the sort of thing I'd never have been able to do before, not even as a teen. But today, I feel as free as I've ever been and I want to make up for lost time. Right now.

As we sit on one of the rollercoaster carts minutes later, moving slowly up together into the ice-cold air, I can't deny I feel a bit nervous – what if the ride breaks down? What if we go flying on to the concrete below? But then I look across at Adam, at the big smile on his face, and I know there's nowhere else I'd rather be in this moment. The cart pauses at the top, and then in a rush of speed and light we're dropping so fast, my hair is flying and Adam is whooping and I'm screaming, but it's not with fear anymore, it's with sheer bloody delight.

And I want to do it all over again.

After going on more rides and playing at the arcades together, shouting out loud every time I beat Adam, the sun starts to set in the heavy winter sky outside and I feel him take my hand.

'Better get going before it snows,' he says softly.

Sure enough, a few minutes after getting into the van, the heavens collapse in on themselves and snow falls lightly, then heavier and heavier as we speed back out of the city. The roads become thick with it in no time and even Adam's robust van begins to swerve about.

'It's pretty bad out there,' I say, looking ahead at the other few slow-moving cars, which veer precariously as well.

'We're all right,' Adam says beside me, but even I can see the white of his knuckles as he grips the steering wheel, and my heart pounds lightly. His eyes are focused hard on the road and I wonder just how long we can keep driving for. But we're back in the middle of nowhere and I can't quite think what we passed on the way up.

We're about half an hour outside the city when it comes into sight – a beacon of light away off the main road, a plume of smoke and a sign at the top of a long-wooded drive that says, 'Eastwick House Hotel'.

Adam slows the van down and I can feel my heart quickening as we reach it, grateful for its presence, yet also excited about what this might mean. He turns to me.

'I'm not trying to suggest anything,' he says quickly, 'I just think it's safer to stay off the road tonight . . . what do you think?' As snow rushes into the windscreen, I turn to him and say, 'I think I agree.'

He sets off down the drive, which is now thickly white. The wheels are silent, as the quaintest hotel comes into view. With its big Victorian windows shining out, I only hope they have space for us.

We jog up the enormous stone steps to a huge old door. Walking inside from the cold, we are immediately met by a wave of heat from a roaring fire. Red tartan lines the floor and a light fixture made of antlers hangs from above. At reception, we're told there's one room left, which makes me think of every bad romcom I've ever seen. But I don't really care – I reckon I'm due a few cliché moments.

And as we're shown the way up to the second floor, I know instinctively what's going to happen tonight, in this body which isn't mine, and yet feels so much mine now it's getting hard to distinguish Maggie from Emily. I can feel that old anxiety still pulling at me, still trying to protect myself and everyone else from getting hurt, but this time, I'm not going to listen to it. I'm not going to let it ruin this moment – this brilliant day we've had.

We're shown into a comfortable double room, which is all tartan furnishings again and tweed chairs. And at the centre of it all is a crisp white bed, turned down already for the night.

As the girl tells us that breakfast is served from seven and politely leaves the room, I can feel Adam glance at me. The tension from the day has built to an absolute crescendo and it takes us seconds after the door has shut for us to fall into each other again, kissing almost desperately now. The strain of this morning, the uncertainty about where we actually stood, buried now by snow.

And as we fall on to the enormous bed, with flakes fluttering against the window, I feel myself floating up and up, leaving the two of us together.

Like how it always should be.

CHAPTER SEVENTEEN

'Merry Christmas you filthy animal.'

'And to you too, Fran,' I say with a laugh down the phone, 'though it's still only Christmas Eve. But thank you already for the most enormous hamper of chocolate I've ever seen. We'll be eating it for the next year.'

Or at least, I hope so.

'Not a problem,' Fran carries on, as Ferris curls around my legs. 'I assume your new *boyfriend* will help you with it.'

I can't help smiling. We haven't spoken about anything serious, of course, but I'm sure he's feeling what I'm feeling. And perhaps that's enough for now.

'I can't believe he made you up an actual stocking for tomorrow,' Fran carries on. 'Jesus, I basically have to tell Toby what to get me.'

'But then you do want very specific gifts, like that star sweater I went to ten shops for,' I blurt out before I know what I'm saying.

She laughs. 'God, yes!'

I stop because that just felt so strange – words falling out of my mouth like that, more than just a random memory of Emily's this time. It was like the words had become a part of me.

'Anyway,' I say, breathlessly now, 'how's it going at your parents?'

'Oh, you know, half-cut obviously, five Buck's fizzes down already. But then the family flew in from Rome yesterday.'

Fran pauses. 'Are you seeing yours at all?'

It's strange because, if she and Emily are cousins, then why aren't Emily's parents included in this family get-together? Where are they?

'I don't think so,' I say eventually.

Which is true – I haven't heard from them after all.

'Well, it's no wonder after the argument you had. I still can't believe what your mum said to you,' Fran says.

I blink.

Didn't Stella also have an argument with her mother before she went up north?

But I'm just overthinking it; jumping to the worst-case scenario like I always do.

'Anyway,' Fran continues, 'do you think you might make it down to London sometime in the new year?'

My stomach flips. I'd like to meet Fran in person, of course I would, but now more than ever, I have absolutely no desire to leave Edinburgh, or Adam's side. This is all I've ever wanted and I don't want to let go for a second.

'Perhaps,' I say eventually, knowing how flaky it sounds.

Fran sighs. 'You're welcome to bring Adam obviously.'

I laugh at the persistence.

'And if this is about seeing Simon again,' Fran continues, 'London is a big city, remember. It's not like you're just going to run into him again, so you can forget all about him.'

'Right,' I say, immediately feeling a little twinge of something odd in my chest at his name. I got another of those random messages the other day, which said, *I miss you so much, Emily, can we please talk? xx.* I still don't know categorically that it's Simon, but I'm not entirely convinced that I can do as Fran says and just put him out my mind.

'I've got a question for you also,' Fran says.

'Oh?'

'I was wondering if you would be the photographer at our wedding?'

'What?' I say, my heart rate rising. 'I thought you had one . . . and I haven't even done a course yet. What do I know about being an events photographer?'

'E,' Fran says sternly, 'if you put half as much effort into photography as you did with your job and your university degree *and* your school exams, then you are going to be an amazing photographer. I trust you, all right? Now say yes so we can all be as happy as you.'

I take a moment to think it through – on the one hand, it will be really awkward and difficult seeing more people from Emily's old life. But on the other, I can't deny that Fran is a part of this life and the two of us have become unwittingly close. I can't just ignore her or the very lovely offer of doing something I'm slowly growing to love.

'All right,' I say eventually. 'I'd love to.'

* * *

After saying my goodbyes to Fran, I head off to do some last-minute shopping. I've already got Adam a new woollen sweater and a book I found about Munro bagging, but I want one more little thing. I've still got some time this afternoon until Sven and Charlie come over for our Christmas Eve celebrations. Sven's doing the cooking, of course, despite Adam and me insisting in the pub last week that we could give it a go. Sven had just looked at us like we'd said something crazy. *No*, he'd said in this horrified way, which made us burst out laughing. It didn't feel totally fair – I happen to love the slightly sketchy food Adam makes me, particularly his over-poached eggs, though maybe that's something to do with who the chef is. We spent a while this morning getting the place all cleaned, setting up the table with a tropical Christmas tablecloth Adam's mum managed to send over from Christmas Island last year. The glasses were a mishmash, the patterned dishes too, but once we'd finished, I couldn't help thinking how perfect it looked – how excited I was to spend Christmas Eve, and even the day itself, with Adam. Lilly was hitting up number 501 on her bucket list – Christmas in Hawaii – and when Adam asked me if I'd be going down to London to see my parents, I'd found myself saying they were abroad over the season too.

Despite a slightly curious look in his eye, he didn't push it again.

I'm desperately sad not to see my own family, particularly at this time of year, especially given how close they physically are in Edinburgh. I think of the boys waking up crazy early, everyone exchanging presents sleepy-eyed before going out for a Christmas walk together; watching rubbish movies on the sofa with Jess later in the day. But at the same time, it was always such a limited experience for me. At least here I get to experience the full thing without dragging other people down too.

Strolling down the busy road a second later, I realise everyone else has had the same idea. But after a little wander around in one of the department stores, I find what I'm looking for – a pair of bright-orange socks for Adam, to match that ridiculous orange headband he gave me.

I'm just heading back along Princes Street when I notice the German markets again – the bright lights of the Ferris wheel, and the twinkling ones from the stalls. I've been to them already with Adam, after we went to a tree farm the other week. We listened to more bad Christmas tunes full volume and drank lattes from the Purple Pineapple. The farm was even snowy when we got there, the countryside gently covered with a powdering of white, and as I stepped out the van into the freezing air, I breathed in that intense scent of pine, that perfect winter day smell, as a memory from my old life fell straight into my mind – Cat, Jess and I going with Mum and Dad to a tree farm just like this (perhaps even the exact same one?) before the diagnosis: drinking hot chocolate from Mum's red, shiny flask and playing tag among the trees, laughing hysterically as Mum and Dad watched happily on. There were some great days too.

Walking by all the trees available that day with Adam, the tall, regal ones and the plump bushy ones, I found myself wandering over to a more fragile tree. Its branches were a bit patchy in places and it didn't look like it would last as long as the others, but I still stopped in front of it.

'Is this the one?' Adam said, taking my hand.

'I think it might be,' I said and then without thinking, added, 'do you mind that it's a bit rubbish?'

Adam looked at me. 'Define rubbish?'

I shrugged, something tightening in my stomach. 'I dunno, a bit frail, with a shorter shelf life.'

'I think,' Adam said, 'that it's not the lifespan of the tree that counts but the life it leads while it's here. It's about the spirit, not the sturdiness.' And with that, he threw my flimsy tree easily over his shoulder and loaded it up on to the van.

Later that afternoon, in the quickly dimming light, we strung the tree up with fairy lights and a few old baubles of Adam's. But after agreeing there really wasn't nearly enough, we set off into town to the markets.

Hot sugar and cinnamon permeated the air as soon as we stepped in, and we went from stall to stall, buying mulled wines and exclaiming over all the decorations. We bought a load, including one that Adam found – a small Christmas butterfly in all the colours of the rainbow.

'This made me think of you,' he said, and as we wandered away off up the road, I couldn't help thinking that this day was something that would just have never happened in my old life. Christmas was something to be got through after Cat – like Mum was scared of enjoying it all too much without her there. Cat really loved Christmas. She would always blast 'Rockin' Around the Christmas Tree' on Christmas Eve, spinning Jess and me around until we all got dizzy and fell down.

It's incredible how great things can just disappear like that.

But looking at the colourful lights of the German market around me now, and thinking about the lovely evening ahead with my new friends, I'm reminded that there is still a lot of joy to be had in the world somehow.

Wandering back up the road eventually, the light is dim as I approach the building. Something looks different though, and my heart starts to thump.

There's a new sign above what was the card shop, and the *To Let* sign has been taken down. I squint as I start walking quickly towards it, unable to take my eyes away.

Moving closer, the words sharpen – focus.

Dee's Bakery.

My heart is racing as I stare at the sign, my thoughts all tangled like flashing Christmas lights, and I don't know what to think. Because surely, lots of people live above a bakery. Surely, it's an incredibly common shop to live above, and it doesn't have anything to do with my heart donor, Stella.

The woman who dies seven months from now.

All the same, I immediately turn and rush back into the building, my stomach twisting and nausea rising as I go.

* * *

Back in the flat twenty minutes later, I've turned out every bit of paper again, searched through every drawer, looking for anything at all with the name Stella on it. Because that was definitely my heart donor's name, not Emily.

It absolutely wasn't Emily.

I've double-checked the passport and driver's licence, even her birth certificate, just in case Stella might be a middle name. But it's Isabella. I've gone back through everything I can recall from the letter too, because I'm pretty sure the name element is the only thing not stacking up now – Stella was thirty when she died, the same age as Emily now. She went to the best university, and from those pictures I found, I think Emily went to Oxford; had an argument with her mother and moved up north.

Individually, all the pieces are fine, but put together like this in my head, it does not feel fine at all. It feels very much like I'm living my heart donor's life.

But how would that even be possible?

How would any of it be possible? another voice says.

But at the end of the day, no matter how many coincidences are happening here (because that's what they *must* be), the name factor still stands. The two are totally different, and I have to look at facts here. So, everything is fine.

Isn't it?

With shaking hands, I eventually wrap the orange socks, before heading across to Adam's. Glancing over the banister to the flats below, I'm briefly distracted by the thought of William – but after one cake drop, two unanswered Christmas cards and three unanswered knocks, I've finally concluded he has absolutely no interest in speaking to me. I know it must seem odd to William, this total stranger trying to befriend him like I am, but there's just something about his situation that I can't leave alone: the way I can see from the door that his TV is blaring into an empty room all day long, and how his mantelpiece is absolutely choc-a-bloc with pictures of what must have been his wife. A wife who died a long time ago from the looks of it.

Outside Adam's, I smile at my rainbow-coloured welly boots sitting beside his green ones, and I take a deep breath. *Everything is fine.*

Letting myself in, I find Sven and Charlie already setting up and I'm amazed at the effort they've gone too – Adam's whole flat is now decked out in ropes of ivy and sprigs of holly. All the candle-holders from the roof have been brought down too, and with every single one safely lit up, it's like Charlie and Sven have created some sort of Christmas wonderland.

'Oh, there you are!' she gushes, and I immediately smile back, despite how hard my heart is still pounding. And as I hug Charlie, hold the sparkling form of her, the panicked thoughts start to ease slightly. She's almost dressed like a tree herself, or perhaps an elf, in a glittery green dress, red tights and a Santa hat.

'So glad we could do this together,' I say.

'Me too,' she grins.

'How are you getting on, Em?' Sven says, coming over and hugging me.

Just as Adam bounds through from the kitchen, a potato clasped in each hand, I hear a knock on the door behind us.

We all look between each other, confused.

'Who can that be?' Sven says.

'The ghost of Christmas past?' Adam tries and I roll my eyes at him fondly.

Turning to open it, I find myself smiling widely at the pale-blue eyes and bushy eyebrows – William. And as I reach in to hug him, my heart overflows with warmth.

*   *   *

'So, what you're saying is, you snuck on to a war ship?' Adam is saying, almost leaning into his Swedish yule log.

'Exactly right,' William says, and takes a small sip of his red wine. His eyes are shining with the night and his cheeks are slightly flushed from the sheer amount of food.

All around us are remnants of the most terrific meal, a true smorgasbord of delights – pickled herring and Christmas ham, pork sausage and a delicious egg and anchovy mix called Gubbröra. There is wort-flavoured rye bread and potatoes and, just in case William showed up, an obligatory turkey crown.

But much to everyone's surprise, William didn't bat an eye at the slightly stranger offering on the table; told us his wife was half Swedish and had a particular fondness for pickled eggs. Ate them all through pregnancy, apparently.

'And on that note,' Sven says suddenly, as everyone looks across to him, 'we have a bit of an announcement this evening.'

A trickle of excitement goes through me, as I realise what's coming. Because I've had this exact conversation before. I'm sure of it. And just as my heart rate goes up again, Sven says, 'We're pregnant.'

'Oh my god,' Adam says, getting up and rushing around to hug them both. 'Guys, this is amazing.'

I do the same, but as Charlie pulls me into another big embrace, I know I've experienced this whole scene before, more than just faint memories and words falling from my mouth – I've felt it, experienced it and lived it.

I just don't know why this feeling is getting so much stronger.

'Congratulations,' I whisper in her ear. My heart is thumping hard in my chest right now, but I have to keep calm.

'We're only about four weeks along,' Sven says, as we all take our seats again, 'and I know that's really too early to tell people, but you guys are like family to us, so . . .'

I feel so bloody happy for them but internally I'm starting to freak out. I think about the letter again, all those individual pieces I was putting together about my heart donor and Emily – the fact her memories are getting stronger. *Oh god*. But it could just be my eggnog-addled mind making me panic. I'm overthinking it, surely.

Because I can't lose all of this.

I won't lose all of this.

'You must be really excited,' I say to Charlie with a smile now, determined to enjoy this evening and stop worrying. *Just let go.*

'Will you dance to due date?' Adam asks.

'Absolutely.' Charlie grins.

It's so wonderfully Charlie, and it's not like dancing is bad for pregnancy, I don't think, but I can't help feeling a little worried too – they've had so many issues, after all. I suspect if it were me in the situation, I'd probably do very little; be panicked the whole time, if I'm honest.

'And then the plan is to do some travelling after,' she continues.

'Wow, that's awesome,' I say.

I think back to how different it was for Jess after. I can't count the number of times she wheeled them around the same neighbourhood loop to get them to sleep. Her life became very small during that time, come to think of it. But despite that, I know she loved it.

'Oh tosh,' William says out of nowhere, and everyone turns to look at him. He's frowning suddenly, his big bushy eyebrows downcast, and it's jarring. He's just been so agreeable this evening, lit up almost.

'Dancing till due date, travelling the world with a baby. . . don't you know all the things that can go wrong?' he snaps.

'We wouldn't go right after the birth, of course,' Sven says to him gently, 'but maybe after a while, if everything is going OK.'

When William says nothing, just looks down at his plate, I want to reach out to him, find out what's wrong. But before I can say anything, there's another knock at the door.

CHAPTER EIGHTEEN

As I'm leaving the room to see who it is, I can hear Adam asking William if he wants to come see the roof terrace one day and I think how kind he is – how he wants everyone to feel completely at ease.

Glancing at myself in his hallway mirror briefly, I smooth down the glittery velvet dress I'm wearing. It's ridiculously short, I have to admit, but if I can't be a little out there at a Christmas party with friends, then when can I be?

A Christmas party with friends.

The words sound so odd in my head, but at the same time, a shiver of happiness goes down my spine.

I'm still thinking about how happy I am and how I was clearly worrying over nothing as I fling the door open wide, stopping short at the sight of a woman standing there.

She's tall and trim, in navy trousers; a smart cream coat on. Her light-blonde hair is neatly bobbed, with pale-blue eyes I've seen before. Except they're much harder up close and now they scan me over from top to toe, an almost shocked look on her face.

I open my mouth to speak, but nothing comes out.

My heart is thudding so hard right now.

'Good to see you've still got your ability to say nothing.'

We stand like that for a moment, me looking at this woman I know nothing about. Yet this dynamic feels oddly familiar, and all those strange déjà vu sensations I've been having come flooding back again.

Glancing behind me briefly, I say, 'How did you know I was here?'

'I tried the other flat first and no one was in, then I heard the racket,' she says firmly.

Uncertain what else to say, I lead her across the landing and let us both into my flat. She immediately starts looking around, at the ceilings, at the floor, at the living room she walks into.

'Can I take your coat?' I try uncertainly. But even I can hear how pathetic it sounds.

Emily's mum turns to me now, eyes seemingly on fire.

'Nine months in my belly and eighteen years under my roof,' she says, 'and you treat me like a stranger, if I can even call it that,' she says.

Heat reaches up my neck, as she moves about like a wasp trapped in a bottle, picking at the blankets on the sofas, and glancing at my still-technicolour wall. And all the while, I stand at the side, uncertain what to say, what to do.

Shit, how long did I actually think I could hold off a mother for? What have I been playing at? Just ignoring Emily's old life like this. I don't know exactly what happened between Emily and her mum, but perhaps I should have taken the bloody time to find out.

Emily's mum finally takes a seat on the sofa, perches there like it's deeply uncomfortable.

'Would you like a tea?' I try, my heart thudding.

'That's obviously not what I'm here for,' she says slightly softer now.

'Then what are you here for?' I falter.

Her eyes widen, something like real anguish in them now. 'How could you just drop your responsibilities like that, Emily? How could you quit your job like that? And that wonderful man?'

She starts shaking her head and I find myself unable to speak.

'This whole life you're living up here is a dream, Emily,' she says, standing up again. 'A child's fantasy. You've always lived in a wonderland, and right now, you're risking all of it, everything we've worked so hard for.'

Something sparks in my stomach at her words.

Because she's right. These past six months *have* felt like a dream to me, a fantasy. I have lived more in the past six months as Emily than I did for my whole life as Maggie.

I have felt more joy and experienced more excitement than I ever dreamed possible.

And I won't let anyone take it away from me.

Emily's mum spies something on the mantelpiece, walks towards it. She picks up a selfie I put up of Adam and me at the Christmas markets – we're on the Ferris wheel, clearly freezing, but we're both grinning away madly, our faces right up against each other. She just stares at it for a long moment, before turning it around to me.

'And who is this?' she says, holding it out to me with both hands, as though I didn't take the photo myself, as though I haven't stared at it in wonder a hundred times already.

'That's Adam,' I say, steadier now and take the photo from her. 'The man I'm seeing.'

Emily's mum looks at me, lost. 'We've just worked too hard for this, Emily. We had a plan. Think of all the schooling, all that work at university and to get that promotion,' she implores. 'I poured my life into your father's business so that you could have every opportunity I never had, and now you're throwing it all away for some photography hobby and some man who looks like a nobody to me.'

The words cut.

How can she say that about someone so kind and wonderful and vibrant? He's the most alive person I've ever known, after Cat. And suddenly, that spark in my stomach turns into a flame.

'Don't you dare say that about him.'

'And why shouldn't I?' Emily's mum says, clearly frustrated too. 'Why should I let you destroy your life like this?'

'I'm not destroying it,' I say steadily.

I look around myself, at the shabby living room, which is popping with colour and life. I look at the picture of Adam in my hands.

'I'm finally living it,' I say then, as though a dam from somewhere else has been opened; as though someone else's words are passing my lips. 'I've spent my whole life trying to live the life that you wanted me to have, I forgot how to live the life that *I* wanted to have. But if I don't go out and give it a proper shot now, then I might as well be dead already.'

Emily's mum walks towards me until she's standing right in front of me.

'Come back with me now, Emily,' she pleads.

My heart is beating so very fast, and I don't know what is happening right now, but it's like I'm here, and also not, as though I have the thoughts in my mind, but someone else's too.

This is the life I was always supposed to have, they're saying.

This is the life I always dreamed of.

'I won't leave,' I find myself saying, 'I won't be scared anymore.'

A long silence passes between us, mother and daughter standing in the shadows without speaking.

'You're a fool,' she says finally. 'A wasteful fool, throwing away everything we've ever given you. Don't come crying to me when none of this works out.'

'I won't,' I say, more forcefully now.

And then as swiftly as Emily's mum came into the flat, she turns on her smart black heels and heads back into the hallway. At the last second, she turns, and I'm not sure but I think I see the glisten of something in her eye; a slight drop of a barrier she's had up the whole time.

And in this moment, I finally understand it all. That somehow, despite all of our surface-level differences, Emily and I were the same. Neither of us were living the lives we actually wanted.

But more than that, I wasn't actually living at all.

Emily's mum opens the door, stares back at me with eyes full of pain and regret.

'I love you, Mum,' I find myself saying, even as those strange sensations start to drift away again, 'but I have to do this.'

She looks like she's about to say she loves me too when she stops herself.

'Goodbye, my Stella,' she says, 'my star,' she adds softly, before walking out.

The door closes behind her, and my whole body stiffens.

My Stella.

And everything I thought I'd just figured out is covered by a tsunami.

CHAPTER NINETEEN

In the very early years, Dad used to get confused between Cat and me. With our matching red heads and pale skin, you could catch us at a certain angle and find that we looked near identical at times – the way we walked, the way we talked, the way we laughed even. That's when he started calling us Big and Small. Cat wasn't that much bigger than me really, but I always felt it still fit somehow because when you were around her, the world just felt brighter and lighter and full of possibility. She would be the first one to try a new flavour, a new activity, the only one to get up and dance in the kitchen at breakfast just because she felt like it. The names helped him to keep track somehow but it was also just his way of being affectionate, I think, of creating that specific link between him and each of us. And as I sit here staring at the screen, it finally dawns on me that Emily's parents had a name for her too, and everything I thought I knew, everything I've fallen for in this life, comes crumbling down. The running in the rain and stomping up hills in the wind, trying new foods and sharing cocktails with friends, meeting the man of my dreams and following where my passion leads me for the first time in my life. All a set design being pulled apart on stage.

Placing my head in my hands, I let out a shuddering sob. Stella.

Star in Italian.

Which means I'm living in my heart donor's life and seven months from now, this body that I'm in – this life I've been living – will all be gone.

And I'll be right back where I started.

The cruelty of it threatens to overwhelm me. There I was thinking the universe was finally helping me out, giving me a second chance at it all, when all it was doing was showing me what I can't have: health, fun, love.

I walk over to my handbag on the sofa and pull out my wallet. Taking some scissors from a side table, I cut straight through the leather and finally tear out the mystery card, which wouldn't budge. And now here it is in my hands – her donor card, fresh and shiny, her absolute confirmation to the world that, in the case of her death, she wanted to donate her organs. Because Emily was just like that, always giving, always thinking of others first and she wasn't going to leave it to anyone else to decide it for her.

'*No*,' I cry, a ragged sob coming out of me.

How is this even possible though? I rush to the computer again, start typing in words like heart transplant and phenomenon, and reports from all over the world come up about organ transplant receivers claiming that they've inherited memory and experiences – even the emotions of their deceased donors. The reasons for it are varied, from the 'little brain in the heart' theory, where the heart has an intrinsic nervous system that might be responsible for memory transfer, all the way to psychometric theory, where psychics claim that the donor heart is an object imbued with the psychic energy of the person it came from; much as a bracelet or other object could carry the memory.

So, what if some way, somehow, one of these theories has manifested fully after my transplant? What if it's been stretched to its limit and I've gone back into those memories, but it's real, it's happening, and it's me instead of her. I'm actually over-writing her last year.

Slumping to my knees, I put my head in my hands.

Oh god, what am I going to do?

How can I possibly tell Adam the truth? How can I even face him? How can I go back over there and face any of them, all the while knowing what's going to happen?

Because now I understand the real truth of it all: this life wasn't going free, Emily didn't want rid of it, she died unexpectedly – that's what the letter said. Not 'she took her own life', or didn't want to be here, or anything like that. She'd made a new life for herself, and now, for some reason I still can't even fathom, I'm reliving the last year of it.

Before she dies.

My phone buzzes and I know it will be Adam before I've even looked.

Is everything OK? Was that your mum earlier?

What do I say to him? No, everything is not OK, and even though we've started to fall for each other, I will have to go soon. I will have to leave you. And so will she.

But how the hell can I do that to him?

How the hell can I do that to me? Because I know deep inside of myself that I will be leaving this life and going back to my old one seven months from now. There is only one heart between us, after all, and it's transferred to me in the future. And if I'm the one here now – walking, talking and moving as Emily – that must mean she's well and truly gone. Fate is fate, like it was for Cat, like it is for anyone, and whatever cosmic glitch has happened between us, I can't start playing God here. No, it's certain in my mind: this body I'm currently in will die regardless of what I do on 25 July this year – the day of the heart transplant – and I will go back to the small, limited space that I came from.

Lying back against the hard wooden floor, I stare up at my technicolour wall, at the swirls and loops and splatters of life and light, and I try to work out what to do; what to say to someone I can never have.

In a life I can never keep.

Time passes, Christmas evening rolls on, and I'm still lying on the floor; still trying to ground myself to something solid. Eventually I hear noises across the hallway, Sven and Charlie and William all talking away. There is laughter and chatting, calls of Merry Christmas as the snow starts outside my window. The noise rises up, lowers again as they all head downstairs, and then a moment later, the inevitable knock comes on my door.

For a moment, I think about not answering it, but I know I owe him more than that.

Pulling myself off the cold wood, I walk slowly to the door and it sort of reminds me of that very first night he came over, when I was so scared and alone, but hopeful too; curious about what else might lie out there in this new world. And I just wish I could take myself back, have it all stretching out before me like that.

Opening the door, I find him standing there like always, his forest-green eyes on mine.

'Are you OK?' he says, then pauses. 'You didn't reply.'

His voice is full of concern.

'I'm sorry,' I start, stop. Because I still don't know what to say, where to go from here.

'Is your mum still around?' he asks hopefully, as though that might explain my radio silence.

I shake my head. 'No, she left a while ago.'

'I see,' he says, a crease forming on his brow.

'Adam,' I start finally, unsure how to word this exactly, 'I . . . have to go back home.'

He looks worried. 'For how long? Is everyone OK?'

'Yes, everyone's OK,' I say slowly, 'and I'll be here for a while longer yet, but I just can't stay here, long-term, I mean.'

'Why not? I don't understand?'

When I don't say anything back, he reaches for my hand, that crease on his forehead melting again.

'Look,' he says, 'I don't know exactly what happened with your mum, Emily, and I can't even begin to pretend to understand your experiences. But all I do know is that in the past five months, I've been happy in a way that even I wasn't sure was possible. I've felt things I've never truthfully felt before . . . and I think I'm in love with you.'

My heart is beating so fast at his words, as other words, my words, chime from just before Emily's mum came over – that these past five months with Adam have been the most perfect of my life. They've been all I've ever wanted, and it's because I stopped being so afraid all the time. And in the time I've got left – in the seven months I've got left – I know already that I have to fit in as much as I possibly can. Not for me, but for Emily. Because I can feel it in my bones – her bones – that this isn't an alternate reality. It's there in the trees and the grass and the air around me.

This is it.

And even though she's gone, what I do will affect Emily's legacy forever.

'Say something, Emily,' he says, his eyes trained on mine, his hand gripping mine too. 'Just please don't do anything we'll regret later . . . I can't lose you now.'

And while all I want to do is throw myself into his arms, and never leave his side ever again, I pull my fingers from his.

Because I can't drag Adam into this; won't drag him into this.

It was different when I thought I could stay, that perhaps I could keep living this life as my own, but there is no doubt now about who it belongs to.

And what's going to happen to it.

I see the love in his eyes, the warmth from his touch. I pull my hand reluctantly from his.

'I'm sorry,' I say. 'I can't.'

CHAPTER TWENTY

The end of Christmas Eve was nothing like I'd hoped for – that look on Adam's face before he went back over into his flat alone, that mix of concern, desperation and then something more like anger. And I get it. After all, I explained nothing – gave him no valid explanation for my coldness, or why I have to leave. But how the hell could I explain anything? How could I explain to him that this body that I'm in – this life that I'm in – is all going to disappear in a few short months.

I called Charlie straight after it happened, made her promise to look after Adam on Christmas Day, and although she agreed, I could still hear the confusion there.

'Did you guys have a fight?'

I tried to hold back the tears, as I said, 'Something like that.'

Then she promised she'd see me soon, said I was as much a friend to her as Adam now and she'd support us both.

So, I spent Christmas afternoon with William in the end, and despite the fact that I felt so awful, so utterly desolate without Adam there beside me, we still managed to make it a little merry – after William gave up cross-examining me. I finally did some digging on Emily's parents that day, realised her father ran some multi-million-pound real estate business, after severing ties years before with his previous business partner and brother – Fran's dad. A family rift it appears, that didn't extend to the cousins luckily. And, more than ever, I understood the pressure Emily must have been under to be something great, to make it all worthwhile.

Some mulled wine and a big bowl of pasta later, I dragged myself back up to my empty flat, before having the most mammoth of sleeps. And then, waking up on Boxing Day, something came over me. Despite the ache in my heart, I looked out through the snowy panes with fresh eyes and knew that I could hide away from the world and wallow in the misery of it of it all – or go do.

Go do all the things Emily wanted to.

Because her mum asked just one thing of me in her letter. To keep her alive.

And after the past five months, I know now that simply staying alive isn't enough; simply existing is not enough. I need to figure out what Emily wanted to do and go where she wanted to go, actually get out there properly and *live* her life, the way I'm certain she did the first time around.

I know it from all the vague memories of being in restaurants and checking out dance classes, from the camera and the clothes and just the whole fact that she made such a drastic change in her life. Because if I don't go and live for her now, while I'm physically in her healthy body – if I let her legacy down like that, and it sticks in time – how could I ever face myself back in my own life?

And even though I won't get it exactly right, I reckon I can get pretty close. I've increasingly felt Emily with me at every step, in those memories and sensations, in the way I started speaking to her mum like I did. And there's just this *feeling* I'm increasingly getting, that I'm not alone.

She's guiding me along the way.

That's why I finally sat down and thought about all the things Emily might have wanted to do in this last year – all the things she must have done the first time around. I make up a list from things I've noticed in the flat and from all the conversations with Fran – a clichéd bucket list, so to speak.

Which is why I'm here now in a deserted car park doing number two on the list – *Learn to Drive*. Number one was figuring out how to apply to photography school, of course, given that will likely take the most time (and I might secretly enjoy it too). I knew I'd missed most of the deadlines at this stage, but after a quick call with Daphne in Aberdeen about courses, I discovered I could send a late application if I put together a portfolio quickly enough. It feels almost wrong, taking more photos for a course Emily will never get the chance to do. But still, I know this is right. I know she really wanted to get in, and perhaps that has to be enough.

But driving was definitely next on the list, because it was one of the first things I noticed when I got here – that she had no licence.

It's something I always wanted to do when I was seventeen, of course, when every other normal kid begged their parents to get behind the wheel. And even though I technically could have done – even though the doctors said that many people with heart issues drove – I decided I couldn't risk it. What if I had a heart attack on the road? Or knocked someone down?

But now, as I sail around the potholed space with Charlie beside me, all of those worries and 'what ifs' just evaporate. It almost seems silly that I thought so much about it before.

'Now release the clutch, and push down on the accelerator ... that's right,' Charlie is saying. As her little red Mini rolls slowly across the empty car park, I grit my teeth, but I don't stop.

'Why don't you make a turn here and we can loop back to the other side.'

'OK,' I say, with more confidence than I actually feel. But that's the thing I've learnt in the week since Christmas. Maybe I'll never feel totally ready for anything in life; maybe I'll always feel a little bit scared of it going wrong. But isn't it better to try?

As I finally pull over to the rusted fencing and bring the car to a halt, I tip my head back against the seat, and smile.

'You did so great,' Charlie says, and I turn to see her holding her belly lightly. I'd suggested it might not be a great idea with the pregnancy and everything, but Charlie being Charlie had immediately waved me off; told me the baby would enjoy a little spin.

'Thank you for taking me,' I say.

'My pleasure, we'll have you joyriding in no time. God, I used to love cruising off with my friends when I was younger,' she says, with a somewhat distant look in her eyes. 'We'd open the windows, blast the music full volume and just disappear off into the sunset.'

'That does sound fun,' I reply softly, realising yet again all the things I missed out on, all the things I kept saying no to. Was it really necessary?

And not for the first time, I think about how oddly similar Charlie and Cat are, or were. That's the sort of thing Cat did with her friends, and then with Fraser. She lived like every moment could be her last one, like every sunset might be her grand finale.

She always tried to get me to live that way too – as much as I could anyway.

'So,' Charlie says, turning her attention back to me now, 'what's with the sudden desire to drive?'

I pause, realising there's truth in what I'm about to say. 'I guess I'm just tired of waiting for it all to begin.'

'Waiting for what to begin?'

'Something,' I say, and look up at the wide-open sky outside. 'Everything. There's so much stuff I've always meant to do, but never actually did. I've got this list actually . . .'

'List?' Charlie says. 'I like the sound of a list.'

'Well, you're welcome to come along for it,' I say, because the truth of it is, I would have loved to have done something like this with Cat, and although Charlie can never be my sister, they have the same energy, the same gusto for life. And I could probably do with some of that along the way.

'What about Adam?' Charlie says after a moment, lowering the paper to her lap. 'I'm sure he'd have been keen to do some of this too.'

I look ahead again, at the way the rusted fence knots in and out of itself.

'I know,' I say, 'but it's better this way. He's better off without me.'

Charlie raises one eyebrow. 'Debatable.'

I turn to her, take a breath in. 'Have you heard from him?'

'Only briefly,' she says. 'He was on some ferry at the time.'

'He just took off so quickly after it happened,' I say, thinking of the sight of him with his backpack out my window, 'I didn't even get a chance to say goodbye.'

'Well, that sounds like Adam,' she says slowly, 'but I don't think he's away for long this time; just seeing some of Norway. He's got orders to complete before he goes further.'

I pause. 'And how was he? When you spoke to him, I mean.'

'Not great,' Charlie replies truthfully, 'but he'll be OK, in time . . . will you?'

I force myself to look up now at the sky above, knowing that I am still here with time to complete my list. And even though my heart is still aching at the thought of Adam, I smile. 'I hope so.'

Charlie smiles back. 'Still on for Friday night then?'

'Absolutely.'

Number three on the list, here I come.

* * *

It takes William and me a little while to get down the stairs of our building a few days later, but I don't rush him, don't say a word. He's a little older, and I know that everyone needs to make their own decision about when they want to change their life.

And for whatever reason, this was it for William. A simple invitation to a dance lesson; a request for the expertise I saw up on his mantelpiece with his wife. It was simple as that – something, or someone as unexpected as a neighbour, coming into your life and making you say, how about now?

We get the bus down through the lamp-lit town in silence and as I watch him stare out of the darkened windows, I realise that this might be the first time he's been on a bus in a very long time. This might be the first time he's gone anywhere in a very long time.

And suddenly, I wonder if the two of us are all that different.

I wish I could have driven us, of course – Charlie and I have been out for a few more intensive driving sessions this week, each time becoming easier than the last – but I still need to actually pass the exam. I've booked it in right after the theory test though, for two weeks' time at the start of February. Even Charlie's eyes went wide when I told her and she suggested maybe I spread it across a couple of months at least. But I don't have a couple of months to waste. I've only got six months left in this life and with Charlie's intensive training, I'm confident that I should be able to pass it.

I will pass it – for Emily.

What came next?

Dancing was next on the list – it was a given from all the little dancing figures around the place and the fact she'd clearly gone to check out Charlie's class almost immediately. And, God, did I feel nervous when I looked on the website and realised what an idiot I'd look like when I went. But so what? If this is what she wanted to do. Though I couldn't help wishing Adam could have come with us too.

I'd have loved dancing with him.

'Where is Emily Perin and what have you done with her?' Fran had laughed down the phone when I told her but she sounded happy for me all the same.

Eventually the bus pulls up at the stop Charlie told us to get off at in Stockbridge, and, tapping William lightly on the arm, we slowly make our way down the bus to the front. Though I offer out my hand to him, he tells me that he's able to get off the bus perfectly well alone, 'thank you all the same'. A second later, he shuffles to the edge of the step and down on to the pavement beside me.

I can't help smiling as he offers his arm to me – perhaps stubbornness can work in good ways too.

'So, tell me why you're here, and not with Adam then?' he says as we walk away to the lit-up building together. 'What happened between you two lovebirds?

I pause, surprised by the abrupt question after the silence. But it is William, after all.

'I'm just . . . not sure I'm the right person for him is all,' I say eventually.

'Oh tosh,' he says, 'who is ever right for anyone? When I met my Connie, I had no money and her parents thought I wasn't good enough for her but I didn't care. Because I loved her with my whole heart, and there's no greater gift, you know. Do you love him?'

My heart beats faster. 'It's just not as simple as that.'

'I think you'll find it actually is. When I met my Connie, I just knew,' he says, and stares up at the sky above. 'Three months, that's all it took before I proposed. And we had the most wonderful, imperfect life together, before she left.'

I pause, thinking about those pictures of her pregnant on the mantelpiece, William's harsh words about Charlie's plans at Christmas.

There's not one photo of her older than the pregnancy.

'Was it childbirth?' I say softly.

His silence tells me that I'm right.

'Our twin boys inside her too,' he says, without looking at me. 'And in that moment, my whole world collapsed. I stopped speaking to everyone, even my brother and his children, because I couldn't face it.'

As we walk along the cobbles in silence, I try to digest what he's said – that the most awful of things happened to him. He took a chance on love and it ended in devastation. The world is filled with so many awful outcomes, so many ways of getting hurt, that it makes me scared to breathe sometimes.

How are you supposed to take any risks at all?

'It just didn't seem right though,' he says, and I turn to look at him sharply.

'What didn't?'

'Saying no to these dance classes. Because Connie adored dancing and I think she would have loved this.'

A beat. He pats my arm.

'I think she would have loved you.'

I'm trying to form a response when I realise we've arrived at the dance centre. A man in glasses walks past, opens the door.

'You guys coming in?' He smiles, holding it open.

I look at William, and he gestures for me to go in first.

Walking into the warm, whitewashed hall, we're immediately surrounded by a bustle of people talking and laughing – all different ages, men and woman. Pin boards hang around the place with flyers about yoga, toddler groups and dance classes. Tables are pushed across to the side for other activities, and there is such a buzz of life here – such a feeling of community too. A second later, a flash of red polka dot comes rushing through the crowd towards me.

'You made it,' Charlie gushes, hugs me tight. 'And you too, William,' she says, turning her thickly lashed eyes on him. 'This is amazing.'

'Thank you for having us,' he says, 'but I will tell you now, I am no beginner.'

'Oh, I didn't think that for a moment,' Charlie says quickly, 'but it's often good to go through the motions for a warm-up, don't you think?'

He seems to consider it. 'I suppose so. My wife Connie and I used to dance, you see. That was our *thing*, as you people say these days.'

Charlie beams. 'And what a great thing to have had.'

'Well, yes,' he says, and Charlie ushers us towards the middle of the honey-oak floor.

Stepping back to her place at the front, Charlie starts up a little swing music, which warbles from the speakers, and everyone almost magically starts to fall into lines across the hall. William and I take a spot in the middle, even though I actually want to go right at the back. A minute later, Charlie takes the class through some warm-up exercises, then a few little dance steps, which are easy enough to follow. My limbs start to loosen, my heart rate starts to climb.

That vision of Cat's red hair, flying around as she loses herself in the music.

For a brief moment, I want to slow right down; stop like I did that time in the speakeasy. But then something new happens – I look down at these healthy limbs, feel this heart beating inside my chest, and suddenly it dawns on me, that instead of stopping for someone, I need to act for them instead.

Just like Cat always did for me.

CHAPTER TWENTY-ONE

Over the next few weeks, I work my way steadily through Emily's list, and Charlie is only too happy to join in too. In a strange way, I've realised we're tracking the same timeline – around August this year, she will have this baby and her whole life will change. Just like mine.

So Charlie and I start cooking classes with Sven and go climbing at an indoor centre. We try new instruments, me the guitar from the cupboard and Charlie the ukulele, because Sven had one lying around from his youth. We go out dancing until all hours of the morning and I try shots for the first time, get properly drunk and eat a 2 a.m. kebab with a more sober Charlie. And I am *so* close to sending Adam a tipsy message but somehow manage to stop myself. We go skiing on the dry ski slope at the other end of town – or rather I do, with Charlie watching happily on. And although it's not quite the Cairngorms, yet, I know I have to start somewhere.

I have to assume that Emily already skied, given the affluent crowd she ran in, but given what Fran said about her working all the time, maybe she never actually managed to go.

I put on those hiking boots at the door and Charlie and I walk up a Munro together one clear, frosty day. And as I stand there at the top, looking out across the beaten green and brown landscape, I can't help thinking how absolutely incredible the world looks from here.

I'm a bit concerned about Charlie overexerting herself during her pregnancy, of course. But as she keeps saying, she's still only a few months along, and the worst of the sickness has already passed, so everything is fine. Sven seemed a little nervous about it initially, but when he sees how much fun we're having, he quickly backs off. He knows I'll look out for her, after all.

At any rate, we're pretty limited with what we can do on the list as it's only February and it's still too cold for some activities. I think about jumping on a flight to continue them somewhere hot and exotic, but I'm not sure if I want to; I'm not sure I'm quite ready to, truthfully. Plus, I'm enjoying doing a lot of it in Scotland, and as I've learnt since I've been here, you don't actually need to leave the country to have big adventures.

It's as I'm walking towards the flat after doing another Munro with Charlie, with mud all over my boots and a lightness inside that's just wonderful, that I see someone coming along the street from the opposite direction. My heart catches.

Adam.

The first I've seen of him since Christmas.

'Hello.' I can't help smiling, as we come to a stop in front of each other. He's in jeans and his old black winter jacket, a scruffy beanie on his head, and attraction floods through my body.

'Hello,' he says, his eyes lighting up like he's genuinely happy to see me too. No annoyance or trace of animosity, but perhaps a hint of sadness.

'How have you been?' I say, once I've caught my breath. 'How was the trip to Norway?'

'Really interesting. Busy.'

He doesn't elaborate on what busy means exactly and I don't pry. It's none of my business anymore, after all.

'And you?' he says, a touch of nerves there possibly. 'How have you been?'

'Oh, fine, fine. Busy.'

We both start smiling at my equally lame reply. It's weird being awkward with each other.

'Where have you been?' he says, looking down at my muddy feet.

'Up a Munro, with Charlie.'

His face lights up. 'Sounds great. Cold?'

'Wonderfully cold,' I grin. 'Freezing actually.'

'I heard you were doing quite a bit with her recently; sounds like fun.'

'It is. And we're going to do a ski trip soon too,' I say, before I can stop myself.

'Oh yes, Sven was saying he was going.'

I pause. 'Do you want to come too?'

His eyes linger on mine. 'I wouldn't want to intrude.'

I feel myself heating up under his gaze because I'm the real intruder here. And I know I need to keep my distance, and I know nothing else can happen between us, but the fact is these were his friends first and I don't like shutting him out of his own friendship group.

Plus, I miss him: his enthusiasm for everything and everyone, the way he makes even little moments seem big, his never-ending encouragement – being close to him.

Would it hurt to spend a little time with him?

'You wouldn't be intruding at all,' I say firmly, 'please come.'

'All right,' he says, 'I'll come then. We can take the van.'

I smile, happy, relieved.

'Do you fancy,' I start, before I can talk myself out of it, 'I mean, do want to want to hang out this evening? Go get a bite to eat or something, just as friends I mean.'

He opens his mouth to reply, when a taxi pulls up alongside us and a man gets out – handsome, sandy swept-back hair, chiselled jaw. It takes a few moments for it to click.

Simon.

And suddenly it's like my heart is exploding in my chest and I'm flooded with all these intense feelings: attraction, panic . . . hurt.

Oh god.

When he spots me, he stops, and I can see he's just as good-looking as in the pictures. Like a different breed of human, in his expensive wool coat and navy cashmere scarf; tanned skin as though he's been in the Maldives for weeks.

'Emily,' he says, stopping in front of me.

'Simon,' I say the name like I'm trying it on, and find it's oddly familiar on the tongue.

And then he smiles an amazing smile at me.

I hear a scuffing noise and turn to see Adam looking between us, and my heart bleeds because I know how it must look, Simon being here like this.

But that's not why I broke it off, I want to cry out. *It's not that.*

Yet at the same time, something is definitely happening here with this man I've never met before. The connection is undeniable.

'I'd better get going,' Adam says to me softly and, with a nod at Simon, he heads back towards the building.

I'm about to call out to him, say something, anything, to explain all of this to him, when I feel a gentle hand on my arm.

'Do you fancy a drink somewhere maybe?' Simon says hopefully, and I turn back to him. 'Or, do you need to get back to . . .'

'Adam,' I finish for him. As I hear the building door swing shut, frustration floods me. 'His name is Adam.'

'OK, I see. But do you think we could just . . . talk somewhere?'

And despite my annoyance at losing that opportunity to spend time with Adam, other feelings are bubbling away now in my chest and my heart softens at Simon's words. He must have travelled all the way from London to see me, after all, and I could be wrong but I swear there are dark circles under his eyes, like he's not been sleeping well.

'I could do a coffee?' I offer.

'I'll take it.' Simon looks visibly relieved, and a moment later, we turn and head along the darkened pavement together. The Purple Pineapple should still be open for a while yet, and at least that's a safe and familiar setting. Because the truth is, no matter what I'm feeling, I don't know this guy at all.

We're quiet as we walk the few metres along the twilight pavement, the general rush of Tollcross filling the void when I don't know how to – cars zipping by, shops closing up and restaurants prepping. Walking into the warmth of the coffee shop, we take a small table at the back and Zoe looks over at us suspiciously as she settles up with a couple at the till.

I told her about Adam, of course, and she was openly annoyed at me – said she had been planning to cater our wedding, which I could only laugh numbly at.

'This place is nice,' Simon says genuinely, shrugging off his expensive coat. But even I can see he's a fish out of water here. He should be in some luxurious restaurant or hotel bar somewhere. Not a purple coffee shop in Tollcross.

A minute later, Zoe is over to us taking our order, glancing repeatedly at Simon as she does so, like he's some sort of movie star. And I suppose he does look like one, really. I'd never have met a guy like him in a million years in my old life.

Once Zoe's loped off to get the coffees, Simon turns back to me.

'Are you . . . dating him? Adam?' he says eventually, and I can see the anxiety on his face.

I think about the question for a moment, almost wishing I could say yes. But that's just not the reality anymore.

'No,' I say finally.

He nods, relief spreading across his features.

But questions bubble up in me now.

'Why are you here?' I say finally. After all, he was the one who cheated on Emily when they were engaged. He was the one who broke her heart and made her feel the need to leave that life, so why the wait? Why now?

He looks at me. 'Because you wouldn't reply to any of my texts, or the flowers on your birthday?'

Oh god.

So that was definitely him – the cardless flowers.

Simon turns to me and I stop, look up into his cobalt-blue eyes, which seem so very full of love right now.

'And I came up here to tell you something,' he says.

'What's that?' I say, heart thudding in my chest.

'The receipt—' he pauses '—you were right: I was with another woman.'

I look up at him sharply, ready to speak for Emily again, when he cuts in.

'But it wasn't what you think at all. It was just a dinner with an old girlfriend of mine, and I should have told you in advance, I know that now. I wanted to explain myself, but you'd already gone.'

I'm curious on Emily's behalf now; can't help but be vaguely protective too.

What possible reason is there to meet up with an old girl-friend and then lie about it?

'What is the explanation then?'

He nods, as though I've given him the permission he's been looking for. 'Everything had just gotten really hard. You were so focused on your work and I felt like I was doing everything for the wedding. It was all on me. You always put your career first over everything, something I totally admired about you, but eventually it completely took over – you know it did, Emily. We spoke about it, several times. And God help me,

I got lonely. Then she contacted me asking for a catch-up, for old time's sake, but nothing happened, I promise.

'And the thing is, Emily,' he continues, before I can interject, 'after you left, I just missed you so goddamn much, and I realised how stupid I'd been, how much I loved you too. I love your big smile and your terrible singing in the shower; I love how you make such a big effort with everyone, even that woman who was lost on that little back street that time in Madrid, remember? I love how determined you are to succeed at whatever you do, but most of all, I love how you had the courage to start all over again like you did, and I'd like to be a part of this new story, in some way. And we could stay in London or I could move up here to be with you, or we could go somewhere else together. Whatever you want, Emily, because all I know is, I'd follow you anywhere.' He takes a breath. 'I'd follow you forever.'

Something bigger starts to grow and expand inside me now. Those strange sensations again.

Because I've heard this all before, seen this all before – his devastatingly handsome face, his sorry words right here in this café.

And suddenly all these feelings come rushing up at me, memories resurfacing like bubbles in my mind, my heart – Simon's face across from mine under white sheets, sitting together on a plane somewhere and feeling so happy I could burst, dancing down some boulevard with Simon twirling me over and over under his arm, laying on some beach with him in a distant land, our hands intertwined on the sand, feeling like the world was at our fingertips.

And there is love there, even after all these months apart. So, maybe it was just a catch-up for old time's sake? A simple misunderstanding as he says.

A curdling of guilt starts in me now, that I should have looked a little more closely at Emily's life from the start. Because what if she was simply taking a break up here? What if she only stayed for a while then moved back down?

What if she got back together with Simon in the end?

Oh god, I'd never thought about that – that the course I'm on now might not be the one she finished on at all. I've been so concentrated on doing all the fun stuff I think she did, that I haven't actually considered any other pieces of her life.

My heart bleeds for Emily, because now I categorically know that this is the end for her; that these are her last months on Earth that I'm using up. I'll go back to my old, limited life, where I've got a bit more time. Emily, on the other hand, will be gone. Absolutely and completely.

So, what did she do the first time at this juncture?

What did she actually want?

I'm searching my mind for more images, more sensations. But it's all stopped again.

'Say something, Emily,' Simon says, and I look up sharply, see him gazing down at me. And I know I can't leave it here.

For her sake.

'Let's keep talking,' I say finally, firmly, 'if that suits you.'

Then he smiles the biggest of smiles. 'That suits me great.'

We talk for the next couple of hours over a bottle of wine about everything and nothing – about what the rest of the gang is up to, how Phoebe and Hector just had their second kid who Simon will be godfather to, how he went to Tristan and Layla's wedding in Cornwall and it was the most elaborate spectacle he'd ever seen. Business is going well with his dad, and his mum says hello to me, and I get another glimmer of a tall, elegant woman who spent a lot of time in spas. Simon is funny and confident and intriguing in this way that fascinates me, and I'm not sure I've met anyone like him before. But he's warm too, and I feel immediately at ease with him in the same way I did with Fran. Then before I know it, Zoe is shutting up shop around us and we slip back outside into the cold. Standing in front of my building, Simon gazes down at me with his deep blue eyes, and I know instinctively we're not done here – I know Emily was not done here.

'Can we keep talking then?' Simon says hopefully.

'Yes,' I agree, realising I actually do want to, and he grins.

After a quick kiss on his cheek, I head back into the building, and run back up the stairs. Standing uncertainly at the top, I glance only briefly towards Adam's door, a pain pulling at my heart, before turning left and heading into my own.

CHAPTER TWENTY-TWO

'Now move back into a parallel park here please.'

Clutching the wheel of the instructor's car, I glance at the woman beside me with her curly black hair and poker face. As smoothly as I can, I pull the car into the space behind us, even as my legs are shaking above the pedals.

I'm almost too scared to check if I've done it right, but when I turn around to the examiner again, I know from the curt little nod that I nailed it.

As the examiner starts making notes on her screen, I look out the window past her to where Charlie is standing. She gives me two thumbs up.

All the same, when the examiner puts her hands on her lap and turns to me, I can't help but gulp air down.

Please, please, please.

'Well,' she says, 'you'll be happy to know that you passed with flying colours, Emily. Congratulations.'

I immediately grin, reach in to hug the lady who lets out a yelp of surprise, until her shoulders soften slightly.

'Well done,' she says again into my shoulder, before pulling briskly back. 'Now go tell that friend of yours out there.' She cocks her eyebrow. 'She's starting to creep me out standing at the window like that.'

As soon as I'm out the car, Charlie rushes up to hug me. 'I knew you could do it,' she says, squeezing me tight.

'But then I did have a pretty great instructor.'

She shakes her head of blonde curls.

'It was all you, Emily,' she says, 'I could never have passed it in a bloody month. So, what now? What are you planning to do with this new freedom?'

'Drive,' I say, 'to our ski trip this weekend.'

We're almost at the end of the ski season already, and I know this is what Emily wanted to do from the flyers I found, so it's now or never. I'll be sad to miss the dance class with William on Friday though, and I suspect he will be too, post-dance dinner included. It's become something of a routine with him these days, and he's really coming out of his shell; staying out later and wanting to go new places. Just like me. But when I suggested he reach out to his brother and family again, he shook his head; told me it really had been too long.

'How are you feeling about seeing Adam?' Charlie says carefully.

'A little confused,' I say, because of course it will be strange to see him up there. Particularly after Simon's visit and all the emotions that's raised in me.

Charlie bites her lip, like she's got something on her mind. I frown. 'What is it?'

'Oh god, I was in two minds about saying anything . . .' she starts, 'but I think it's probably better that you know. Because I love both you and Adam, and I just want the two of you to be happy.'

'Does this have anything to do with Claire?' I say now, my heart thumping.

And she nods. 'They were engaged, you see.'

My heart plummets.

'Then he called it off,' she ploughs on, 'a few weeks before the wedding. Claire was absolutely devastated and I feel awful telling you this, but I'm just not sure Adam's got it in him to stay in one place. He had a difficult time growing up—'

'I know,' I cut through, feeling all sorts of strange again – another sort of déjà vu feeling when she mentioned Claire – and not for the first time, I wonder what happened exactly with Emily and Adam. There was something, I'm sure, I just don't know what or how much. A moment later it is gone, leaving me still reeling from Charlie's revelation about what happened with Claire.

'You OK?' Charlie says now, looking concerned. 'It's just that, after what you've already been through with Simon,

I'm not sure being with someone who struggles to commit fully is a great plan for you. But I feel really bad for saying anything now . . .'

'Oh, it's fine,' I say, even as my heart thuds, 'thanks for looking out for me.'

Charlie looks relieved.

'You still keen to come too, even if you're not skiing?' I say finally, willing her to say yes. Because I really need her there – I need her support more than she even knows.

'Of course,' she says brightly. 'I'm looking forward to getting some mountain air before the baby comes.'

'Great,' I say. 'It's going to be epic.'

'Truly epic,' she agrees, a big smile on her face once again.

* * *

The two of us set off early doors on the Friday in Adam's van, except this time, I'm driving. I can't help feeling a little nervous driving something this big – wonder if I should have practised in the city first, as Adam had gently suggested. But there's no time like the present and, clutching the steering wheel, I keep my eyes on the road. With the glittering cold Firth of Forth rushing away behind us, I can't help thinking of the last time Adam and I drove up north.

That first incredible night we spent together back in November. Things are so different now.

But still, I'm just happy to actually be doing this. We talk away about the activities I've been doing, what pieces he's making at the moment, until we eventually fall into a comfortable silence listening to the tinny radio together. He doesn't raise Simon's visit and neither do I, but I can't help wanting to explain what happened.

Which was ultimately nothing in the end.

But at the same time, I feel very confused. Simon's been messaging more and more since we met and I'm scared to admit I've been enjoying it – that I feel this rush of delight when I get one. Because ever since that evening in the Purple Pineapple, I've been getting so many more memories back – of those years at Oxford together, always hoping, always wondering if Simon Carmichael might feel the same. And then finally it happened . . . not at university, but in London. A rainy work night out with Fran right after I turned twenty-five and the three of us had far too many, and then that kiss I had with him at the end of the night. He was exactly the person I'd always seen myself with – exactly who my mother had always seen me with too – and he'd taken me on a 'proper' date to a Michelin-starred French restaurant the following week: champagne, red wine, his startling blue eyes on mine. I fell hard and fast, and by the end of the month, we were in love.

So many sights and sounds, so many glimmers and flashes and sensations, which are getting under my skin almost as though they're my own. And I'm becoming convinced Emily must have been torn about what to do – receipt or no receipt. Because I remember more about that too now, why it triggered me to go. And it wasn't just about a little bit of paper. It was about a growing distance between us as I worked all the time; how sometimes I would come home late to find him not yet in either; how sometimes I would catch Simon texting in bed late at night before he would hurriedly put the phone down and say it was work. But at the same time, I can't help thinking about the look in his eyes in the café, the warmth from him. He still loves me, I know he does – he wants to marry me. So maybe it was just in Emily's imagination. Maybe she was tired and stressed and struggling, like I already know she was. And no matter the electric pull I have towards Adam, this isn't about me and what I want anymore. This is about Emily and figuring out what she wanted at the end – and who.

I spoke to Fran about it all, of course, and while she listened to all the details of my meet-up with Simon, I could tell she didn't approve that we were still in touch – thought I should close a door on the whole thing and move on. *You deserve better*, she'd said, a particular firmness to her voice. And I found myself wondering if there was anything else Fran knew about Simon. But then I reasoned with myself that after everything Emily and her had been through together, she would surely just say.

Now, as we drive past tumbling snowy fields and the odd puffing chimney, with the Cairngorms looming up in the distance, I have this soothing feeling of coming home. We used to come up here twice a year, after all – it was easy enough to drive to, and more importantly, not too far from the hospital in Inverness.

But was this really such a good idea? I haven't been since Cat died and, to be honest, I'm really not sure how I'll feel about it. Will I cope?

Everything else was booked in the area when we checked though, and I had this feeling that the cottage might be free – they don't rent it out all the time. So, I'll just have to get on with it.

I'll just have to be fine.

Bumping down the country track towards the loch now, I concentrate on the driving, trying my best not to skid off to the side. But Adam's van holds steady beneath me and I feel his reassuring presence beside me.

'Where exactly are we staying again?' Adam says as he looks out at the tall, white-powdered trees above him.

'You'll see,' I say, spotting a sign up ahead finally with the name 'Inch Cottage' on the gate.

'Here we go.' I swing the van right down a final track and there it is, right by the loch – all thick white walls and red iron roof, set in its own rambling garden. Just like I remember.

'Wow,' Adam exclaims, 'this place is amazing.' He squints out the window at the smoke puffing up from the chimney.

As we get of the van, the red kitchen door opens up wide and Charlie tumbles into the snow, closely followed by Sven.

'You're here!' she cries, running towards me in the most enormous furry winter boots. She's wearing a sparkly pink sweater, her bump beginning to slightly protrude from it, and as she envelops me in a big hug, I feel the firmness of it pressing against my abdomen.

Sven walks out now in just a t-shirt and jeans, and in seconds the four of us are chatting and exclaiming and hugging. As we head into the warmth, I catch Adam's eye at the last moment, feel electric sparks rush through me.

Inside, Charlie and Sven have already got everything sorted after they picked the key up from the rental agency in town a little earlier. The ramshackle kitchen is stuffed full of fresh bread, fruit, wine and biscuits.

'You didn't need to do this,' I say, walking in.

'Oh, don't be silly,' Charlie tells me, 'I'm the one eating for two anyway. Coffee, guys? Or are you ready for cocktails?' She grins.

'Cocktails would be amazing,' I say, feeling a buzz of excitement. With all the activities and nights out I've been doing recently, I've come to love that rush of adrenalin coursing through me, this absolute high that comes from seizing the moment.

It's all so different to my old life.

As Charlie and Sven get busy in the kitchen, I find myself wandering around the space I used to know so well. The scent of old books and rugs, the clementine soap Mum used to use. It's still around me and it takes all my strength not to flinch at the family photo hanging beside the old red Aga – of Mum, Dad, Cat, Jess and me, up here about six months before it happened. Mum and Dad are in the background near the loch with Jess, smiling away, while I stand somewhere nearby. And right up at the camera is Cat, so close that her features are huge and she's grinning like mad down the lens – a rare weekend away from Fraser.

'Nice family,' Adam says beside me. Hurriedly wiping tears away, I move forwards into living area, dump my bag on the floor.

'How did you say that you knew them again?' Adam asks, doing the same.

'Oh, just family acquaintances,' I say quickly, before taking in the cosy room. Still the same stripy rug, still the small ketchup stain down the back of the cream sofa – from a game of pirates Cat insisted on us playing when we were younger. My parents have updated a few things, I guess – that trendy standing lamp in the corner and the new armchairs by the fire. But it's more for the rental guests than themselves. After all, they don't come up here anymore either.

Everyone crying. A darkness like no other.

Suddenly I feel a little strange; I'm not sure this was a brilliant idea after all.

'You OK?' Adam says and I open my eyes. I didn't realise they were shut.

'Yup,' I say quickly and turn to him. 'I'll show you where the bedrooms are.'

'Oh, just to say,' Charlie calls over, 'we dumped our bags in the double downstairs, but it looked like there were two rooms under the eaves upstairs, if that suits you guys?'

'Yup,' I say, a little breathlessly, 'that works fine for me.'

'Suits me too,' Adam adds, and I'm sure he sounds a little breathless too.

* * *

Later in the evening, we're all sitting around the table, laughing away over wine like nothing much has changed. Sven made the most gorgeous roast, with locally sourced venison and an outrageous amount of side dishes – potatoes, winter greens, cauliflower cheese and more, all washed down by the bottles of Malbec Adam picked up from the little French place in Tollcross. We go pretty heavy on the alcohol (other than Charlie) and I know I'm topping up everyone's glasses a bit too regularly but I just really want to have fun on this trip – the real sort of abandoned fun that I've never had before. I instigate a game of Flip Cup and we dance around the living room and I laugh so much it hurts. Charlie and I chat through every possible crazy baby name we can think of and demolish a box of Celebrations together, and I have such a sense of warmth and headiness that makes me want to do this all over again.

'Oh god,' Charlie says eventually with a yawn, 'I'm sorry, it's not even ten o'clock and I'm already turning into a bloody pumpkin.'

'Come on,' I say, unwilling for the fun to stop, 'before you know it, you'll have a baby in tow and these sorts of nights will just be a dream.'

She nods in defeat. 'OK, maybe one more of those mock-tails for me please.'

'There you go,' I say as I bounce off with her glass. After all, there's no need to have a super-quiet pregnancy like Jess's – all she did the whole time was watch TV on the sofa while looking out for the boys' alien-like belly kicks.

The rest of us have another real cocktail, of course, and I can see Sven and Adam's eyes start to blear. I'm feeling pretty woozy now, intoxicated by all the drinks, but it doesn't matter if we stay up late – we'll just dose up on caffeine tomorrow morning. You only live once after all, and in Emily's specific case, for only four months more.

'All right, guys,' Sven says about an hour later, and hauls himself up from the table, 'I think that's probably enough for us. I need to get this tiny dancer to bed.' He glances at Charlie briefly before looking around at all the dishes and glasses still out. 'I can just . . .'

'Never mind that,' I wave him off sloppily, 'we can deal with them in the morning.'

'All right.' Sven wobbles on the spot a little again, before Charlie guides him towards their bedroom.

After they've disappeared, Adam and I stagger up the stairs to bed too, and once again, I breathe in that soothing scent of home.

'Well,' Adam says, turning to me at the top, 'I had a fun night.'

Blinking back the thoughts, I look up into those amazingly kind, if somewhat bloodshot, eyes; trace down those solid shoulders I know so intimately under his black fleece. If I leaned in two inches I'd be able to kiss him.

'Me too,' I swallow.

A pause; his mouth parts.

'Well, goodnight, Emily,' he says eventually, and with a final glance, he heads into his room.

'Goodnight,' I whisper, still standing in the hallway. My lips are aching for him, the rest of my body too and I'm not sure if it's the alcohol or not, but I want to be with him so badly right now, it takes all my effort to not follow him. A part of me can't help wondering, yet again, if something happened between Emily and Adam the first time.

Could she have fallen for him too?

A beat.

Could I be with him again if she did? Even if Emily isn't actually here anymore, I still want to honour what *she* would have wanted, and who – if it's going to stick in time forever. So what if that someone was Adam?

But then I think about Simon, the way he looked at me – the fact that we were actually engaged once, and he openly wanted to be with me forever, something I'm really not sure Adam can give. Not after what Charlie told me about him leaving Claire like he did. So, I know that I'd only be getting with Adam for me.

I go through to my dark room eventually, flop down on the bed to see if it helps, but it only feels worse somehow. I stare at the wall and try to imagine what Adam's thinking right now, what he's feeling. My whole body is firing with a mix of longing, frustration and drunkenness, and I wonder how I'm ever going to be able to sleep, knowing where I am and just how close he is. Although we live right across the hall from each other, there's still something separate about it. But in this place, our doors are wide open.

Beckoning to each other.

Eventually, as with everything, my body takes over, and my eyes finally shut.

Sleep comes.

CHAPTER TWENTY-THREE

The next morning, I wake groggily. My head is splitting and my mouth tastes like sandpaper left out in the sun. Reaching to find water, I find that I have none, and looking around the room, I suddenly realise where I am – in our old room, in the cottage. It's all here again in the daylight – the eaves, the little Scottish paintings, the matching quilts at the foot of the beds, the lamp with the beaded tassels Cat found in a shop up here, her old reading books on the shelf: *The Secret Garden*, *Little Women* and *The Baby-Sitters Club* collection and, for a moment, I can't breathe from it all.

The last day Cat existed on this planet.

Those final steps she took just outside this house.

Oh god, oh god, oh god.

But then I look down at my hands – Emily's hands – and my heart rate slows as I remember why I'm here: to spend time with good friends, to eat and to ski, and do all the things I never permitted myself to do before. Because I can't deny that all of this isn't largely for me – I remember so clearly watching as other people in the area piled into their lodges and chalets, loaded up with booze and ski gear, and I would wonder what it felt like, living to the max like that. Now, finally, that gets to be me.

Getting out of bed slowly now, I feel a bit hellish and regretful of quite how much we drank, how late we stayed up, but I manage to get my base layers on and brush my teeth before heading downstairs in search of sustenance. It's already nine o'clock and I curse myself for missing the best part of the morning on the mountains. Down in the kitchen, Adam is already dealing with the mess we left last night.

'Hey,' I croak, a touch of guilt kicking in as he looks at me coming down. He looks pretty jaded too, and I know I played a part in that. There are shadows beneath his eyes, and his hair is ruffled like he's been tossing and turning all night.

'Good morning,' he says in a deeper voice than normal and places a very welcome pot of coffee on the table. 'How are you feeling?'

'Rough,' I say truthfully. 'I'm not sure I've ever had that much alcohol before.'

'Well, just get some coffee into you,' he says gently, 'and you'll be fine. But let's maybe take it a bit easier tonight, Miss Party, all right?'

'All right,' I smile ruefully as I take a seat at the table. He pours us both a cup, putting milk in mine while leaving his black.

'Do you fancy some eggs too?' he says, pointing at the stove. 'I could poach them, if you like.'

I pause, feeling all kinds of emotions rushing at me – breakfast together, coffees together, eggs on the stove.

Just like before.

'That's OK,' I say, eventually. 'I'll get some toast in a bit.'

'All right,' he says, and takes a seat across the table.

We drink our coffee in the comfortable silence we've always had – just two hungover friends up early, but content with the other's company.

Our eyes meet and I feel he's about to say something, when footsteps sound from somewhere. We both look around sharply to see a very dishevelled Sven walking towards the table in his boxers and a stained Scandi Pizza Man hoodie.

'Morning,' we both manage to grunt.

'I feel like wild animals attacked me,' Sven says, 'and then I got run over by a truck.'

I can't help laughing, even if I feel a little sheepish. 'I'm sorry, that was my fault. I got a bit carried away.'

'No shit,' Sven says, heading to get two mugs from the cupboard. Bringing them over to the table he takes a seat. 'Ah, it was all good fun. Nothing a little ski won't fix, once Charlie's up.'

'Charlie's not going skiing, is she?' I say, a trace of worry kicking in.

'No, no,' Sven says, pouring himself and Charlie a cup, 'she'll just hang out at the bottom of the slopes. I feel sort of bad leaving her but remember what you kept saying last night?'

I frown, my memory of it all blurring somewhat. 'What did I keep saying?'

'YOLO,' Sven and Adam say at the same time.

You Only Live Once.

I feel myself cringing. 'God, sorry *again*.'

'Don't be,' Sven says, taking the cups back to the bedroom now, 'it's all good. We'll catch you guys back here for dinner later, OK?'

'Sounds like a plan,' Adam says, and meets my eyes across the table again.

It dawns on me in this moment that I'll be spending a whole day with Adam, out in the mountains. And I don't know if it's the caffeine flooding through my system or knowing I get to be close for him for all that time, but my stomach does the greatest backflip – twice.

* * *

It's a clear day up on the slopes and I can feel the pain in my head starting to ease off with the freshness of it all, plus about

232

a gallon of water. The snow is light and powdery-looking under the chairlift we're on, which Adam insists is a rarity in Scotland – it's usually sheet ice and rock, apparently, and he saw it all in his childhood – skiing in Japan, snowboarding in the Canadian Rockies. But as I lower myself off the lift at the top, I feel a pleasing bounce beneath my skis, totally different from what I experienced at the dry slopes back in Edinburgh.

It all looks quite different to the trips I've organised in the Alps, none of the outrageous peaks or huge stretches of woodland. It's a vast range of glittering white, vulnerable and exposed to the elements. But there's something so glorious about the way the slopes meet the sky like that.

There's nowhere to hide out here.

As Adam leads me slowly down the run, a slight hitch of nerves hits my chest, and I think back to the first time I tried it a few weeks ago. It had felt pretty unnatural at first, of course, and my whole body had braced as I'd slid slowly down the synthetic hill away from the instructor. And then I was going faster and faster.

'Shit,' I'd said, as the toes of my skis had pointed together then crossed. My heart rate had shot up as I'd flown through the air, landing with a thump on my side. I'd started laughing because the funny thing was, it hadn't hurt, not really. Not enough to take away from how awesome it had been, that feeling of flying.

The next time, I'd followed the instructor's line, imitating what she'd done as best as I could. I'd managed to make the turn for a moment only, before my skies seem to run ahead of me and I was flying backwards through the air – cold ground again, skis tangled in front of me. But this time I hadn't laughed. I'd just picked myself up and dusted myself down again.

Let's go, I'd said.

We'd kept doing it, the instructor swooping down in front and me following behind with a new sort of determination, the type where all I could see was the bottom of that run and the only way I could get there was to move. I'd fallen a third time, a fourth, my skies either crossing in front of me or me just simply losing my nerve when I started moving too fast. But then I'd managed to make two turns in a row, then three. The final time I'd fallen, I'd looked back up at where I'd come from and suddenly I'd realised just how far I'd skied. After that one go, I was hooked. I returned several times with the instructor or by myself, determined to get the hang of it. It was expensive, of course, but since I knew how short Emily's life would be, I didn't feel bad about spending the money she'd saved anymore – no point in saving for a rainy day when the days are running short.

Ahead of me, Adam pauses now on the slope we're on, and I pull up alongside him.

'You were ace up there,' he grins. 'Did you seriously only begin a few weeks ago?'

I smile, knowing he's only being nice – I'll never be a pro but I'm still proud of myself for giving it a crack, for even getting to this stage.

'You would love the summer skiing in Canada,' he says, pauses. 'I might do some when I go actually.'

My breath catches. 'You're leaving?'

'Not forever,' he says steadily, 'but yeah, I'm planning on going out in May and then spending the summer there, I'll be leaving in a month or so.' He looks softly at me. 'There's nothing holding me here right now and I've completed a bunch of orders, which should last me for a while money-wise.'

I swallow as I realise the enormity of what he's saying.

I'll never see him again.

But not just that, it's also confirmed what I suspected about him all along – he was always going to leave in the end, and I would have only have gotten hurt. He didn't even fight for me, not really. It only took one quick push for him to go to Norway the first chance he could after Christmas. It's just as well I called things off when I did.

'Sounds like a great trip,' I say, my voice slightly strangled.

'Hopefully,' he replies, and we just stand there for a moment, uncertain.

Eventually he nods down at a significantly steeper section. 'You game for this last stretch?'

I take in a lungful of cold air, smile. Because what else can I do?

'I'm game.'

'Good. Well, you go ahead this time; I'll go behind.'

'You might regret that when you're skiing over me.'

He tilts his head, a soft expression on his face. 'I think you've got this, Emily. Just remember to head forwards every time you turn,' he says, making a slicing action down the mountain with his gloved hand.

'All right,' I say firmly, and before I can dwell on it, I'm off down the mountain again, except this time, I go forwards when I turn. The wind rushes at my face before I push down with my boot. It still feels slightly odd to plummet headfirst in order to change direction, but as I turn into the slope and soar across, I wonder if this is maybe where I've been going wrong in my own life. Because you have to just give things a shot, and maybe you fall down, but maybe you'll fly. And isn't it worth the risk? Isn't it worth falling a hundred times to finally get that soaring feeling in your soul?

Then suddenly we're close to the bottom and I've actually done it. I've skied down a mountain and I didn't fall. It's not hurting me, or anyone else for that matter, and all I want is to do it all over again.

Because this is living.

This is everything.

A whooping noise behind me makes me smile, and I finally come to a stop at the bottom. Adam pulls up alongside me and, as we look out together at the white ridges, with the dazzling sun glinting above it all, I think I've never felt more alive in my life.

* * *

Driving back to the cottage with Adam, with the sun setting rosily in the sky, my whole body feels pumped from the experience. And as we chat away easily about which slopes we'll attack together tomorrow, I get that overwhelming pull towards him again – this electric feeling spreading through me when I catch a glance at his hands, which once ran across the entirety of me.

My heart is beating wildly at the thought as we pull into the driveway. Charlie and Sven will already be back, the fire will be crackling and no doubt Sven will have started putting together some incredible canapés like last night. Perfect.

It's clear something isn't right though, as soon as we pull up to the house. All the lights are out and the chimney is still. Suddenly that setting sun in the distance, which had looked so rosy before, is looking blood-like in its redness.

The two of us immediately get out, look around the area. There's no sign of Charlie's red Mini.

I can feel this strange sense of wrongness swelling inside me, which I've felt only once before.

'Let's check inside before we start worrying,' Adam says, reading my mind as he unlocks the cottage door.

It's clear when we enter that someone has spent a while tidying everything up. The breakfast dishes have all been put away and the chequered table wiped clean – the fire in the living room has even been swept and reset for the evening, and both of us heave a sigh of relief.

'Maybe they came back early and went out somewhere,' I say.

'Or they did something else entirely today?' Adam suggests, and heads to put the kettle on for a tea.

It's just as I'm pulling down a couple of mugs for us that Adam's phone rings, and as he pulls it out his pocket, his face lights up.

'Sven,' he says, answering it, 'where are . . .'

His face falls again and he glances at me. Then he walks across the kitchen, stops at the window. So I can't see his face, can't hear what's being said.

'Oh god,' he's saying, placing his hand on the island. 'Oh god.'

My heart is pounding. What's happening?

Adam finally turns, takes a breath in as he says the words I was dreading, 'Charlie had a fall on the mountain this afternoon and she's been airlifted to the hospital.'

He pauses.

'I think we should go quickly.'

CHAPTER TWENTY-FOUR

It takes us longer than it should to get to the hospital because of the ice, but at least Adam's driving this time. I was just too jittery, my legs shaking from a combination of skiing and shock, but I was still able to direct him before he'd even turned the satnav on. I knew how confused he must have been at how well I knew the route, how I could even tell him which back roads to take.

This isn't the first time I've raced to the hospital here.

This isn't the first time I've been at risk of losing someone I love. But it's simply not the time to be concealing my old self from him.

Because Charlie has to be OK.

The baby has to be OK.

The words go over and over in my head as we approach the bright lights of the hospital. Parking up as quickly as possible, the two of us jump out and run across the grey car park to the tall beige buildings at the centre. Inside, Adam goes up to the reception desk, as I stand back a little, trying to process what is happening.

A million thoughts are running through my head. How did Charlie fall if she wasn't skiing? Did I cause this to happen by suggesting we all come up here? By keeping everyone up like that. If Charlie hadn't have come here, would she and the baby still be OK?

William's family were not OK.

Cat was not OK.

Before I can process it any further, however, Adam is telling me which ward we need to go to. I follow dumbly, heart pounding in my chest.

'They've been given a private room apparently,' Adam says, but I can only nod, panic surging up inside me.

'You all right?' Adam says, turning briefly to me with worried eyes, and it's enough to snap me out of it. Because this isn't about me right now. It's about Charlie and the baby.

Arriving outside the room, we pause briefly at the sight inside. Sven is sitting with his back to us on a hospital chair, beside Charlie on a hospital bed, seemingly asleep. She's lying on her side, a slight bump still protruding out from the covers, thank God, but her usually active body is now hooked up to all sorts of wires and monitors. It's an experience I know only too well, though seeing it on Charlie seems different somehow. She's supposed to be up dancing and laughing and moving. And now one mistake – just one – might have destroyed everything.

As though sensing our presence, Sven turns sharply. His usually calm-looking eyes are red and swollen and he's still wearing his black salopettes and skins from the mountain. He gets up and walks over to the door. Immediately Adam pulls him into a hug and Sven shuts his eyes. A small noise comes out.

'Thanks for coming, guys,' he says eventually, stepping back before hugging me too, and as he does, I think about how much I truly love Sven and Charlie. I can't bear the thought of them suffering.

They're like family to me.

'How is she?' I ask, just as Adam says, 'What happened?'

Sven shakes his head. 'She was just so excited to be close to the mountains; you know how she gets sometimes . . .'

I nod. I really do.

'She convinced me to take her up in the end, just for a quick ski on a green slope. But then she fell out of nowhere . . . she was so tired.'

'But how is she?' I repeat, heart beating fast. 'How is the baby?'

Sven's face darkens and he looks back in through the glass at Charlie. 'It's too early to tell at the moment, apparently . . . the way she fell caused some internal bleeding,' he says, tailing off.

He covers his face with his hands and I immediately go to put my arm about him.

He takes a few breathes in.

'You guys should get home and get some sleep,' he says after a few moments.

Adam and I shake our heads at the same time. 'No way,' Adam says. 'We'll hang out here tonight, see it through with you.'

After a moment Sven nods. 'OK,' he says, putting up no further fight.

*   *   *

Light, corridor walls, the clattering of plates, the scent of toast. I look blearily around when I wake the next morning, feel something soft against my cheek – Adam's fleecy shoulder. I lift my head up to see we're in another part of the hospital, having slept on a couple of stiff plastic chairs through the night. It's dimly lit, though doctors and nurses are still rushing by. An alarm is going somewhere. My heart beats faster and, just like that, I'm back there again.

The day my whole world collapsed.

*   *   *

It was me who suggested we come up to the cottage for the weekend, at the tail-end of that balmy summer – for 'old times' sake'. Cat was now living with Fraser in Edinburgh, and I would be off to art school soon. Already I felt like there was something precious about this moment in time, like it was a hazy peak that we would never get back again. Maybe because of that, I allowed myself to relax a little, be the 'doer' for once. I remember Cat smiling across at me in the car as she drove: 'What's come over you, sis? Is this the new Maggie?'

I laughed, but perhaps it was? Perhaps I could start doing more – living more. So, we bought a tonne of stuff from the supermarket: wine, crisps, pizzas, sweets and everything we could think of for our final hurrah together. Stuff I would never normally be allowed but on this occasion, I thought I could relax a little – after all, Mum wasn't going to be there. And we weren't going to go completely nuts – just enjoy ourselves. I knew how happy it made Cat, seeing me let go of the reins slightly. Stop worrying quite so much for everyone.

That first night we ate crap and drank wine and watched brat-pack movies until the wee hours of the morning – *Pretty In Pink*, *The Breakfast Club* and our favourite, *Ferris Bueller's Day Off*. That was always our thing: watching eighties movies and escaping to that safe, fun-only era where the hardest thing you had to deal with was getting a great dress for the prom. The next morning, groggy but happy, we went for a long walk around the loch together, ambling our way under the tall pine trees, the sun glinting down through the branches at us.

The water on the loch was calm that day, inviting in the clammy summer heat, and we paused when we found the high bit we used to jump off as kids. Mum had banned it years ago due to my condition but it probably wasn't a good idea anyway, given the lower water level in recent years. We laughed about how we used to do synchronised dives, and I said we should do it again. Cat laughed (at the idea of me doing it clearly) and, in a moment of defensiveness, I smilingly suggested that perhaps *she* was the one not brave enough to try it. Then we walked on, talking about all the things I would do when I got up to Aberdeen, all the art I would create and the experiences I would have. And it felt lovely for a time, to feel like I would get a few years of normality: at some point, we agreed, I would get a new heart, and everything would just work itself out.

She told me her plans too, that she was applying to do nursing – it had been her secret dream apparently, after seeing how much they did for me in the hospitals, and when she said it, it made absolute sense. Of course she would be a fantastic nurse. Of course she would make everyone feel better, with her cheer and spark, just like she'd always done for me. Then she admitted she and Fraser had had a fight, and suddenly I realised why she was only too happy to disappear off with me. It was over something stupid, she said, but she'd gotten angry and walked out. And I felt awful for her, knowing how much Fraser meant to her, how serious they'd become. 'It will be OK,' I said gently, 'just speak to him when you get back,' and she nodded; said she would do that.

Said she loved him so much.

That evening, we had dinner together again, some chilli I cooked up for us over the course of a lazy afternoon, then we just lay on the sofa together, reading magazines and scrolling through my fresher's week itinerary. We had a few too many glasses of wine and I fell asleep on the sofa.

When I woke, she was gone, and even though I felt a twinge of worry, I just put it down to the alcohol; after all, Cat disappeared off to do stuff all the time. In the end, it took me an hour to fully realise something was wrong, and I will regret that hour for the rest of my life. I will forever regret falling into an alcohol-induced sleep on the sofa and not trusting that kick of worry when I woke. Because, instead, I went upstairs and had a shower. I took a while drying my hair, sent a message to Mum saying we were having a great time and not to worry. And then I headed back downstairs and waited for her to reappear.

But she never did. My darling, wonderful sister, the person who made me tick, the person I was supposed to grow old with.

My other half.

I will never forget that image of her floating face down out on the water, below the high bit we used to dive from – *for old times' sake*, I could imagine her saying as she leapt up high, eyes shining. But now, her usually bright-red hair was splayed dark, and my gut twisted when I realised what she'd done; what I'd done, by goading her like that before. I ran in screaming, pulled her limp body out, then I shouted as loud as I could for someone, anyone to help. But there was no one was there.

No one heard me.

I went into some sort of auto mode next – called emergency services, administered the CPR we'd both been taught until they got there, and then when the ambulance finally arrived, I rode with her all the way to the hospital just praying that it could all be taken away; that this was all an awful, awful dream.

But it wasn't a dream, and they couldn't revive her.

And it was me who had to call home and hear my mother's wails down the line when I told her what had happened.

Just a simple trip, just a moment of fun was all it took to destroy everything.

And I knew in that moment that it was all my fault – despite what anyone said later on about her knowing the water levels were shallow and it being a reckless move. If I had never suggested that trip, if I had never encouraged her to jump, my sister would still be here. If I had simply stayed being careful, stayed being grateful for the small life I had, nothing bad would have happened to her big one.

But it did.

I took her life.

And she'll never get it back.

* * *

A stirring beside me, and Adam wakes.

'Is that an alarm?' he says, looking around. Then before I know it, he's jumped to his feet, and he's walking away down the corridor. Dazed and tearful, like I'm coming out of a watery dream, I follow behind.

Sven is in the corridor outside the room when we get there, and he is hunched over himself, head in his hands. My heart stops.

Oh god, oh god.

Not again.

Not Charlie and the baby. I'll stop doing my list, I won't push it any more than I already have. Because if I really think about it – this list was never about Emily; it was about me and all the things *I* always wanted to do. I went around her flat and made blind assumptions based on some flyers she probably thought nothing of, some hiking boots she maybe had no intention of ever actually using – an atlas she likely never looked at and one solitary chat with a dance instructor. But this is what happens when I take chances.

Everything goes wrong.

Everyone loses.

'Sven,' I say, putting one shaky hand on his shoulder. He looks up sharply, his eyes filled with tears.

And then, out of nowhere, he smiles.

'They're going to be OK,' he says, grabbing my hands in both of his own. 'They're both going to be OK.'

* * *

A few minutes later and I'm ushered into the room with Charlie, as Sven speaks to Adam outside. Sven looks incredibly relieved but there's a new strain on his face, which I've never seen before.

Charlie's still lying in bed, looking just as out of place as the night before – her blond hair too bright for the room, her face devoid today of her usually spunky make-up.

'Charlie,' I say, walking towards her slowly, 'are you all right?'

She takes in a breath, looks at me, but her eyes are suddenly blank. 'What do you think?'

I'm a bit thrown by her tone but I also know she's been through a lot in the past twelve hours.

'Is there anything I can get you?' I say. 'Some water maybe?'

She shakes her head and I feel something uncomfortable rise up in me now.

'I'm really sorry this happened . . .' I start.

'Yup, me too,' she says, rubbing the bump in front of her. A silence.

'Was it a rock?' I ask.

She shakes her head. 'I really don't want to talk about it, Emily. And I won't be doing anything on the list anymore either, OK?'

'OK,' I say softly, thrown by her abrupt tone.

But at the same time, I know I deserve this. This is all my fault – if I hadn't suggested the trip and kept everyone up so late, then none of this would have happened. If I hadn't thrown caution to the wind, then we wouldn't be in this position. Just like with Cat.

'I'm so sorry,' I say, swallow, 'but the good news is, you're both healthy, right?'

She shrugs. 'Maybe, maybe not. Who knows, though, if there's any lasting implications?'

'But Sven said—'

'Sven isn't a doctor,' Charlie snaps.

'Charlie I—'

'Just stop,' she says now, holding her hand up, and she looks so very exhausted in this moment. So utterly spent and I feel awful.

'I just need to be alone right now,' she says, her voice cracking.

I'm about to saying something, anything to help, when Charlie turns to face the other wall. I don't move, too upset about what's happened – what I've caused – but after a moment, I realise there is nothing else to do but go.

Go home.

* * *

The journey back down to Edinburgh with Adam is much quieter than the way up, the shock of the accident still ricocheting through us. I don't tell Adam exactly what was said with Charlie, but I think he knows it was fraught. 'She just needs a bit of time to recover,' he says gently at one point and even though I try to be reassured by his words, I can't quite feel their truth.

When we finally get back to our building, I stand sadly on the pavement, just taking it all in.

Reaching the top of the stairs with our backpacks a few minutes later, I turn to go into my flat, when I feel him reach for my hand. I look back to see his eyes on mine, warm and searching.

'Don't go,' he says. 'Come travelling with me.'

My heart catches in my chest. 'Why? So, you can have someone to hang out with?'

'No,' he says, frowning lightly, 'because I want to be with you.'

I half laugh, still exhausted by today's events. 'Today you might, but what about tomorrow? Or the next day? What if I wanted to stay exactly where I am. Would you stay too?'

Adam doesn't answer immediately and I find myself nodding. 'See, you were always going to leave eventually. You always do.'

'That's not true,' he says firmly.

'Oh, isn't it?' I say, my heart thumping now. 'What happened with Claire, Adam? That's right, Charlie told me.'

He swallows. 'That was different, it felt different with her. I told you that.'

'Nothing seems very different to me,' I find myself saying wearily. 'People need you here – Charlie, Sven, me – but you're still just going off anyway.'

'That's because the world never let me down,' he says gruffly now. 'The world was the only consistent thing in my life. Do you know what it was like, never having anyone to depend on? Being left to fend for myself like that.'

'No,' I start, 'but—'

'So you don't have any idea what I went through with Claire. Do you know she said if I didn't settle down and stop travelling completely, she would leave me?'

'No,' I whisper now, feeling awful for him.

'So I knew she would ultimately be happier with someone else, and it also just confirmed to me,' he says, 'that the only person I can depend on to actually show up for me, is me . . . until I met you that is, and I wondered if maybe, just maybe, you might be that person to show up for me too.'

Tears prick at my eyes because I want to show up for him, I do. I want to follow him to Canada and travel the world and go everywhere I can with him. He's the most vibrant, warm, enthusiastic person I've ever met, after Cat.

Adam reaches for my hand and a lump starts in my throat, as I wonder what it would feel like to just jump on a plane with him – live in the moment, like he always does.

Even if this is all going to end.

But after everything that just happened, I have to stop thinking about me and start thinking more about what Emily would have wanted in her last months; keep her alive and honour her legacy like I'd planned – in the important ways. And not just that, the closer I get to the day of the transplant, the more I'm recognising that I can't just up and leave the UK. Emily has to be here for my other self to receive the heart, and I'm not entirely sure I want to risk throwing anything off-course. Because something about Charlie's accident has shaken me and I have this innate sense that that didn't happen the first time. I just know it – in the same way I've known that some other things definitely *did* happen the first time – this growing awareness that I could change something here.

Change the outcome.

The thought makes me shiver and there's something else about it all too, something knocking at my brain. Like a puzzle piece I'm not quite fitting into place – or my brain won't let me fit into place.

Adam takes a breath when I say nothing, holds my hand tighter. He smells of warm fleece and joy and light, and everything I've fallen for about him.

'Say something, Emily,' he says. 'Don't do this for the second time ... I don't think I can go through it again. I won't go through it again.'

Those words. The way he's looking at me now, so very full of love.

But I have to see this through for Emily, and my other self, to the end.

'I can't, Adam. I'm sorry.'

CHAPTER TWENTY-FIVE

The next month goes by in a blur as I finally put together my photography portfolio for Emily's college application. I feel certain this was important to her – just like Cat with her nursing training. Except, because of me, Cat never even got the chance to apply, let alone get accepted.

And I won't let that happen to Emily too – I won't ruin her legacy like that.

I can't deny I'm enjoying the application process, though, and like with everything I've done so far, I find my soul come alive as I stretch myself; seeing what else I can do in this healthy body.

And perhaps when I'm back in my old life, I could become a photographer too. There was nothing physically stopping me, I'm realising.

I feel a little bad when William comes calling, asking if I'm coming to dance classes, but I really don't have much time left – I have to get this done for her. Anyway, I know he's had his eye on a woman called Ruth who goes every week; even joked he might ask her out for a tea. So maybe this could be his opportunity to do something about it?

I struggle a little with the application, figuring out exactly what kind of story I'm looking to tell with my pictures; what I'm trying to say with all these images I've taken around the city. In the end, I just take the plunge and do it – finish the project and send it off. I know that at the end of the day, there's no perfect way to do anything. You just have to take a shot.

I wish I could talk it over with Charlie but she's made it abundantly clear she doesn't want to see me right now, and anytime I've called the flat, Sven gently tells me she's not up for company right now.

I can't even talk to Adam about it, the person who actually put me in touch with Daphne in the first place, but I know it's not appropriate now – not fair on him either. We haven't spent any time together back in Edinburgh and, although it hurts, I know it's still for the best. Sometimes I catch myself glancing across at his door when I'm back from a run or see him from my window heading off to the workshop and I feel something I don't even want to think about. Can't think about.

Because falling for him now, when I've realised who I need to see next, is even less of an option. And, just like with Cat and Fraser, I'm starting to think that what happened between

Emily and Simon was a simple misunderstanding – something stupid which didn't mean anything.

But unlike with Cat, I can actually tell Simon that. I can make it right again, if that's what he wants too, which I'm assuming he does from the amount he's been messaging. I worry about him a lot in all of this, of course – the devastation he'll feel when Emily goes. But the truth is, I know from seeing Fraser after the funeral that he'd have given anything to have had those final days with Cat. And even though Simon is going to lose Emily at the end of all of this, I'm pretty sure he'd still want that final time with a special person like her – even if that time is short.

I'm just placing the last of my clothes in Emily's fancy suitcase, zipping it up, when my phone starts ringing.

Fran.

'Hello.' I smile.

'E! You all set?'

'Just about; still deciding on how many ball gowns I need for this wedding weekend.'

She laughs, her genuine, warm one. 'Don't be silly, we only need your wonderful self . . . and on that note, are you bringing anyone? Adam perhaps?'

I sigh because we've been over this already. 'You know we're not together anymore.'

'But why not?' she says. 'It was all going so well before.'

'I'm just not sure if it's the right thing for me.'

A pause. 'Is this about Simon? I thought we talked about that – about him not deserving you.'

'I know,' I say eventually, 'but I think it might have all been a misunderstanding. I just need to spend a little time with him while I'm down – see if we can fix it.'

A silence follows, and I can tell she really doesn't approve, which irritates me slightly but then I guess she's just looking out for me. There's something else there too – a tingle in my chest, a sensation I can't quite put my finger on.

'Well, I guess you have to see him at the wedding anyway,' Fran concedes eventually, and the tingle fades away. 'When are you coming anyway?'

'Today, actually; I'm getting the train down this morning.'

'Oh, amazing,' she says, 'do you want to get drinks later? I can let Toby know—'

'Not today,' I say quickly, 'I've got something else I need to do first but I'll see you at the lunch tomorrow.'

'All right,' Fran says happily, 'tomorrow then.'

* * *

It's as I'm heading out the building to the train station a little later, that I run into William again, coming back in.

'Oh, hello,' I say breathlessly.

'Hello yourself,' William says. He eyes my suitcase. 'Off already?'

I nod. I eventually told him I was going to London; asked him to look after Ferris while I was gone, and while he begrudgingly agreed, I can tell he secretly likes that cat.

'Lovely,' he says, 'and will we see you back at classes when you return?'

'Possibly,' I say faintly, 'But I don't actually know when I'm coming back right now.'

William frowns, a slightly hurt expression on his face. He starts to walk by, when I say, 'how's it going with Ruth?'

'How's what going?' he says gruffly, looking back. 'Such nonsense, I'm too old for any of that anyway.'

'No, you're not,' I start, surprised by the turn in events. 'Why don't you just give it a shot?'

'Why don't you give it a shot with Adam?' He fires back, and I close my mouth.

'That's what I thought,' he says, letting himself into his flat now. 'But run away back to London now, don't mind us.'

'William,' I start, moving towards him.

'Just remember it's three months' notice on the flat,' he says before shutting the door firmly.

And all I can think is, *I'll be gone by then*.

* * *

A little later, I'm on the train, cream cheese bagel and hot coffee on the table in front of me. People are still walking into the carriage, checking the tickets above the slightly cramped seats, saying 'sorry, sorry' as they stuff bags up on to racks and slide into seats.

Taking a sip of the rich liquid, I lean my head back against the headrest, try to calm myself after that tense chat with William. He just doesn't understand what I'm going through, how hard this all is for me too. I barely slept last night; tossed and turned until the early hours as I thought about Adam, thought about Simon, until I finally woke up drenched in sweat. Because it still feels so wrong, leaving Adam like I am, like some invisible bit of string is holding us together somehow. And even the thought of going to London in itself is causing some discomfort I can't quite explain, but I know I have to explore this for Emily. I have to see Simon again and find out if there's still something there between them.

If that's what she wanted.

I suppose, when I really think about it, why would Emily not have loved Simon still? They had the most passionate of starts and he's everything any woman could possibly look for – and not just in terms of the glamour and the wealth. From that short meet-up we had, from all the glimmers of the past, I know that he was kind too. I can feel it. Plus, maybe she realised that she'd played some part in it all too, what with her awful work hours.

But what about Adam?

What about *my* list?

Because it really is clear now what I was trying to do before – and it wasn't about Emily. None of it before Charlie's accident was really. It was me who wanted to drive and to dance, to go out till dawn and ski down a mountain. But although I might wish I could go travel the world now and have those big experiences I always dreamed of, this is not my life to mess up, and I have to think about Emily and her loved ones too. Make sure nothing else gets thrown off-course.

The thought unsettles me and I can feel something else prodding at me. But a moment later, the whistle sounds, and the thought is gone. The carriage jolts forwards and then we're off, slowly at first, then faster and faster, out past the great Georgian structures of Edinburgh I know and love so well, out past trees and houses and gardens, out past washing fluttering in the breeze, out past trees and fields towards the unknown. I turn to the glass, see my reflection looking back at me, and for the briefest of moments, I see her smile back at me, and I get one of those sensations again, that inexplicable feeling that our tracks are aligning perfectly: Emily and I, together on the train, down to London.

Then, just as quickly, our tracks diverge in a rush of metal and noise and the moment is gone. I turn back to the table, feeling all shades of strange, but confident at least that I'm going in the right direction again.

The train bullets down the length of the country – past the Millennium Bridge at Newcastle, Darlington, the ancient city of York, all the way down to the country's capital, and all I can do is stare out the windows, thinking that in all my thirty years, this is somehow the furthest I've ever been. I don't know why exactly, given my parents liked to travel so much before they had kids. Mum used to tour the world with the orchestra after all, but then three girls and one heart condition later, I suppose it got harder to go away. But I wish she would. And perhaps she might again, if I branched out first – showed her that I can live differently too.

I just wish I could talk to Mum properly – I *will* talk to her about it, when I'm back in my old life.

An announcement on the tinny speaker ahead; the iconic King's Cross Station suddenly emerges outside. The train pulls to a stop and, after collecting my suitcase from the luggage rack, I step down on to the bustling platform, in the heart of the country's capital. I feel a rush of anxiety at the prospect of what's ahead of me, but also a buzz of excitement too, this sense of coming back to somewhere special.

And as I walk up the platform, I put all thoughts of my family, and of home, away again.

* * *

Sunlight glints through the blossom trees as I walk along the neatly kept pavement. To both sides of me, beautiful white and sandstone houses sit back in closely cropped gardens, pastel flowers lined orderly up their driveways. A mother and daughter dressed in matching white summer dresses and beige sunhats walk smartly past me. Even the bus that goes by seems shinier somehow, and I try to swallow down my nerves.

Then I see it, the street number I scribbled on a piece of paper before I left Edinburgh. I'd found Emily's parents' address eventually in a floral address book at the bottom of a box, and although I knew the area would be affluent, I'm not sure I really got how much. Looking up at Emily's pristine childhood home, behind wrought-iron gates, I feel incredibly intimidated. It exudes money and power, in a way I've never really seen up close before, the name *Morton House* etched on a gold plate. Going to press the fancy-looking buzzer beside the gates, my heart catches in my chest and I feel sick. Because why the hell would I put myself through this again, after that awful argument at Christmas? After Emily's mum made it perfectly clear that she didn't want to see me. But then, I really am running out of time now – there's only three and a half months left, and if there's one thing Emily must have wanted, I've got to think it's making peace with her mother. But even though I know they never made up, I've still got to come here, so her mother always knows Emily tried.

A second later and the gates start to open. As I walk up the perfectly paved red drive, I can't help but feel like an imposter here. It was one thing going about my business in

Edinburgh but quite another actually coming down here to Emily's world. As I stand on the step of the grand entrance, all stone arches and golden door knockers, I tuck my hair behind my ear and smooth down my sky-blue blouse. I thought jeans would be OK for today but after seeing that mother and daughter combo, I feel underdressed suddenly.

I'm about to knock again, when the door opens up, but instead of Emily's mother, I'm surprised to see someone else, someone I don't know initially, until I tilt my head to the side, and as the sensations wash up and over me again, I see it: strawberry hair now flecked with grey, beady green eyes that crinkle at the side from years of laughter.

'Jackie,' I say slowly, as the name falls from my mouth.

'Darling, girl,' she says, rushing to greet me, and as the familiar form of her presses against me and I smell lavender and peppermint around me, it all comes rushing back.

'You came home,' she whispers into my hair.

* * *

A little while later and I'm settled with a tea by a vast marble island in an extensive kitchen. Everything in the open-plan room is white and cream and glass, a sort of New England look mixed with something shinier; harder. And the rest of the house is largely the same, like it's trying to be inviting but falls flat in its neatness. As Jackie stirs a large vat of soup on the shining

Aga, I recall how she always used to warm up the place somehow. She was who I came home to every day, after all.

It didn't take long to realise that no one else was here, and when I asked where Mum was, she told me they'd just left for one of their European social tours again – partly to do with the business and partly just to 'schmooze', as she put it. They had obviously not been invited to Fran's wedding, and I got the feeling that these trips were a fairly regular feature of life – a memory too of being left here with Jackie for long stints when I was a teenager.

I was always so alone, a voice says from somewhere within, and I shiver.

'Here you are,' she says, coming over with a bowl of something delicious smelling, and I look down to see a thick red-ish broth.

'Thank you,' I say.

She sits down with her own across from me, some buttery baguette slices on the plate in front of her.

'Would you mind if I stole one of those?' I say, without thinking.

Jackie stares at me quizzically for a moment, before pushing the plate across. 'Of course. Edinburgh's clearly been quite the change for you, then.'

I swallow nervously, before starting to eat.

'This soup tastes . . . like I'm nine years old,' I say eventually, and Jackie smiles.

'You always did love minestrone.'

I take a breath. 'Do you know when they'll be back? Mum and Dad, I mean?'

'In a few weeks, I'd imagine. That's the usual really, as you well know.'

'I see.'

'So tell me,' Jackie says, 'what happened between you and your mother?'

I pause, as I remember the awfulness of it, those all-consuming feelings of anger and frustration. I don't even have to lie.

'She wanted me to go back to my old life but I wanted to stay,' I say eventually.

'So why are you back then?'

'I told you,' I say, not quite meeting her eye. 'Fran's wedding.'

'Are you sure that's it?'

'Yes,' I say, but my voice is wavering.

A silence settles.

'You were always such a dreamer when you were younger, you know?' Jackie says finally.

'I've heard that before,' I say wryly.

'Yup, you were four years old when I started working here, after my Colin passed, and, oh boy, you were always in a world of your own. Always drawing and creating things. Always taking pictures with those—'

'Disposables,' I say softly.

'That's right. You said they captured real moments better, even as an adult.'

Her face falls slightly. 'But then you started at that fancy school and everything became serious so quickly. Homework every day for hours, it was all work, work, work, even at the age of five. And suddenly, all those fun activities disappeared. That dreamer disappeared.'

'But why?' I say. 'Why did Mum hate it so much?'

'She didn't hate it; she just thought it was frivolous,' Jackie says steadily. 'She wanted to give you the big life she never had – she was determined to. Poverty does strange things to people, and your mum really did come into a tough version of the world. Do you know that she used to work three jobs before she met your father? Including one in a fish factory, if you can possibly believe it.'

I shake my head. 'I didn't know that.'

'So, now you do,' Jackie says firmly. Then softer. 'She only ever wanted the best for you.'

'Funny way of showing it,' I say, as I fiddle with the spoon in the soup bowl. I pause. 'Do *you* think I should come back then?'

I don't know why exactly but I already feel I can trust this woman who I've technically just met, but feel insanely close to, in a way I just couldn't with Emily's mum. And if she says it's better for me here, I think I have to listen.

'It's not my decision to make,' she says eventually and her expression softens. 'You know Colin and I always wanted kids . . . but it never quite happened for us. You were like a daughter to me, Emily, so all I want is for you to be happy. And if that's here in London, then that's lovely. You achieved such an incredible amount in such a short space of time, and you have great friends too. A great life. But if it's Edinburgh, or anywhere else you pick, then that's also wonderful. The main thing is to make your own mind up about your life, whatever that may be, and stop doing what someone else thinks you should.'

'Even you.' I say, mischievously.

'Even me.' Jackie grins, and if you do that, then you'll never have anything to properly regret. Things can go wrong – they will go wrong – but as long as we know we followed our heart, and weren't just dictated by fear, we can rest easy. Because this life goes by much quicker than you'd think . . .' She reaches for my hand now. 'Your mother will get there eventually. Just give her time.'

I squeeze her hand back. 'Thank you,' I say, even though I want to say that we're running out of time much quicker than she knows.

She looks at my hand, up at me, squints. 'You seem different somehow.'

I swallow. 'Well, I suppose I have been away for a while.'

She shakes her head. 'No, it's not that . . . oh, I'm just being silly, aren't I? You're still my darling Emily and always will be. Just maybe give me a call the next time you disappear, even if you can't call your mum.'

I look up to see tears in her eyes now and realise in this moment, just how loved Emily was, by so many people. I can't bear the idea of putting them through more grief.

But it's not my choice.

'I'm sorry,' I say. 'I won't do it again.'

'Good.' Jackie says, wiping a tear away. 'Now, will you stay overnight then?'

'Sure,' I say, curious to spend a little more time here.

Jackie nods, pleased. 'Well, your room's all made up. I'm just popping out to meet a friend for coffee,' she says, getting up, 'but I'll be back for tea later. Maybe we can watch one of those silly—'

'Horror movies,' I finish softly, as that new detail about Emily drifts back to me, and she smiles. 'Sounds great.'

She gets up to clear the bowls away, before I stop her. 'I'll sort this out.'

Jackie cups my cheek with her papery hand. 'You were always such a thoughtful girl.'

* * *

It feels odd once she's gone, as though I'm a stranger in someone else's home, but it doesn't take long before it all comes back to me fully – the cream, untouchable drawing room to the right of the entrance hall; the shiny, mahogany dining room to the left; the study and the cold conservatory;

the annex for Jackie at the back, and the six huge bedrooms upstairs, including Emily's childhood bedroom. When I walk in, I immediately feel her, not in the ivory walls or the perfectly neat white bed (both chosen by her mother, I can tell) but in the colourful jewellery still hanging off one of those branch things, in the butterfly cushion sitting on a beige chair and the turquoise rug by her bed; the general warmth in this room, which lingers on.

A solitary print hangs on the wall with a quote that says, 'Every adventure requires a first step', from *Alice In Wonderland*. There's a photo on the bedside table too, which I go to pick up now. It's of Emily with her parents when she was younger – maybe eleven or so – and she actually looks really happy in it; they all do. Emily's pulling a silly face and her mum has her head tipped back in laughter. Her dad is grinning to the side, and just behind it, I see something I think I know. The outline of a cobbled archway, and a sign.

Dunbar's Close, I whisper, as the memories finally trickle back – coming up to Edinburgh and visiting the castle, skipping down the Royal Mile and going down all the little closes, until I found the one I loved the most. It was a rare weekend my parents weren't working, so they let me choose any activity I wanted and eat wherever I pleased. We grabbed pizza slices for lunch and waffles for tea. We stayed up watching movies together at the hotel, and for just a moment in time, we slowed down.

It became my favourite place.

So that's why you went up there, I think at the exact same time. Almost as though the two sets of thoughts are merging into one, and I shiver.

But did you stay?

Flopping down on the bed, I stare up at the ceiling, only to find a dreamcatcher floating gently above my head.

And as I look up at it, I get the sense that she once lay here, debating what to do too.

CHAPTER TWENTY-SIX

'E!' Fran says, running across the private dining room towards me at lunchtime the next day. The place is incredible, with murals across the ceiling and heavy gold drapes at the tall Georgian windows. A long table down the middle of the room is covered in silverware and candelabra.

'Oh my gosh,' she gushes, pulling me towards her, 'I can't believe you're actually here.'

'I can't believe I'm actually here either,' I say into her silky hair. She smells of expensive perfume and something else that I instinctively just know.

Pulling back from me, I take her in, the beautiful knee-length green dress, with its silky wraparound front and capped sleeves, which highlight her lean, tanned arms, the golden brown of her eyes.

'This place is amazing,' I say now, looking about myself in awe. I knew Fran's side of the family was wealthy too, but still.

Fran grins. 'Of course it is; do you remember how many times we came here for cocktails that summer? God, Dad almost threatened to have the club bar us,' she says with a laugh.

A memory of the two of us falling through the door, propping ourselves up at the bar in the other room – drinking something pink from tiny gold-rimmed glasses.

'The Elton,' I say, the memory catching faster this time. 'I can't believe how many of those we drank.'

Fran lets out a burst of warm laughter. 'Oh my god, right?' She clutches my arm. 'We have to have one today for old times' sake.' A second later, and she's speaking merrily to a passing waiter, who nods and immediately disappears to the next room.

'Great idea. Not that I want to be *totally* sloshed for all the relatives but one might help.' She grins. 'Come on, I'll show you where we're sitting.'

As she guides me across the floor on her arm, the memories drift away again, but I'm aware they're getting stronger the more time I spend down here.

I just don't know why.

I don't have long to dwell on it as we're soon surrounded by the family – uncles and aunts and cousins all fussing over us, exclaiming '*tanto tempo*', and it's bizarre because I realise I somehow understand what they're saying to me – *it's been too long*. And it should feel strange and awkward how familiar they all are with me but it's not. Just like Fran, I feel I know these people. The women are neatly quaffed and in stylish dresses, and I feel a little self-conscious that I chose the butterfly dress to put on in Emily's childhood bedroom this morning. Jackie thought it was fabulous, of course, said softly, 'this is *so you*', but from all the photos I've seen, and the people in here, I can only assume that Emily used to dress quite differently.

Suddenly I'm highly aware how much she transformed herself. Fran, being Fran, hasn't batted an eyelash about it at least, and I know instinctively that she doesn't actually care what the hell I wear. Just as long as I'm here. She'd already told me I'm her only chosen bridesmaid, and I realised how big a part of her life I really am. 'I can't be bothered with the drama of selecting anyone else,' she'd said a few months ago. 'You're my favourite cousin, so it's just easier this way.'

I'm not totally sure how it will work with being the photographer too but I suppose the flock of other female cousins will probably help.

A tall, thickset man with salt and pepper hair and a clumsy smile appears beside us now. He's wearing a loud blue blazer and a crisp white shirt, and automatically I know that this is Toby. As he leans in to hug me, exclaiming loudly, 'She's here!' I get flashes of memories – of him and Fran meeting at a charity masked ball and finding out they only lived streets apart, of the hundreds of jokes he tells and the way he puts everyone at ease, and the fact that I adore him too.

'Toby,' I say, hugging him back, and the words, 'I've missed you,' fall from my mouth.

I touch my lips in surprise.

'Well, look what the cat finally dragged in,' Toby says, stepping back. 'Speaking of which, did I hear you have an actual cat now in this Scottish life of yours? What's it called then?' He grins, oblivious. 'Fluffy? Tom?'

'Ferris,' I say with a laugh.

'Original.' Toby says. 'Where are you staying before the wedding anyway?'

'Oh shit,' Fran says, flustered. 'Sorry, I totally forgot to check, what with all the wedding madness and everything.'

'It's fine,' I say immediately. 'I booked into a Travelodge nearby.'

Fran and Toby look at each other in a slightly shocked way.

'You will most certainly not,' Toby says. 'Are you forgetting my family own hotels? We can just put you on the wedding floor a night early.'

I'm about to protest when I see somebody else coming over. Simon, looking devastatingly handsome as usual. He's wearing perfectly fitted navy trousers and an expensive-looking white shirt with a beige jacket on top. His skin has that gorgeous suntanned hue, and he looks at me in a way that makes my heart genuinely flutter.

'Hello.' He passes one glass of champagne to me and one to Fran.

She takes it from him with a stilted look and I wish she would just forgive him.

I have.

'Hey, where's mine?' Toby says, letting out a guffaw of a laugh.

Fran's eyes flicker between Simon and me, and I know exactly what she's thinking – that I'm making a mistake.

'Come on, Toby,' she says, taking hold of his hand, 'let's go check my mum hasn't started on the Martinis.' Then shooting me a final 'be careful' look, she wanders off, leaving the two of us alone, or as alone as we can be in a room full of people.

Suddenly my mouth feels dry, and my legs are a bit shaky. *I always had such a huge crush on him.*

And oh god, I feel it, that pull I've always had.

'How have you been?' he says.

'Good.' I smile, heart still racing. 'And you?'

'Better, now you're here.'

I take a breath.

'What have you been up to lately?' he says.

'I went skiing up north recently, actually.'

His face cracks into a grin. 'You actually did it? I tried so many times to get you away the past few years. Do you remember that one time you made it out to Zermatt for a couple of days?'

And the funny thing is, I sort of do – vague images of a luxurious wood and glass chalet, Fran, Toby, Simon and me looking out at a snow-covered world, champagne in hand.

'You made us all s'mores on the hob,' I say, laughing at the image.

I was really happy. And then work just started getting busier and busier, and I cancelled the ski trip two years in a row, while the others went on without me. I'd travel a lot internationally, get all the stamps in my passport, but only ever actually see the inside of hotel rooms. I lost sight of things.

I lost sight of us.

And the way he's looking at me right now, with this hope in his eyes, steals my breath.

'Hey,' he says quietly, and reaches for my arm, 'how about we go have a day out together tomorrow? Just you and me.'

I pause. 'Won't we have wedding stuff to do? I'm sure Fran and Toby will probably want me to help out with things.'

He shakes his head. 'I've already cleared it with them.'

Glancing over at the bar, I see Toby looking back and he gives me a big thumbs up. Fran looks less convinced beside him, but then she smiles at me, nods.

'Please say yes,' Simon says, and I turn back to him, 'I've got something to show you.'

Even though an image of Adam flashes across my mind, there's a strange pull happening here too, this growing feeling like everything in Emily's life comes back to this guy right here – this incredibly handsome man, asking for a simple day with her.

And I know I have to explore this.

'All right,' I say eventually and his shoulders relax slightly. His whole face comes alive.

'Brilliant,' he says, just as Fran's parents walk over. My aunt starts hugging me, and then my uncle, and suddenly I'm enveloped in warmth and love, and a distinct feeling like I'm back where I belong.

CHAPTER TWENTY-SEVEN

The next morning I'm sitting in the lobby of the hotel Toby put me in. It's all turquoise velvet and polished marble, and as I sit sipping the most delicious Turkish coffee, I think about how incredibly well I slept on the fluffiest of beds, in the most sumptuous of suites – thank you, Toby. The lunch went on for the whole afternoon, a lavish feast put on by Fran's parents – antipasti, pasta course, sorbetto, meat course, and what felt like a never-ending stream of desserts at the end. And then as the older generations drifted away, the four of us eventually tumbled into a little bar we used to frequent along the road. Fran even simmered a bit about the whole thing with Simon; actually got up and did some terrible karaoke – Elton John's *Tiny Dancer*, of course – and we ate greasy burgers and drank cheap pints (two max for me after the skiing incident). I've realised it's not all glitz and glamour down here; it's solid and real and delightfully grubby too. It was a whole host of experiences and events and life; a life that worked really well once, and maybe could again for Emily, at the end.

A movement at the doorway. I watch as the top-hatted doorman opens it with a flourish, and Simon walks confidently in. He's more casual today in jeans, trainers and a lightweight navy jacket. But somehow he still looks like a million dollars, and I know that every inch of his outfit probably cost more than my rent each month. But then he looks at me in this way that puts me absolutely at ease, and I wonder for the hundredth time what he has to show me today. Coming to a stop in front of me, he holds his hand out.

'Ready?'

I smile. 'Totally.'

* * *

A few minutes later and we're standing on the sunny street outside. The buildings are grand around here, with Hyde Park right ahead of us and the luxury hotel behind, and I can't help but feel stupidly excited by it all.

'You have to tell me now,' I say, 'what's this thing you want to show me?'

Simon smiles mischievously, glances at something over to the left. 'You'll see,' he says, 'in exactly one second.'

And then, as if by magic, this huge shiny truck-like vehicle comes to a stop right in front of us.

'What the . . .?' I say, trying to peer in the darkened windows.

The driver's door opens and a man in a black suit and cap gets out, goes to open the passenger door. Then he looks at me expectantly, his bushy grey eyebrows raised.

'Miss,' he says, ushering me in.

I look at the man, look at Simon, who takes my hand in his.

'Here's the thing,' he says, and I immediately feel the tingle of his touch, this real familiarity about it. 'Before you left, things were crazy, with your work, with our lives – I think we forgot why we were even in London in the first place, what we wanted from this place. And as I said before, I'll follow you anywhere, Emily, but more than anything, I'd just really love for us to pick up where we left off.'

'So,' he continues, turning to the plush seats inside, 'I thought we could go around the city and be tourists for the day, see some of our favourite haunts too.'

And even as he speaks the words, I think of all the sights I never went to see, and all the big cities I experienced only through a screen.

'What do you say?'

'I say yes.' I grin, and climb into the car.

'You've got that camera of yours at the ready, I see,' Simon says, getting in beside me.

'Yup,' I reply, feeling for it around my neck.

'Best present I ever got you,' he says, clipping himself in.

My heart skips slightly, and as I look at it with surprised realisation – the camera from Simon, attached to the lens from Adam – we speed off down the road.

* * *

Moments later, we're cruising through London in our very own tour car while the driver, Alex, merrily fills us in on titbits of history – how London was the capital of Roman Britain for most of Roman rule and over 8.7 million people live here. It is a city full of life and activity and opportunity, and just seeing fragments of it sends a thrill through me. We stop at Big Ben ('did you know it's actually the clock that's called Big Ben and not the tower?'), the houses of Parliament, Buckingham Palace and London Bridge. I get my camera out and start snapping away at it all, and not for the first time, I wonder about coming down here when I get back to my old life. Seeing everything I can.

We head to old haunts of ours next, jumping out at Holborn and finding the little frozen yoghurt shop with the amazing mango flavour. We head to Borough Market and wander around the stalls and restaurants. We end up at the Singapore street food place we love and I start laughing suddenly, remembering that the last time we were here we were dressed up as pirates for a party after. We get iced coffees at our place nearby where the dog always wears a bow tie. We have a couple of drinks at the wine bar at Embankment where we had our particularly drunken and hilarious (due to the unfortunate name of the wine) third date, before heading across the water to a little fair. We wander through the people and the happy music, talking about absolute nonsense, and I get a flash of something in my chest – this feeling like I genuinely enjoy hanging out with this guy and we've experienced some great times together. It wasn't all about the money and the lifestyle. We actually loved each other too.

We end the day at a gorgeous little Bistro in Bermondsey and, as I take a last perfect mouthful of the crème brûlée Simon knows I love, I feel him looking across at me.

'What is it?' I say, feeling suddenly nervous.

'Nothing.' He pauses. 'Just ... you seem happy; more relaxed than before. Maybe the time away was a good idea, after all.'

'Maybe it was,' I say softly.

But as I take a sip of my champagne, I can't help thinking about that night up on Adam's terrace. How, even though we had no roof above our heads, and there were no fancy waiters and no two-hundred-pound bottle of champagne, I was still happier than I've ever been.

'Everything OK?' Simon says.

I look up at him. 'Yes, of course.'

'Well then,' he says, 'how about I take you back to the hotel?'

'All right,' I say.

Ten minutes later and we're back where we started. Simon jumps out with me to say goodnight in front of the grand entrance, and as soft music floats out the hotel into the late March air, I feel so nicely full and tired.

'So,' he says, standing in front of me, 'have you had a good time today?'

'Of course, what wasn't to like?'

And I mean it. I've had the most incredible experience – seen all the best sights of London in style, and with great company too. Because Simon is a brilliant man and maybe he and Emily just needed some time apart. Maybe she did still love him, and it would be very easy now to slot back into this life. To see out Emily's last few months, right here in London. Her friends are all here, her old job, Simon – the life, all right at my fingertips.

A pause.

'Shit, Emily, I promised myself I wouldn't do this, but I have to know,' he says.

'Know what?'

'If you see this happening again; me and you, I mean.'

He looks so very vulnerable suddenly under the hotel's light, and my heart goes out to him.

A second later, I'm kissing him, and it feels strange and familiar all at once. I hear him gasp at the surprise of it, and then he's kissing me firmly back, and his arms go around me and I don't know what's happening exactly, but it's as though I'm not even in control of my own body anymore.

After a few moments, I pull back. My heart is racing and I have no idea what's going on, but what I do know is this is another moment that's happened before.

And I must be on the right track.

'I'll see you at the wedding tomorrow,' he murmurs finally, dropping my hand.

'I suppose you will,' I say, and with that I turn and head back into the hotel.

* * *

The day of the wedding is gorgeously sunny, as though somehow Fran's family has managed to make it so. I woke up alone in my suite feeling a little confused and dazed from last night, but I've barely had time to process anything when Fran runs in ranting and raving about a spot. 'Jesus F-ing Christ,' she says, examining her face in the mirror, and I instinctively go to order ice from reception.

Then come the mothers and the nonnas all flapping about and telling tales about their own wedding days, and I can't help thinking back to Jess's more intimate wedding – how subdued it all felt in contrast. We were missing someone big, after all.

Once Fran's sorted her spot and the make-up artist appears, I start to take the pictures and I'm so thankful to her for this experience, for supporting my dreams like this, for just being a great friend. In no time at all, Fran has stepped into the most gorgeous antique dress of lace and silks. There are 'oohs' and 'ahs' from everyone and snaps on my camera and then we're off to the ceremony in the church. It's a traditional yet light affair in an exquisite cavern of stone, and as the priest starts taking us all through the vows, I catch Simon's eye from the front pew. He's not one of Toby's groomsmen, given Toby has his three brothers standing beside him already and he said a fourth might be a bit 'JLo' of him, but I can sense his proximity just as much. And finally, I allow myself to think about last night again.

Because where did that kiss come from? Was that me who kissed him, or Emily? And why does it keep happening, the increasing memories and actions of hers?

I'm starting to worry I'll eventually disappear completely.

But perhaps this also means I'm on the right track with figuring out what she wanted, and I have to think, if Emily experienced anything like what I've experienced in London so far, there's a high chance she would have wanted to come back here. Because isn't this a great life? Isn't this all pretty special, like something from a dream?

Like a version of the life that I wanted too?

I don't have long to dwell before we're all throwing rice over the happy couple and crying '*auguri!*' outside the doors and then heading back along to the reception down the road. And as I ride along in the wedding car next to Simon, I feel him take my hand – and I don't immediately let go.

It kicks off in style with aperitivo back at the hotel, then yet another never-ending Italian feast followed by speeches, then digestifs and dancing, and looking around, it's clear that most people here are 'something'. From the incredible dresses, to the smart suits and eye-watering expensive jewels, I'm surrounded by a sea of success, fame and style.

Simon always makes sure I've got a champagne in hand or some delicious canapé as I take the photos. But just occasionally, he gives me this strange look, which confuses me a little.

'Will you excuse me for a minute?' he says eventually.

'Of course, everything OK?'

He looks at me softly, but I'm sure there's a trace of concern there. 'Yeah,' he says, 'everything is great.'

A number of people run up to me while he's gone: Sofia from the company, Tess and Mira from school, Hugo and Chloe from the office, all charging over to ask about my 'life sabbatical', and asking when I'm returning to London, inviting Simon and me over for dinner or to some weekend away. And I know there could be something great here at the end for Emily, coming home and slotting back into everything.

But still, something is pulling at my chest, poking and prodding at me, and as the sun dips outside and the party really gets started, I find myself wandering into the cooler entrance foyer for a quick breather. It's quiet here, except for a few guests moving through.

Hushed voices from somewhere, urgent and sharp. I look over to where they're coming from – behind a large table of flowers.

And I don't quite know why, but I find myself moving in their direction. I know I should be taking photos right now but I really have been snapping away all night, and Fran would want me to take at least one actual break, I'm sure.

Then I see them, Fran and Simon speaking to each other. I'm about to say hello when I stop. Because there's something about their body language that's off – the strained look on their faces, the way Fran is gesturing at him. 'Don't do this, please,' she's saying. 'Not now.'

Then he's saying, 'she's going to find out eventually, you know. And I can't keep doing what I'm doing without telling her the truth about what happened with us.'

My heart stops.

Fran and Simon.

Simon and Fran.

Oh no.

Oh no, no, no.

I must let out a noise because Fran and Simon both turn to look at me sharply.

'Oh my god,' Fran says, her face washing out completely. Simon's face just falls sadly, like he knows it's all over.

But then Fran starts coming towards me. 'E,' she says, and another memory rushes up, finally pushes to the surface. Standing in this exact same spot, seeing Fran and Simon together. A dawning realisation that all the chat about an ex-girlfriend was a lie.

It was Fran he was at dinner with that night. He really was cheating.

With my best friend. My cousin.

And without another thought in my head, I sprint away from Fran towards the exit. I hear her calling sharply behind me, but I ignore it.

They betrayed me.

'Emily, stop!' she cries out to me again.

But I can't stop, won't stop, and running down the pavement, I see it, a lit taxi on the other side of the road. Without another thought, I immediately go towards it.

A honking sound then screams.

The bright lights of a car rush towards me.

CHAPTER TWENTY-EIGHT

Light above me, faces, people asking, 'are you OK?' over and over, as the scent of perfume and aftershave surrounds me. And then a figure in white, Fran; Simon too, both crouching over me, and Fran is hugging me into her, and saying, 'oh my god, oh my god, oh my god.'

My heart is racing, and yet I feel the oddest sensation coming over me again, hot and strong, as pieces fall together in my brain. Seeing Fran and Simon talking like that, running out and on to the road, the fact I almost killed myself but then someone pulled me back – they stopped me going over into traffic.

They stopped it happening.

It's been growing since Charlie's accident, I realise, this dawning awareness that I could change things.

Change the outcome.

But there was something else I couldn't put my finger on – some missing piece of the puzzle.

Then at the sight of those car lights, the life-ending metal milliseconds away from me, that beautiful lifting feeling as someone pulled me back from it, I realised what I've known all along. What my brain clearly wouldn't let me consider before: that I could accidentally kill Emily before the day of the heart transplant – which means maybe I can save her too.

CHAPTER TWENTY-NINE

The train back to Edinburgh goes by in a shell-shocked blur. I barely look out the window, barely touch the chicken sandwich I made myself buy at King's Cross. And as the train rushes northwards under the leaden sky, it all sinks in.

Maybe this was why I was here all along, and it wasn't a glitch. Maybe Emily isn't properly gone at all – and I could stop her dying at the end of all of this.

Which would mean, I'd die instead.

Me, Maggie.

Because there is only one working heart between us – this one here in my chest – and I need it in the future or my old self will die: it is a medical certainty and I knew how lucky I was to get that call. But what if I simply stop whatever happened to Emily from happening the day of the transplant? What if I change things?

Because I know that the skiing accident didn't happen the first time with Charlie, I felt inside myself that that was a proper deviation from Charlie's life, so why not for Emily too? The evidence is right there, staring me in the face: people can be killed here, like they can normally, and if they can be killed, surely they can be saved too. My mind was just in complete denial of it all. There I was, simply assuming that Emily was still going to die at the end of this, when the truth is, I might have a choice.

The biggest choice of my life.

The letter said she died unexpectedly – so that's either an accident or an illness. If it was an accident, I know I can avoid it (I'm very good at avoiding death, after all) and if it was an illness, I can get it checked out – maybe do something about it. As long as it's not something terminal, perhaps I could prevent it getting worse.

But ultimately preventing it would mean *I* die. Suddenly I feel so utterly lost – so utterly desolate.

I didn't actually see Fran in person this morning at least, thank god – she was up and away early on her honeymoon, not that that stopped her trying to call me; send a million messages saying how sorry she was and how bad she feels, and I imagine how confused Toby must be by her behaviour right now. But I just couldn't face it; couldn't face her, not after what she did.

What they did.

Simon came to see me this morning, of course, waited in the lobby for me.

'Please don't let one mistake ruin everything,' he pleaded, as I walked towards the exit. 'I love you so much, Emily.'

I shook my head. 'No, you don't. And it wasn't just one mistake, was it?'

He said nothing, his eyes forlorn, but the answer was in his silence.

'We could still make it work,' he tried.

'No, we couldn't. Not now.'

As I stare out the train window, I think how wrong I was. About everything.

* * *

Five hours later, and I'm sat in a private health clinic – it's amazing what you can achieve with a little extra money and a desperate plea for a cancellation. I'm guided through the private health assessment for the first hour, then for the second, tested: bloods, body fat percentage, height, weight and bowel screening. I'm told I'll get the results in just forty-eight hours. A part of me can't help hoping it's something terminal (as unlikely as that would be before donating a heart) because then the choice will be out of my hands. But I already have a suspicion I'll be fine – from the vaguely surprised looks on the doctors faces at a fit and healthy thirty-year-old girl doing this sort of check-up, from every burst of energy I've felt in this life. And for the first time since I've been here, this healthy body makes me sad – because I know it will most likely have been a preventable accident that killed Emily; know that ultimately, the decision will be in my hands – as long as everything else is still the same.

So, the next stop is home, of course – my real home. Just in case, somehow, the other version of me is doing better. Because isn't that another option? That we both survive, somehow?

Then I see Mum coming out the door, wheeling me down that awful ramp, and I'm as pale and sickly as can be, my red hair tied limply behind me. And I know in that moment that nothing is different. I am dying, and it's the most painful thing to watch, but at least now I know the truth.

The decision about who lives is mine. And how can I look away from it? There Emily was, going through something terrible, yet still having the courage to change her story, change her life, and there was me with her healthy heart doing absolutely . . . nothing. And perhaps that's why it all happened when it did – I always wondered about the timing.

Her mother asked me to keep her alive in her letter but maybe the universe is telling me to keep her alive quite literally. Emily wanted to live so damn much. I can feel it.

But oh god, my family – Jess, Mum, Dad, the boys.

My life.

Later, I let myself back into my building and trudge up the stairs. No one was waiting for me at the station earlier, of course – not Charlie, not William. At least Sven messaged this morning, to see how I was and to tell me that Adam's gone away already, and as I read the words on the screen, my heart ached. I pushed him away one too many times, and now he's gone.

When I finally arrive at the top, I stare across at his flat, which seems so silent and dark now – no happy clattering around, no light above the door telling me he's in, no sound of him bouncing down the steps to his workshop. I see a thousand moments we've had in such a short space unfolding like ghosts behind that door – cuddled together on his sofa or cooking something terrible in his kitchen, that night under the stars on the terrace and lying tangled together in his bed, decorating our first Christmas tree and laughing with friends. Good times. The best of times, which I may never get again, because in just three months, I might have to go.

For good.

Pulling down the blind to the world, I slide under the covers and, with my clothes still on, I press my face against the pillow and shut my eyes.

* * *

Days and nights pass in a blur and I spend most of it in bed either sleeping or putting on a movie like I used to in my own life on darker days. I wander to the bathroom when I need it, or to the kitchen for the leftovers of whatever takeaway I've ordered, then back again – after all, I doubt a month more of eating shit will actually do anything much now.

I should probably feel better equipped to deal with the possibility of dying, given I lived in this exact way for years, never really going anywhere or doing anything. Simply existing. But then all of this happened, and I experienced everything the world had to offer, every shiny glittery wonder in store.

And just when I'd fallen in love with it all, I find out it might be snatched away completely.

It's perhaps on the third day that I get the test results by email – and with bated breath I sit up in bed and open it.

All clear – as suspected.

Which means there was nothing wrong with Emily, and the choice is mine: keep her safe on the day of the operation and save her, or save me.

I hear the knock on my door a few moments later, a familiar male voice saying, 'Emily, are you in? It's William.'

I'm surprised to hear from him after the last time we spoke. But then I feel that overwhelming sadness take over me and I sink back down in bed. Pressing play on the film I'm only vaguely watching, I lie against the pillows once more.

But he comes again the next day, and when I still don't answer, I hear something drop on to the hall floor. Once I think he's gone, I tentatively go to see what it is – a red envelope. Ripping it open, I find a Christmas card inside with a reindeer on it. *Just like I did with him.*

To Emily, it says inside, *please come dancing with me, Best, William.*

Although my heart catches briefly, I just don't see the point in any of it anymore. Not if I might die anyway. Placing the card on the side table, I head back to bed.

On the fifth day, I receive one with a snowman on it, which feels a little odd in late March. *To Emily, please come on a walk with me, Best, William.*

And while my heart begins to thump at the prospect of fresh air, I quickly push the thought away.

I start to think about my family while I'm doing nothing; what they'll do if I die in the hospital. No heart, no second chance. What kind of legacy would that leave the boys with anyway? To have one aunt die, then another?

I know Jess has never actually had them tested because it absolutely terrifies her, the very idea that they might have the same condition as me. And maybe if I had had a second chance in my old life, I could have shown them that there was life after diagnosis; life in the face of death.

But I might never get that chance now.

On the seventh day of being inside, I get another card with a lonely Christmas tree in a forest. *To Emily*, it says, and I instinctively know this will be the last, because there's only so many times you can try; only so many times before it starts to break you a little bit too.

Please come back into the world, it says, *like you made me do. Love, William.*

My heart is thudding in my chest but he just doesn't get it; doesn't understand what I'm dealing with.

A few minutes later I hear a shout of pain, then the words, 'Emily, help me!' echo up from downstairs.

Immediately I'm back on my feet, pulling on a grey sweater. Then throwing myself out the door, I'm leaping down the stairs two at a time.

Please be OK, please be OK.

Shit, I should have gone to see him quickly, I should have just popped my head out the door even, I should—

But when I get to the bottom, I'm surprised to see him standing there in the hallway, very much OK. A tiny box sits in front of him and his eyes twinkle when he sees me.

'Sorry,' he says, his mouth twitching, 'I just thought I could use a little help with this very heavy package here.'

Frustration bursts through me, from all the time alone in the flat, from him making me feel worried about him like that.

'What the hell do you think you're playing at?' I start, heat blazing behind my eyes, 'don't you ever . . . don't you ever . . .'

And then out of nowhere, I am crying, big heaving sobs right there in front of him, as though the simple act of speaking to another human has broken down my walls, and all I can do is stand here and weep with the relief of it.

'Oh Emily,' he says.

*   *   *

Twenty minutes later, and I'm ensconced in Connie's old chair, hot tea in hand. William puts a custard cream on the saucer too, *to get my sugar levels up*, and I find myself nibbling at it slowly. As he walks back from the kitchen, I can't help noticing how much quicker he's moving these days, as though dancing's revived some part of him that had never truly gone away. And when he hugged me in the hallway earlier, I could feel the strength of him around me still, the exact support I needed in that moment. Eventually, once I'd calmed down, he told me to come over for tea, but first to go shower because I looked like, 'a creature from the deep'. Despite everything, it made me laugh, and as the water poured over my skin a few minutes later, I realised I hadn't actually washed since London. And it felt sort of good, that simple exercise of cleaning myself.

Sitting down opposite me now, he places his tea and saucer purposefully on the little table to the side – next to a new mobile phone, I note.

'So,' he says, leaning forwards slightly, 'let's hear it. What's going on, Emily? Why the hell did you let that man go to

Canada without you? And why the hell did you disappear on us all?'

I can't help smiling; there's never been any beating about the bush with William. Still, it's hard to form the words, impossible to tell anyone what my real issue is. But he's right in one way, I did sort of ditch them, these people I've grown to adore, in search of something else. And where did that leave me, trying to follow someone else's heart? Sad, alone and miserable. Emily even tried to tell me: I felt those mixed emotions with Simon and on the train to London, and that tingle speaking to Fran before, but I didn't listen.

So, I probably do owe him – all of them – an explanation.

'I might have to leave . . . in a month,' I say, tracing my finger over the blue beading of Connie's chair.

I don't need to look up to know that William's face has dropped and I feel awful again – for upsetting Adam, for upsetting William. But also for upsetting myself. Because I've had the best time of my life and I really don't want it to end.

Of course I don't want it to end.

I've only just got started.

'Why?' he frowns.

I pause as I try to form my words. 'I can't tell you the reason exactly, just that I have a big choice to make.'

And it really is a big choice – an impossible choice. Because this wasn't even my heart to start with and now I'm here, back in the past, with the chance to right it for her. To let her physically live again.

But equally, this is my life too – this part of me alive in the world somewhere – and now I've experienced so much of it, I'm just not sure I can bring myself to end it all. Not yet.

'I might have to leave in a few months,' I repeat, 'for good.' And I could be wrong but I'm sure something crosses his face. Some glimmer of understanding – almost as though he *knows*.

But he can't know, can he?

'So, that's how you want to play it,' William says and I look up, not to see him sad, but to see him angry.

I find myself frowning now too. 'Play it?'

'That's right,' he says, jabbing his finger at me. 'Play it. Because if I've learned anything since you bloody well moved into this building, it's that life is completely ours for the taking. It is our choice what we do with every second, every minute left of it. We're all leaving sometime if you weren't aware, some of us sooner than others. So, if you want to sit around here for these last few months doing nothing because you're scared, then that's all on you, Missy.'

'I'm not even going to push you on what's actually happening here,' he ploughs on, 'But after everything you've achieved this last year, I'll be damned if you throw it all away now. Because it's not the length of time we're here, it's what we do in that time. It's about living your life, every single day to the end, or it's an utter disservice to those who can't. And I don't care what your reasoning is for doing nothing because the only truth is that you're letting fear stop you, and that's just not good enough.'

A tear falls down my cheek.

'And yes, maybe you will have to go,' 'he continues firmly, 'but wouldn't you rather go out on a high?'

Suddenly everything he's saying starts to make sense, like choppy waters finally settling in my mind. Because this is where I've been going wrong all along, always doing what I thought other people needed or wanted, always being too scared to just get out there and live out my dreams. I even went to London and considered rekindling with a man I didn't love. And what happened?

My heart is threatening to burst from my chest and I can see in this moment how very foolish I've been.

For so long.

'I've got to go,' I say suddenly, the words unexpected even to my own ears.

But William just smiles a watery smile, as I stand up.

'Bloody glad to hear it,' he says.

'Thank you, William!' I shout, as I run out the door.

CHAPTER THIRTY

Four months to live

The bus journey to the airport is strange, knowing that, for the very first time in my life, I'll be leaving this country; something I've never even entertained before. And as I stand outside departures, I look up in wonder at the powder-blue sky and the planes rushing up into the ether. In no time at all, I'll be up there too.

As high as I can go.

I check in my bag before heading through security. It's hectic, and yet I kind of like it, how I feel just like everyone else going on holiday, or flying off to see a relative, or doing some business elsewhere.

Even the airport shops are exciting to me, this strange world of cafés and clothes shops and restaurants, open at all hours. So I decide to make the most of it. Taking a seat at the champagne bar, it doesn't take long for a young-ish waiter to take my order. Then I just sit there with my glass of bubbles and think about what France will be like, and all the other places I manage to get to after. I'd like to go everywhere, of course, see everything possible, and maybe I should be able to in the time I'm here; maybe I've made some great error by staying here in Edinburgh for so long. But somehow, I don't feel like that, given how very different it's been to my old life in the city. And if Adam's taught me anything, it's that there are brilliant adventures to be found and perfect moments wherever you are. But for the next four months, it's time for me to fly further, see everything I can in the time I've got left. For me and no one else.

Because this is my life too and I'm going to make damn sure I live it.

Pulling the list out from my pocket, I look to the next item on it and smile.

Experience the world.

I can still remember all those tours I booked for other people, all those images of bungee jumpers and surfers, ancient monuments and temples I only saw on a screen.

I think about all those experiences I missed out on because I was too scared. Because if you live a certain way for too long, it becomes very hard to change it. And life *is* scary and messy at times, and we can get hurt. But we only get one, and it's shorter than any of us realise, so now is the time to stop thinking and just go do.

Eventually, my flight is called, and wiping an unexpected tear from my eye, I place my empty glass down, before heading on over to the gate. The word *Paris* flashes on the board above, and my heart starts to thud. It's time.

And with a last look back at the airport, I show my ticket and my passport, and head up the walkway.

* * *

For the next while, life really is a wonderland. When I stepped off the plane on the other side of the Channel, the scents, sounds and even the air all felt different, but in a good way, and I found myself loving hearing the different accents all around me. Everything felt new and wonderful, and my heart came alive with it all.

So I climb the Eiffel Tower, each and every step to the top, before drinking a little wine by myself at the bottom. I stand in front of the Mona Lisa at the Louvre and wonder what she's smiling about. I sit in a café in Montmartre and watch Paris go by. I go to St Peter's Basilica in Rome and actually look up at the Sistine Chapel in person. I stand on Juliet's balcony in Verona and smell hot paving stones in the air. I walk the old city walls in Dubrovnik and sit quietly on the rocky cliffs overlooking the sea. I touch the Berlin Wall and walk up to the topmost tower in Neuschwanstein Castle.

I go to 'Dracula's Castle' in Romania and shop in Krakow's cloth hall.

Then I finish up my first leg of the journey in Amsterdam, where Jess had been trying to get me before, and as I wander down the glittering canals and stare up at all the colourful canal houses, I wonder why I didn't just go when I had the chance. I could have definitely managed a slow-paced city break with some preparation. What was I so scared of?

Because now I realise that it wasn't just me trying to protect other people, I was trying to protect myself.

From the world – the very place that excites me the most.

I've already been away for a month by the time I fly to India to see the Taj Mahal and the holy city of Varanasi, the Ellora Caves and Mysore Palace. I eat street food of kachori and aloo chaat, and message Sven to say he needs to add new toppings to his pizzas. I get a call from Charlie moments after and answer tentatively – I wasn't sure she wanted to speak to me ever again after the accident.

'Hello,' I say from a hot dusty street. It must be breakfast where they are.

'Emily,' she says, and I can hear the nerves in her voice, 'William told me you'd gone travelling . . . so London didn't work out then?'

'No, it didn't, in the end.'

'Good,' she says, and I can hear the smile in her voice too.

'How's the pregnancy going?' I say, concerned now.

'Fine . . . better,' she says. 'Look, I won't keep you long, but I just wanted to say I'm sorry.'

A scooter honks its way past me down the busy street and I cover my other ear. 'What have you got to be sorry about?' I shout down to her. 'I was the one who suggested skiing in the first place.'

'What happened up there on the mountain was a pile of bad luck,' she shouts back, 'and it was also my own goddamn fault.'

I start to protest again.

'Yes, it was,' Charlie cuts through. 'I'm an experienced skier who took a calculated risk during pregnancy, and it went wrong. And the truth is, I was angry at myself, not you.'

'For what, though?'

'For not listening to my body, for being so focused on living my life to the full still, that I forgot about this new life Sven and I have made. So maybe, for a while, I need to take the slower lane for a bit, for Sven and the baby's sake. But you,' she says, urgently, 'you need to keep doing your list because this is your time now, so you need to stop worrying about everyone else and go follow your heart.'

A beat passes, as I process everything she's said. That, perhaps, what happened to Cat also wasn't actually my fault. That she was just living fully like Charlie, like Cat had always done – and she took her own risk that day at the loch because she loved life, because she needed to make the absolute most of her short time on this planet. And yes, that need was maybe heightened by my condition, and yes, she made that jump after I'd suggested it, but it was the sort of thing she always did and always would continue to do. And there was nothing I could have done to change that. If it hadn't have happened there, it may well have happened somewhere else. And this guilt I've been carrying around since, which has been affecting everything I do, every way I look at life, has been mine and mine alone.

Maybe it's survivor's guilt or maybe it's just fear, but it's time to put it to bed now. Stop following someone else's plan. Because while Mum might have been right about a lot, I need to live my own life now – take my own risks. Or I'll regret it forever.

'I will,' I say to Charlie finally, smiling.

I keep pushing further into Asia after that, to the misty mountains of Yangshuo and the strange Avatar-like rocks of Zhangjiajie National Forest. I explore the Forbidden City in Beijing and walk along the Great Wall of China, before ending up in Hong Kong. And as I go on a junk boat and hang out with monkeys at Kam Shan, I think about where my next stop should be in the last designated month of travelling. As vaguely planned, I've come on a meandering line around the globe – there's only so much time, after all. So, I head to the States next, to California. Cat always wanted to see what it was like to be in a place where the sun always shone, where you could be staring into the ocean in the morning, then up in the mountains by the afternoon. I take surf lessons in San Diego and then fly over it in a biplane. I taste wine at the oldest winery in the state and go backpacking in Yosemite, and it's everything I've always dreamed of.

Almost.

Because as I stand there at the top, looking out across the rocky landscape, I can't help wondering if I should go to Canada. Adam just made it all sound so great when he spoke about it. There are tonnes of experiences to have there too, and perhaps I could stop in on him.

While I'm here.

Before I can overthink it, I've booked the flight for the next day. San Francisco to Calgary, here we go.

CHAPTER THIRTY-ONE

Four weeks to live

The sun is starting to set on the road ahead as I approach my final destination, warm yellows and berry pinks blinking through tall pines at me. The air smells almost sweet with the windows rolled down; the remnants of a hot day in the air around me. I'm still a bit tired from all the activities I've been doing during the last week in Canada – hot air ballooning across tree tops and golden cornfields, white-water rafting down rushing rivers and caving into dark crevices – but as I look out around me at the seemingly endless road, flanked by the alpine larches and incredible mountains beyond, I feel myself come alive again.

I thought about travelling up to Alaska for a bit, or even over to the bustling west coast like most people would.

But most people have more time than me.

Or they think they do at least.

All I knew was, I suddenly wanted to see Adam now. And not over the phone, or on Zoom, or any of these old ways

I might have used before in my old life. I wanted to see him in person, and I had the strongest pull to go do it.

I can't deny that I was incredibly anxious, that there were moments on the plane when I wondered what the hell I was playing at. After all, he asked me to go to Canada with him and I just threw it back in his face.

So why the hell would he want to see me now?

But that feeling won't budge, and I know instinctively I'll regret it forever if I don't at least go and try. And if he isn't interested in seeing me, then I'll just go on my way – travel around this beautiful country by myself.

Eventually I see a sign, a turn at an enormous pointy-shaped boulder, which Adam perfectly described to me when we daydreamed once about visiting this place together, and I glance down at the satnav. Sure enough, I'm almost there, and before I know it, I'm bumping down the track towards where I assume the lake must be.

The lake Adam told me about once as we lay in each other's arms. The one he said I would love.

A few seconds later, I see it – a shimmering blue through the trees which gets larger and larger as I approach. And right on the water beside it, just as Adam said it would be, is the cabin in all its rustic glory. Lights are on inside and my heart begins to hammer.

A figure appears in the back doorway of the cabin – Adam, in jeans and a black t-shirt. And he's standing so still, as though he can't actually believe it's me.

'Hello,' I say, take a breath in. 'I'm sorry to just appear like this . . . but I was just doing some travelling around the area so . . .'

A moment later, he walks towards me silently, and I can't help wondering if he's mad at the intrusion. Doesn't he come here to be alone, after all? Yet here I am, interrupting the peace. After everything I've already put him through.

And then he's standing right in front of me, and I look up into his eyes, which match the trees by the lake behind us, see his firm chest rising and falling beneath the black material.

'You're here,' he says, like he can still barely believe it.

'I am,' I barely whisper.

His eyes flit across mine. We're so close now, our hands are almost touching, and I find myself reaching for them. As I do, I see a spark ignite in his eyes, feel it between our fingers too. And as the blush sun glints over the mountains in the distance and our lips find each other's, I close my eyes and decide there's no point overthinking the how or the why.

Because right here, right now, is all that matters.

* * *

Later in his bed, we lie tangled together under the covers, my head resting on his warm chest, his hand gently stroking my shoulder. The first time we had sex, it was hurried and fevered, happening what felt like moments after we got ourselves into the cabin; his arms around me, my hands all over him. But the second time it was slower, more achingly deliberate. It was like he was savouring every part of me, every second of me being there, and I let my mind drift away and forget everything else. Just focus on the now. So, I tell him about all the things I've done, all the amazing sights I've seen, and he tells me about his fishing trips out on the lake and the climbs up the mountains nearby, and the way he says it tells me he's been trying hard not to think of me too. And as his chest rises and falls so peacefully, I realise that, somehow, I might have become the person who finally shows up for him.

Then eventually, as the sun starts to sleepily droop down into its rocky bed outside the window, we drag ourselves from the bed and throw our clothes back on.

'See what I mean about rustic?' Adam smiles, as we finally head back into the main part of the cabin again.

'I totally see,' I say softly, and look around the place properly now. It's not particularly big, all rambling sofas and armchairs set against shabby pine walls and scattered with colourful rugs. A wood-burning stove sits in the hearth and up in the lakeside corner, there's a small kitchenette beneath the red curtained windows. To the back of the room, a big table sits with a patterned cover pulled across it, a teetering bookshelf behind it. And across everything is this intoxicating scent of pine and wood smoke and something homely too.

It's so very him, but it also reminds me of the cottage, which makes me love it even more.

'And you're just out here alone for months?' I say, turning to him. It seems so remote.

'Well,' he says softly, 'It doesn't feel that alone really, with all the memories. It was the one place I actually settled into for a while, in between all the travelling.' He looks around. 'It's not so bad, I'm realising, enjoying one place like this for a bit.'

As Adam heads to the fridge and pulls out a bottle of chilled white wine, I can't help looking around the room and imagining those family scenes together. A younger Adam playing cards with his grandmother at the table, or heading out to do some fishing with his grandfather.

'Tomorrow, I'll show you around the area,' Adam says, as he pours the wine into two glasses. 'But tonight,' he smiles, passing me one, 'tonight, we chill.'

'Just chill?' I tease, moving towards him, and his jaw flinches at my words, his eyes sparkling. I lean in to kiss him softly, then firmly, and he groans into me.

'Let me show you something great first,' he says hoarsely, and I laugh.

'OK,' I say, looking up at him, 'I will permit that. But we're in a cabin in the Rockies – it's all pretty good.'

He grins, before taking my hand again and leading me back towards the door we came in through. Pressing a second light switch, he opens the door.

In the now twilight evening, I can see the whole porch is actually lit up with string lights, which loop around the entire decking – just like the terrace. With my hand still in his, he leads me around to the front of the cabin, which juts out on to the water.

And even though I didn't think it could all get any more perfect, it just did.

'Right here, m'lady,' he says, and indicates at one of two porch chairs.

With my wine in hand, I sit in one while he fiddles with the little radio on the decking. It crackles for a bit before he eventually hits on lazy guitars and sits down too.

We stay like that for a little while, just staring out at the darkening water, the snow-capped mountains behind, late-night birds swooping across the twilight blue sky. There's no need to talk, no need to fill a void, because we are completely at ease with each other.

Just here, now.

Together.

I feel odd suddenly though, lightheaded. A tingling begins, then those sensations surge through me – snow-capped mountains, late-night birds.

Oh god, oh god.

I've seen all this before. I've been in this exact same situation before. And now my body is flooded with stronger-than-ever memories of the wedding and the grief of the betrayal, of lying depressed in the flat, of getting on a flight somewhere and flying into the unknown, of surfing in a turquoise sea I've never seen before and zip lining over the most incredible landscape – of being absolutely dazzled with it all. And there is happiness and there is sadness and there are tears running down my face now, because everything is coming together – everything is coming full circle.

Emily and I might not be doing the exact same things at the exact same time – but in some way, somehow, we've tracked the same story.

Which means—

Emily was here too.

She was here with Adam.

I close my eyes for a moment as the enormity of it all hits me; find that I'm gripping the side of the chair. Because I don't even know what to do with this all, don't know what any of it means. Then suddenly, I sense a movement, and he is there above me when I open my eyes.

He looks a little concerned at first but then he extends his hand to me.

'Will you join me for this dance?' he says, and the sensations start to ebb away, the memories are fading, and all I can do is let him pull me up from the chair. Walking out with him on to the decking, I try to just concentrate on the now – on the rippling lake in front of us and the radio behind us. Because that's what Adam does – he seizes every special moment like the last and pulls me back into the present.

And as we dance away under the starlit sky, I realise that by eventually following my heart, I have in some way, somehow, followed Emily's too.

CHAPTER THIRTY-TWO

The next couple of days are a hazy blur of waking up late in each other's arms and drinking coffees out on the deck. And as the most glorious sun comes up over the mountains, washing this new world over in pine greens and sapphire blues, I feel a strange sense of calm – as though, for a moment, the strands of my and Emily's lives have connected again somehow and I can just settle for a moment – enjoy this part, right here. And I suspect Adam is feeling some of that peace too, as he tells me more about all the times with his grandparents, and I think he's starting to realise that if they could have been there for him now too, they would have.

Then, on the third day, we start to go biking along local leafy trails and hiking up craggy rocks. We visit Lake Louise and stare out at the incredible blue at the basin of steep cliffs. We go camping up in the mountains, lay out beneath the stars and, eventually, we go cliff diving. My heart is thumping with each step up the pebbled path, thinking of my sister floating in that shallow water, knowing exactly how quickly life can be extinguished in a moment. But I also know that, in this scenario, we've checked it all out: the water levels are good, the jump isn't particularly high, and it's an established safe spot to do this. In fact, Adam has made the jump many times already this summer and has run me through best-practice techniques. So when he says, 'you game?' at the edge, I'm as prepared as I'll ever be, and I don't let fear hold me back. Because I might not get another chance. I simply take a deep breath, say, 'I'm game,' and jump high into the air. And it is joyous and exhilarating, and when I resurface from the water below after, I realise everything is still fine – even better than fine.

And I can finally start to let the pain of my sister's final moments go, and remember the true joy she had for life instead.

When we're back at the cabin, we have dinner out on the deck and chat away about everything, like we always did. Then we go to bed and make love, lying wrapped in each other's arms until the morning. He doesn't ask me about why I decided to come here, and I don't raise it – I think neither of us want whatever this spell is to end.

But on our last night, as we're dancing slowly out on the deck together under the stars, Adam says, 'Have you had a good time?'

I smile. 'What do you think?'

He looks down at me with a soft expression, and I can sense what he's thinking. I can feel it now, that question from him. And suddenly, I'm not sure if I can fight it anymore. Before I've even thought it through, I say, 'I love you, Adam.'

'I love you too, Emily.' He says, as though this is what he still truly wants.

And it doesn't feel scary anymore – it feels good and right and amazing and I wonder why I've never allowed myself to get here before. It is the best part of my trip, and I start to realise that nothing about my old, seemingly limited body, was actually stopping me having moments like this – going to new places and experiencing new things. Because the cooking classes with Charlie and the dancing with William and the slow walks I took in the hills with Adam were some of the fullest moments of this past year, even if they did seem small at the time.

I was lucky to be in my old life as Maggie; to have the potential to meet amazing people like Adam.

And it was only my heart I was scared of risking.

Eventually though, as with everything in life, it must come to an end – Adam has to get back for his work in the UK, and I need to get back too – for different reasons. I have to try somehow to come to a decision – let Emily die however she did that day in Edinburgh, or not. I'm fully aware that maybe I've got this all wrong and I'll automatically go back to my old life regardless of what I do, which would also be a privilege, I'm realising now. But even as I think it, a sensation in my stomach tells me that that is absolutely not why I'm here, and there's a reason why all this happened; a reason I was brought here in the first place. Emily died, yet somehow the universe brought me back to her life. Which means she wasn't done with it. There was something, or someone, holding her here – Adam perhaps? And if I stop her dying on the day of the transplant, she'll return to however I leave it, and I – Maggie – will die in hospital instead.

I can change the outcome for her, just like I did for Charlie.

But frustration slams me again now, because the truth is, I'm not done with life either and I don't want to go at all. I want to live and breathe and experience everything I can, for as long as I possibly can.

I'm so desperate for it, it hurts, and as much as I want Emily to finish whatever she was trying to do, I don't want to give my life up for her.

I'm pretty quiet on the way back to Scotland, and I feel Adam keep looking across at me, in the taxi to the airport, in the coffee shop at departures. It's like we've been in this bubble the past week together and suddenly reality is hitting hard.

I have a choice to make and I don't know how to make it.

As Adam sleeps on the plane beside me on the way back, I find myself tracing the shape of his forehead, his nose, the swollen pout of his lips, which I have kissed so many times now, and I wonder – did Emily love Adam as much as I do? Did she cherish him like this? Because she actually had a proper relationship before, one that spanned years, and there was real love there, once. Whereas I'm only just finding this; I'm only just experiencing this incredible sensation for the very first time in my life. What I had with Nick didn't come close. And though I know I'd go back to my old life if I got the heart, I can't help wondering if I could find Adam again, somehow; this person who means so much to me. Whether it could be the same.

But as I rest my head against his shoulder, I know instinctively that Adam meant so much to her too. She loved him, just as much as me. And those amazing feelings whenever I'm around Adam were hers also.

* * *

A jolting sensation.

'We're here,' a gentle voice says.

Opening my eyes, I blink around to see we've landed, and the plane is taxiing along the runway to a halt.

I look around to see Adam just above me, a soft expression in his eyes.

'You slept the entire flight.' He says, kissing me lightly on the forehead, and I smile faintly back at him. Because a knot of reality has been growing in me since we left Canada, and I'm not sure what I'm thinking; what I'm feeling right now. Immediately I see the worry in his eyes, and I feel like the worst person in the world for causing that, so I try to act like everything is OK. I've already put him through enough, after all, and I just try to remember William's words again – that I need to make each day count.

Walking out of Edinburgh Airport a little while later, Adam reaches for me again in the evening air, and holding his hand tightly, I go with him to the taxi rank.

Twenty minutes later and we pull up outside our building, a sight so very joyous for me, with our two flats side by side at the top, dear William downstairs, and Ferris padding softly around somewhere. It's only as we're stepping out of the taxi that I see her, standing outside the building in fitted jeans and a white shirt.

'Fran,' I say, my heart immediately racing.

I haven't spoken to her since the wedding, of course, despite her emailing and calling several times during her honeymoon. I felt bad for the stress she must have been under during what should have been the most relaxed time with Toby, and then I got mad at myself for feeling bad about it. Because this was all of her own making. And after the years of friendship she and Emily shared, and how close I felt to her too, I just couldn't bring myself to speak to her.

Yet, seeing her standing right here outside the building, with those wide remorseful eyes, I can't helping feeling some of that same pull I've always had to her.

'E,' she says, taking a small step towards me. But I don't go to hug her. I don't try to make this easy for her.

'I'm sorry I've come with no warning, but I really needed to speak to you. . .'

Her eyes flit nervously to Adam, who offers her a polite smile, and a 'hello' as he would for anyone. Then he turns to me. 'I'll just take the bags up, all right?'

'Thanks,' I say, all the while wishing he wouldn't leave me. But he knows what happened, and he knows that I have to deal with this alone.

When he's gone inside, I turn to Fran again.

'How did you know I'd be back today?' I say flatly.

She pauses. 'I contacted that friend of yours at the dance school.'

I frown. 'Charlie?'

I can't blame her obviously – of course Charlie wouldn't have thought there was any issue telling a friend the dates. She was just so ecstatic to hear that Adam and I were coming back from Canada together; that we'd found a way to make it work.

'I'm sorry,' Fran says, her voice wavering, 'I didn't know what else to do, and I'm so, so sorry about everything, but I really need you to hear me out on it all, and then you can decide to hate me forever, if you want to.'

For a moment, I think about turning her away, telling her to go back to London with all her lies. But something stops me – memories of us playing as small kids at each other's houses, swapping our sandwiches in the playground and drinking Eltons in the hazy London light, laughing until our stomachs hurt.

I can give her a few minutes of my time, surely.

'All right,' I say finally, 'do you want to come up?'

She nods her head, her eyes hopeful. 'That would be great, thank you.'

* * *

At the top of the stairs, Adam has kindly left my bag in front of my door and I lug it into the hallway, as Fran trails quietly behind me. I hate having to part ways with Adam again after so much time together; feel this almost desperate pull towards him, like I might lose him again if I let go. But he reassures me by text that we'll catch up as soon as we can tomorrow, and after admitting our true feelings to each other in Canada, I know inside myself that nothing will stop it happening this time.

We can't go back now.

I dump my bag in the hall before ushering Fran through to the living room, where she hovers uncertainly at the centre. It's just so unlike the usually punchy Fran that I almost feel bad for her.

'Take a seat and I'll put on some coffee,' I sigh, realising there's no easy way out of this now. I just need to get through it.

'All right,' she says, sitting down on the sofa and looking about herself. 'I really like what you've done with the place,' I hear her call out, and realise she must be looking at my messy paint wall. I go about boiling the kettle and pouring coffee granules into cups – I don't have any milk in yet, so I just serve it black for both of us.

'Smells delicious,' Fran says, shooting up to take one from me. I sit down on the chair opposite her; wait for her to start.

She takes a couple of careful sips first, as though gearing herself up for whatever she's about to say, then she places the mug down on one of the little dancing coasters I bought at a market.

'I like these,' she says, as though stalling for time. I don't reply, don't make this any easier on her than I already have, because I feel annoyed on Emily's behalf. Eventually she takes a breath.

'We never meant for it to happen,' she says. 'I just want you to know that I'd never thought about it at all before. I knew you were with him and I was with Toby. But then you started working all the time – you disappeared on Simon, and me.'

There it is, that weird reverse blaming that Simon did too – he made me feel like it was all my fault. I start to feel frustrated again.

'So, you're saying you don't want me to feel bad about working too much, but ultimately, that's what you're blaming it on?' I say.

Fran starts to shake her head. 'No, that's not what I said.'

'Well, you sort of did.'

Why shouldn't Emily have worked hard if that made her successful and independent? No one would have batted an eye at a man doing it. I don't see why that means her fiancé had no option but to cheat on her with her best friend.

Fran is silenced for a moment.

'You're right, E, you working hard wasn't to blame . . . but it wasn't just for a bit,' she says, and I look up.

'Those last two years in London, you were basically always in the office or on work trips. No one actually saw you. You never made it to any dinners or parties. You even missed my birthday, and Simon's . . .'

An uncomfortable feeling starts to form in my stomach.

Emily missed their birthdays?

'And I promise I'm not trying to make you feel bad about what we did,' Fran says quickly, wipes a tear away, 'I promise that's not it, because there are absolutely no excuses, but I just wanted to let you see how it came about in the first place. We really didn't mean to hurt anyone.'

I feel sick thinking about it; can't imagine what Emily must have gone through. But I need more information.

'How long?' I say.

Fran pauses. 'A few months,' she says, wiping another tear away, and I feel like I've been punched in the stomach.

A few months?

'I know, I'm a horrible person,' she says quickly, seeing my face, 'but I bumped into him at the pub one night and he was drowning his sorrows, and I'd been having all these worries about how different Toby and I were. One bottle led to another and . . . oh god.' Fran puts her head in her hands. But almost immediately, she lifts her head up again, looks at me dead on. 'The next morning, I was physically sick so many times for what I'd done, and I told Simon we needed to tell you the truth straight away, tell Toby too. But then, everything sort of drifted on. You kept working more and more and Toby went away on all those business trips . . .'

'Then you and Simon drifted on too,' I say steadily, 'and I found the dinner receipt.'

Fran nods. 'Yes, and I was sure you'd see right through it. I was fully prepared to come clean, to get it out in the open. But then you decided to leave for Edinburgh and I just. . . .' She takes a breath. 'You and Simon had already broken up anyway, and you were starting this new life, so I figured, maybe we'd let sleeping dogs lie?'

'But then he came up to see me,' I say.

'Yes . . . and I was terrified you'd find out.'

'So that's why you were pushing me towards Adam.'

'Not just that,' Fran says, eyes widening. 'I genuinely wanted you to be happy.'

'Funny way of showing it.'

She shuts her eyes briefly. 'Then at the wedding, Simon started saying he couldn't continue with you again without being honest about what happened, and oh god, I just died inside. But I wanted to say thank you . . . for not saying anything at the time.'

I don't reply initially, as I try to gather my thoughts, as the full picture emerges clearly in my mind. Emily suspected Simon was cheating on her and that was the trigger for her to finally try a new life. Because sometimes you just know something deep inside and you don't need proof. So she did it – left it all behind and started again. Then she went down to Fran's wedding in London, deliberated coming back to it all, coming back to Simon, but we both found out the same thing at the same time – it was Fran he'd been cheating with. And suddenly it all came crashing down.

There would be no going back.

That was it – that was Emily's clincher.

'And I love Toby, I really do,' Fran is saying. 'It's the worst mistake I've ever made, and I just can't . . .' she lets out a sob now, 'I can't handle the idea of telling him. He'll definitely leave me, you know he will. What am I going to do?'

As Fran rambles on about how sorry she is, my mind starts to clear suddenly, settle. We might not be friends again but

I know just how terrible she feels – how she's paid for this a thousand times over in her head, like I did with Cat – and maybe somewhere beneath it all there was a silver lining for Emily; the first push she needed to get out there and change things. And although I could shout at Fran; rant about what a horrible friend she's been, sometimes there really is nothing else to be done – shit happens in life and there is no way back. But you can still go forwards and hope the light eventually shines through.

'What you're going to do,' I say steadily, 'is stop living a lie, Fran, because that is no way to live. And don't make Toby's life a lie too. At least give him the chance to decide what's right for him.'

Fran looks up at me, tears in her eyes, but then finally, she nods.

'And what are you going to do?' she almost whispers.

I pause, suddenly uncertain.

'Because despite what you might think,' she adds, 'I really did mean it when I said I wanted you to be happy. When you moved up here, I was panicked, of course, but it was clear quite quickly that it had been a good choice – you really doing it finally.'

'Doing what?' I ask.

'All of it; all the stuff you never had a chance to before. And you're right about the work, E – you genuinely did so great with your career. But this new Emily is great too . . . this new, slower, Emily seems happier.'

'And Adam's not too bad either,' Fran adds with a glint in her eye, and I can't help letting out a laugh.

A bubble of light passes between us, the old dynamics coming through again. Then Fran sniffs; looks at me.

'Will you ever be able to forgive me?' she says, with tear-stained eyes.

I pause, realising my future right now is still really quite unclear.

'Maybe,' I say eventually. 'Let's see what happens.'

And with a tearful smile, she finally gets up and leaves.

CHAPTER THIRTY-THREE

Three weeks to live

For the next week, I try to just focus on living my life here as much as I can, while I can – so Adam and I cook together or go out for food most nights, and I seem to have this insatiable hunger for it all. We go up Munros, and camp under the stars again in the Pentlands, and I really start to understand what William meant by simply picking one place, one person, and just loving that life. And I think Adam is starting to understand it too, and that constant restlessness in him is calming, for now anyway. Emily's old memories and feelings have stopped appearing for a while and I can't help but wonder why. Will they come back?

And what will they show me if they do?

But for now, I'm appreciating the break. It's only when I find myself in a quiet moment during the day, or last thing at night in bed with Adam lying peacefully beside me, I feel this other ripping sensation inside of myself – and I can't quite catch my breath. That thought I had on the plane, about the love Adam and Emily shared first, starts to play on my mind again. From the glimmers that came back to me, I know they met across the hall, like we did, and got together, like we did.

But what does that mean for me? For Adam and me? Does this connection we share, this love, mean anything at all? Or is it all some carbon copy of what they had? Something that had already happened before I even got here and I'm now just experiencing secondhand.

I'm about to head into our building after meeting Adam for lunch when I see an elderly couple coming along the street and I beam.

'Hello,' I say as William and Ruth come to a stop in front of me. They're a handsome pair, Ruth in her pink coat and William in a red sweater, his hair neatly combed back – and I realise they might have just been on a date.

'Well, well, well,' William gives me a shrewd smile, 'you've returned. And how was it? Those mountains looked fantastic.'

I'd emailed William on his new laptop along the way, of course. After all, he was the one that got me out there – the one who gave me the courage to keep going until the end. And I'd sent him a photo too, of Adam and me, together on the cabin porch, the fairy lights all around us.

William had sent back a smiley face.

'It was great,' I say, but even I can hear the strain in my voice, and William frowns.

'Well,' Ruth says, looking between us, 'lovely to see you, Emily. I'd better get going, though. I'm looking after my granddaughter after school today, you see, and I need to go get those biscuits she likes, the chocolate ones with the cream she licks off in the middle. What are they called again?'

'Oreos,' I say softly.

'That's it.' She grins, and grips my arm. 'Thank you. Well, I'd best be off. I'll see you at class on Friday?'

William nods. 'Of course, wouldn't miss it.'

And as she walks away down the road, William turns to me.

'More tea?' he says, his eyes sparkling. 'Or perhaps a walk this time.'

*   *   *

Wandering towards the Meadows a few minutes later, I'm struck by how limber William is these days. I can barely keep up with him. He's dancing so much, I guess, but perhaps there's something else bringing him to life – something more to do with Ruth.

'So, let's not beat around the literal bush,' he says, as we wander along the path underneath the leafy trees. 'What's happening now? After everything you two stupid kids have gone through.'

I smile at his words; try to vocalise what it is I'm thinking. Because it feels almost petty in a way at this point, wondering who Adam actually loves, which love is the truest. But still, I can't think how else to make my choice. Emily was the one who had the amazing life and made the big move up here; she was the one Adam first fell in love with.

So, why the hell should I keep the heart, and potentially her great love? If I ever managed to find him in my old life, that is. He wouldn't know me, of course, but perhaps he would feel a trace of something. Would that connection between us still be there, though? To me, Maggie?

'I just wonder sometimes . . .' I start, 'if it's really me Adam loves, or if his heart belongs elsewhere.'

William frowns briefly, then softens again in some sort of understanding. 'You're meaning Claire, aren't you? The one he was with before.'

It's funny because there was a point a while back before Christmas when I would have said yes. Now I realise, it was never Claire who was the other person in all of this.

It was Emily.

I nod, just as William gets his wallet from his pocket and opens it. He pulls something out, holds out a faded and creased snapshot of Connie for me to take. It's not one I've seen before but it's still that same woman with her wavy fair hair and excited eyes. She's in a blue dress, at a party, I think. Looks like the nineties.

'She was beautiful,' I say, looking back at him.

'She was indeed,' he says. 'Everyone said Connie was out of my league but I knew something they didn't know.'

'What was that?'

'Love. Sometimes it just happens whether you like it or not, and we adored each other.'

I smile, but I'm not sure where he's going with it.

'The thing is,' he says softly, 'that was then, and this is now. And I'd be lying if I said I wasn't besotted with Ruth too. I've never met anyone quite like her before, and I know it's a bit silly – the two of us at our age, but I love how happy she always is and how she wears pink all the time. I love how she always wants to go see something or do something, and the truth is, they're two very different relationships. And not just in looks, but who they are – their soul. So even if Adam loved someone else before, that doesn't mean he doesn't love you just as much.'

I sit with the words for a moment as I digest them because he's right. All those little things I found out about Emily in London – the love of minestrone soup and horror movies and fancy-dress parties: she was different from me in so many ways.

So even though we might look the same, and even though we might have started off the same, I'm starting to feel that maybe this life wasn't all one big fake.

And the love Adam has for me is actually real.

'And you know what else?' William says, stopping by a lovely spot in the Meadows now, which looks up on to Arthur's Seat.

I turn to him, curious.

'It may be a cliché but when you find that sort of love . . . you don't let it go.'

CHAPTER THIRTY-FOUR

Two weeks to live

Suddenly there are only two weeks left and there is somewhere I need to go; somewhere I've been avoiding up until now because it would make everything far too solid – far too real. But I'm almost out of time so when Adam mentioned he might go on a hike with Sven, I immediately said that was a great idea: Charlie's due date is still four weeks away, after all, and I think it will be good for Sven to have some time with his friend up in the hills before it all begins for them. And I need to spend some time with someone important too.

The crematorium is quiet when I arrive; empty. The summer air is warm against my skin, so very strange in a place that feels like it should be cold and dank, and I weave my way down the pathway I know like the back of my hand.

Then finally, I see it, the rose bush we had planted in her name. It seemed like the right thing at the time, eternalising

Cat as a flower. Because she was always so alive and kept growing til the very end. My brilliant sister.

My heart.

And as I stand in front of her grave, I finally allow myself to cry: I weep for me, for all the future moments we lost – laughing over TV shows, talking for hours on the phone as we got old and wrinkly together, having meals together with our partners and possibly even children.

I just wish I could ask her what I should do – what she would do in this situation. Because she loved living more than anyone, so wouldn't she choose to keep living back in her old life, surely?

And suddenly, faced with the prospect of being in the ground like this, turning to dust like this, I know I can't do it; won't do it. Not now that I know that this love between Adam and me is real and true – the most perfect thing I've ever found and could perhaps find again in my old life.

How can I just give it up for Emily? When I think about it, the past is the past, and what really gives me the right to go and change any of it? And yes, I didn't make the most of it as Maggie, but does that mean I don't get a second chance?

Does that mean I have to die for it?

A noise behind me makes me stop – turn.

And there she is – Jess, and she's looking at me with this slight air of confusion, like she's trying to work out who I am, this stranger crying by her sister's grave.

But why is she here? I didn't know she ever visited other than anniversaries with me.

Wiping away my tears, I turn to her, my heart thudding like crazy in my chest. This is the first I've seen of any of my family in a while.

And I've missed her so much.

'Hello,' she says.

'Hello,' I reply, pause. 'I was just . . .' I wave vaguely at the rose bush, uncertain what the hell to say. It feels like she must be able to see right through me.

But then Jess gives me a curious look. 'Did you know her? Cat, I mean. I've not seen you here before.'

'Oh,' I say, 'well, I moved away, to London.'

Jess stares down at the rose bush. 'She had a lot of friends, I suppose, and I was a bit younger . . . I didn't really meet many of them, in the end. But she told me about them some-times, all the fun you guys would get up to on weekends away and stuff.'

It's so strange hearing Jess speaking about Cat like this, like they had their own little dynamic between the two of them. And I suppose they did – and it was just as awful for her. Losing a sister like that.

Cat was a guiding star for both of us – I can see that now. That's why Jess was scared to move to Amsterdam and uncertain of her big choice. All she really needed was a little push, a little inspiration from someone following their heart too. And I could still do that for her; I *will* do that for her, when I get back home. If I get back home.

'You had another sister, I think?' I say, before I can help myself.

Jess nods, somewhat sadly.

'How ... how is she?' I say, swallow. 'She had a heart condition, I think?'

Of course I know exactly how I was at this point, but I still need to hear it out loud. Just in case something has miraculously changed.

But then Jess shakes her head. 'Not good,' she says, as a fat tear falls from her eye, and in that moment, I know that it's no different.

My old heart is starting to fail.

As Jess covers her face with her hands, in an unexpected display of emotion from her, I find myself walking over and enveloping her in my arms.

'Oh god, I'm sorry,' she says, pulling away sharply, in a way that is so much more like Jess – strong, guarded, resilient.

'That's all right,' I say, aching to hold her again, to breath in that family scent of home again. Real home.

She sniffs, wipes her nose with a tissue. 'Anyway,' she mutters, like she's been caught out, 'I'd better get back to my boys; they're waiting for me with my husband in the car.'

As she turns and walks up the pebble pathway, I think, *I love you so much, and I miss you so much it kills me – our aimless chats, our movie nights and how you always kept pushing for me to live – and I'm sorry for the pain you're going through, because of me.*

Suddenly I know I have to survive so I can have more of those seemingly small moments with Jess and the boys again. Even better ones, now I know how big they truly are.

And what the hell would my family do if I died? How could I do that to Jess, to all of them, after everything they've already been through?

My phone vibrates in my pocket and I pull it out.

Charlie calling.

For a moment, I'm not sure if I should pick up here – I'm in a crematorium after all, in front of my sister's memorial.

But then, Charlie's pregnant and alone today – I was thinking I should pop over anyway, and I get that horrible jolt again that I'll never actually get to meet her baby.

'Hey,' I answer. Holding the phone to my ear, I start to walk towards the exit.

Silence, and then a groan.

'Charlie,' I say, walking faster now, 'are you OK?'

Another pause, then, 'No, the baby's coming, I think . . . but it's too early and Sven's not—'

Another groan.

'OK, stay where you are,' I say, 'I'm coming for you.'

'No,' she says sharply, 'I'm in a taxi already. But can you meet me at the hospital? Oh god, I'm so scared.'

'Of course,' I say, 'I'll be there as soon as I can.'

* * *

I'd thought that after seeing Charlie in the hospital up north, I'd be more prepared for this. But as I run quickly through the corridors, it all comes rushing back to me – the white walls, the blue linoleum I've tread down so many times before, for tests and appointments, discussions with doctors.

And I know that somewhere else in this building, my other self is lying in another bed right now, dying.

But just for this moment, I push it all out of my head again, as I round the corner on to the ward reception gave me. I jumped in a taxi as quickly as I could, leaving Adam a voice message for whenever they came into signal again. And I just pray that they'll get it soon. Because this baby has to be OK – I don't know what I'll do if it isn't. I don't know what Charlie would do if it isn't, and I can't help wondering why life has to be like a horrible game of Russian roulette at times. Why some things go well and some things go so very wrong. There's no rhyme or reason to it, no way we can always mould things to what we want. Life is fragile and precarious and can be extinguished in an instant. And as I see the ward number, I can feel my heart thumping, *please be OK, please be OK*, all the while knowing that if the worst happens, I will be there for her no matter what.

Walking into the room, I can see Charlie already on a bed, her face contorted with pain; several doctors and nurses around her.

I rush up and take her hand in mine.

'I'm here,' I say, as she rides through what must be a contraction, 'I'm here.'

Eventually she opens her eyes again, which are red and swollen. 'They're saying we need to get the baby out now,' she says, her voice ragged. Sweat pours down her face and her hair sticks to it. 'Will you come in with me?'

'Of course,' I say. 'I'll be with you the whole time.'

'Heart rate's dropping,' one of the nurses is saying now, and Charlie grips my hand even harder.

A moment later, the doctor signals that it's time to go and they're moving the bed out on its rollers along through corridors. And then we're running along them, with the most surreal feeling tearing through me. I've been the person on the bed before, the person to be rushed through the corridors. Yet right now, I'm the one who's OK, who can be here for Charlie when she needs it.

Moments later, we're in an operating theatre. It's large and white and it feels as though hundreds of medical people are in here, even though it's probably only more like ten. They move around with quick, deft movements in order to prep Charlie for the C-section. I get into scrubs while they administer her epidural, and then she's lying back on the bed as they pull up the sheets at her middle.

'Ready to make the incision,' one of the doctors says, and I look into Charlie's eyes.

'You're going to be OK,' I say, with more conviction than I actually feel. 'You and the baby are going to be OK.'

Silence, as the doctors move behind the sheet.

More silence and muttering.

Then someone says something about the baby's head being impacted, whatever that means, and I'm not sure if Charlie heard it too but I hold her hand even tighter.

Minutes pass, and there's more movement from the other side of the sheet, people changing position and Charlie is jolted slightly. I just thought this would all happen so quickly – aren't C-sections supposed to be fast?

I can't bear it if it goes wrong at this point. On this fault line between life and death.

'Baby's out,' someone says, and I try desperately to see something, to hear something.

Why isn't it crying?

Surely it should be crying.

Oh god, oh god, oh god.

As tears fall down Charlie's face, all of William's words come flooding back to me, and I feel scared. Because maybe it was all a false win up north and the baby actually wasn't OK.

Perhaps this is where we were headed all along, and no matter how much we want things to work out, we can't make it happen from willpower alone.

And then I hear it.

The smallest of whimpers, the lightest of cries.

Charlie's eyes go wide. 'Are they OK? Is everything OK?'

Then a nurse walks over, a baby in her arms, and she is smiling.

'It's a healthy baby girl,' she says, before laying the baby on Charlie's chest. And my heart explodes with happiness as I look at Charlie looking at her daughter in amazement.

'Hello, little one,' Charlie whispers.

There's commotion over at the door, people talking, and then suddenly Sven appears in the room. His face is ravaged with shock, his brown eyes wide as he stares over at us.

'Oh my god . . .' he says, moves quickly over. 'Is everything all right? Is it . . .'

But Charlie just smiles up at him, their daughter in her arms.

'Everything is great,' she says. 'I'd like to introduce you to someone.'

Sven crouches down to look at her, tears welling in his eyes, and then he gently lifts the baby into his arms. He grins at Charlie, at me.

'Thank you, Emily,' he says eventually, frown lines appearing on his brow again. 'Thank you for being here.'

I swallow. Because it was an honour really, seeing life be brought into the world like this. Playing some part in it.

'My pleasure,' I say, as Sven brings the baby back to Charlie, and they hold her together.

'Hope,' Charlie says, looking down at her, then back up at Sven. 'Hope Emily.'

And then my heart is melting all over again, and I clutch Charlie's hand a final time. 'I'm going to give you guys some privacy,' I say, before gently slipping from the room.

* * *

Out in the corridor, I find Adam sitting on a chair, but he immediately stands up straight when he sees me, his eyes searching mine. When I checked my phone finally, all I could see were phone calls from him and Sven.

'A healthy baby girl,' I say immediately, and his face melts with relief.

'Oh my god,' he says, dragging one hand through his hair. 'When we picked up all the messages down the mountain . . . I've never seen Sven move so fast. It was the tensest drive of my life, after that other one up north.'

'But everything is OK,' I say, holding on to his hands now.

He smiles at me, holds my hands back. 'All because you were here.'

I swallow. 'I didn't do much really.'

He shakes his head. 'But you did, you really did. I just can't imagine life without you in it, Emily . . .' he tails off, like he's going to say more, but doesn't.

My stomach twists.

347

'Hey Adam,' we hear Sven call behind us, 'you need to see her.'

'Absolutely,' Adam says, looks back at me, 'you coming?'

I pause, my emotions all over the place.

'Do you mind if I go do something quickly?'

'Sure,' Adam says, tilts his head slightly. 'You all right?'

He just looks so happy right now, so full of this moment too, and I don't want to spoil it at all. But there's something I really need to do while I'm here.

Someone else I really need to see.

'I'm great,' I say, 'And I won't be long, I promise.'

'All right,' he says with a grin, before heading into the room.

* * *

Walking away from obstetrics a few seconds later, I feel drained suddenly, so very tired from the events of the day. But I don't have time to rest right now, and head quickly in the opposite direction, towards a ward I know much better – an area that was always my destiny really. Because of course my old heart would eventually fail me. I don't remember much about the moments before I collapsed – all I know is that Dad found me on my bedroom floor and called 999. And when I woke up in the hospital sometime later, I knew there was a good chance I'd never leave again.

I'd been in the wheelchair for a good six months by the time I was admitted here, on oxygen too. I spent all my time at home, in my room largely, drawing or sleeping but still hoping somewhere inside of myself that I might get that elusive heart, that I might get a chance to live a little longer.

But then I did get it and I did nothing with it – nothing at all. Because all I saw were my limitations, and how I could hurt people just by living my life.

And as I head towards the ward where I know my other self will be, walk the length of the corridor with this healthy body and all this life flowing through me, I see how misguided I'd been.

About what keeping Emily alive actually meant, and also how little I was helping anyone by doing nothing. Because the truth is, what people actually need help with, is pushing out their comfort limits, not just staying in them. Like with Jess in Amsterdam, and Mum revolving her whole life around me. When Cat was around, she did that for all of us. And by breaking free of my own boundaries, I could help them do the same.'

Coming to a stop, I take a breath as I walk up to the window, which looks into the ward. I have the strongest urge to suddenly turn and run away from all of this – just pretend it's not happening, pretend again that this is my life now and it's all just going to keep going. But that would mean I was letting fear reign still, and as I finally look at myself on the bed through the glass, I know with certainty that I won't let it anymore, and I need to make my decision very soon.

My other self appears to be sleeping, her face so pale now it's almost wax-like. Her red hair spills like blood across the pillow and she's hooked up to a number of machines, which limp painfully along.

A large bunch of flowers lies on the desk beside her, from Mum, of course, because she always liked to make sure I had fresh flowers. I think she thought she could will me back to life somehow, make my heart bloom again. And as I hear a quick tread of feet down the corridor, I brace myself for seeing her.

I don't know how to explain why I'm here but I turn to Mum anyway, smile gently at her surprised expression.

'It's you,' she says.

'It is.'

There are a number of other patients on the ward, so I suppose it doesn't seem all that strange that I'm looking in. Still, I should probably try to explain myself, and I never could lie to her.

'My friend just had her first baby,' I say, 'then I went for a wander and ended up . . . here, somehow.'

Mum nods, and I notice how tired she looks suddenly, how utterly drained.

'I've not seen you at the shop lately,' she says after a moment.

'I know, I meant to come down but I had a lot of things on my plate and—'

She holds her hand up quickly. 'Don't worry at all, I thought you'd just been out and about . . . having fun.'

She looks through the glass now, and I try to decide what to do.

I suppose I could make my excuses now; walk away. But something stops me and I know it's now or never. After all, this might be the last time I speak to Mum before I die. Or it might not.

I don't know yet.

'Is she your daughter?' I say, as she gazes at my other self through the glass. It's funny because I never remember her watching me like this; she was always right there above me, close to me. I suppose I never saw all these other moments when I was asleep – the ones where all she could do was worry and wait.

'She is,' Mum says slowly. 'Heart failure . . . she needs a new one now, or . . .' she tails off and I swallow.

How can I put them through more pain? Here she is, right in front of me, and I know without a shadow of a doubt that it will kill her if she loses another child. I can't do it.

'She seems . . . peaceful, right now,' I say eventually, unsure what else I can possibly say – what comfort I can offer.

'She is peaceful, yes,' Mum replies, sighs.

A beat.

'I just wanted more for her than that.'

I pause, look at her. 'I'm sorry?'

'It must have been a terrible thing,' she continues quietly, as though she's not even talking to me anymore, 'losing her sister like that, but she let it dictate everything. I'm not sure she ever knew she was allowed to go out and live, and I don't think I helped with that, if I'm honest. I just couldn't stand the thought of losing her too . . . and now here she is, an inch away from death, and she can't die now. I won't let her die. Do you know why?'

I shake my head, alarmed almost by this openness from her. In the shop we always just talked clothes and nothing else, like it was her little getaway place from the real world.

'She hasn't experienced all the great parts yet . . . all the best bits,' Mum says finally, 'so that's why we have to get her a heart. That's why this can't be the end for her.'

I find a small tear spilling from my eye, as I fight back my surprise – that she wanted me to live big as much as anyone. Then I got the transplant, and nothing changed, but maybe that's also because I didn't try to change. I let Mum run the show because I felt guilty. And I just wish I could tell her right now, that if I get that chance again, I'll take it. I'll take it and run with it for everyone's sake. I can have just as big a life as anyone else, limited heart or not, because in the ways that mattered, it was never limited at all, I'm seeing now. And I don't see how I can die on them now; don't see how I can rip their lives up again.

Two lives.

One heart.

No one should have to make this choice.

I'm starting to feel a little dizzy from it all, a little light-headed – the lights above are shining too brightly and everything sounds a bit muffled around me. Suddenly it's like my legs are giving way beneath me and I hear Mum saying something like, 'Are you OK?'.

* * *

I'm groggy when I wake sometime later, somewhere in the hospital. I'm in a bed at the end of a ward it seems. There are patients in the other beds. My head hurts and my mouth is dry.

What the hell happened?

I shouldn't be in a hospital bed because there's nothing wrong with me. Is there?

With some panic now, I push my hand up shakily as a nurse with a streaked grey bun passes.

'Oh, you're up.' She smiles and turns briskly, makes her way over to me.

'What happened?' I say, as she flicks through a chart.

She lowers it and looks at me. 'You fainted, dear. We didn't see any bands on your wrists about any sort of condition and you appeared fine otherwise, so we popped you in here until you woke. The woman you were with keeps asking after you though.'

I feel confused. 'I fainted? How long have I been out?'

'Oh, not long, only ten minutes or so.'

This is all so odd. Adam must be wondering where I am.

'Well, I feel OK now,' I say, keen to get going as soon as I can.

'I'm sure you are,' the nurse says, 'but I'll need to check you over quickly before signing you out.'

'All right,' I say, still feeling lost.

'Oh, and I just wanted to check.'

'Yes?'

'You're not pregnant, are you?'

'No,' I say immediately, 'of course I'm . . .'

Then it hits me, like a giant wave rearing up and over me, and this deep sense of 'knowing' settles in my womb and in my heart; this overwhelming love and affection for what's there.

What they created the first time too.

And I know instinctively that *this* is the sensation I've been waiting for. This is what it's all been building to, and in this moment, surrounded by the most peaceful and joyous of feelings, I know exactly what choice I will make.

Which life I have to choose.

CHAPTER THIRTY-FIVE

One week to live

'Like this?' Adam says, and I pop out of his kitchen to see him up on a chair, surveying the bunting he's strung down his hallway towards the open terrace door. Soft summer wind drifts down to us, ruffling the material in its wake, which reads, 'Welcome to the world, Hope'.

I smile widely. 'That's perfect, they'll love it.'

'Anything else left to do?'

'I don't think so,' I say, as I take the plate of warm sausage rolls into the hallway. We have lemon cake and strawberry tarts from Dee's, coffees on order from the Purple Pineapple. The roof terrace is decorated with more bunting, a few more chairs and a table set with plates and saucers – all we need now is to make sure the sun keeps shining in the sky.

Adam reaches in to kiss me, even as I'm holding the sausage rolls, and I close my eyes and allow myself to melt into this moment, just like I did this morning when we found each other again in the dawn light.

The doorbell rings and reluctantly we pull apart, foreheads still tipped against each other.

'We can continue this later,' Adam murmurs and I feel warm all over.

Adam goes to open the door and everyone pours in – William with Ruth on his arm, Charlie and baby Hope. And at the sight of her, I can't help thinking again how relieved we all were when we heard that, despite being four weeks premature, Hope would be absolutely fine; a touch of jaundice maybe, but nothing that couldn't be sorted within a few days.

'Sven's just bringing up the nappies we forgot,' Charlie says, passing Hope to Adam for a cuddle.

Another couple from dancing are next in, one of the girls we met climbing too. Everyone traipses through the hallway, and we begin the tangled process of hugging each other with bursts of, 'such a good day for it,' and 'thanks so much for having us,' and just at the end as everyone starts to head up the stairs, William turns to me, clutches my hand, and I swear it's as if he knows.

'You coming up?' Adam says, holding my hand still.

The door to the terrace is open wide to the spring sun, shafts of light dancing on the floor below. From somewhere up above I can hear the notes of Mumford & Sons starting up and I breathe a sigh of happiness, for this moment with him.

And the child inside me.

Because I didn't even need to take a test to know the truth.

There are some things from this past year that I've known deep down, on some instinctive level.

Emily was pregnant too. This happened to her too.

Perhaps she didn't find out in the hospital with Charlie, but she found out. She knew. Because now that I know it, the signs are as clear as day to me. In the increased appetite, in the sharpened taste; the tiredness.

And any thought I'd had about picking me over her vanished; evaporated entirely, and I knew without a shadow of a doubt that I was going to die. Because this is my clincher.

This is why I was here all along – to keep Emily alive, and then let her keep living.

For her child.

And there in the hospital, I knew exactly what the outcome had to be, because sometimes life is bigger than us and we can't just think of ourselves. I will die and Emily will come back to the life I've been living in her stead. People might be a little confused about things for a while, the small differences between the two of us, but eventually that will fade; they will forget that anything odd happened, or that I was here at all. And I also know that in the remaining few weeks I have, I will live them absolutely and completely – down to the last second.

Adam's face when I told him in his kitchen that evening.

Just sheer joy and elation.

He picked me up and twirled me around the room, kissed me passionately in front of the kitchen sink. There was no shiny ring and no promises about the future, just the feeling that we were inextricably bound together in this life, in this moment.

And we needed no more than that.

Because the other thing I've learned whilst living as Emily is that nothing is black and white, particularly love. Just because someone stays put or does what you think you need them to, doesn't always make it the right thing. You have to meet people half way and get out of your comfort zone too. And more than that, nothing is permanent anyway – people change and people leave; people die. But we can't let that stop us diving in and tasting it all. Making the very most of whatever time there is. And when you do that, the black and white fades to grey, and then technicolour, and then we are surrounded by it. Everywhere.

And even though I don't know for certain what Emily would have chosen right now, I know in my heart, that all of this with Adam is what I want.

For me.

Then, with that thought in my head, I walk up the stairs finally, up and out into the glorious light.

CHAPTER THIRTY-SIX

The Day

The morning starts like any other. I open my eyes, see early golden light reaching in under the blind, then I turn to look at Adam who is still asleep in bed beside me. Except today I really look at him, at the slightly lighter strands in his dark hair and the freckles across his nose, at the tan on his face and arms, that more vulnerable paleness across his torso. And I think of how we made love, not only last night as the summer sun finally sank down on my last night of this life, but once again a few hours ago at dawn.

But I didn't cry, didn't alert him to the fact that there was anything wrong. Because the truth is, there sort of isn't, and in this one year, I have experienced more joy than I ever thought possible. The past week has felt like one long celebration of life, first with baby Hope's party, a perfect day filled with laughter and light. We didn't tell anyone about the pregnancy yet, of course – it was far too early for that at only a few weeks along, but the following day resulted in another celebration anyway, as we found out about William's engagement to Ruth. And so we had another picnic in the Meadows with bubbly and good food and good company, and as I looked around the blankets, filled with all our friends, I realised how very perfect life could be.

Just this, right here, in a place I loved, with people I loved – or some of them at least.

Then the day before came, starting with a run at dawn, before the world woke up, and as the sun glinted over the rooftops, I saw a beauty in the pink and gold clouds I'd never seen before. I got a coffee from the Purple Pineapple, the best tasting of my life. Then Adam met me for breakfast and we chatted away about everything and nothing, before going for a hike into the Pentlands. We took cheese sandwiches, crisps and lemonade for lunch, and ate it all in a grassy sun spot under a perfect blue sky. Later in the day, I called Mum just to hear her voice, then Dad, then Jess, and I whispered goodbye to each of them. Because they'll be in the hospital all day today, watching, waiting, and I'm so desperately sorry for what they're about to go through, so devastated that I can't say goodbye properly, but I can't do anything about it. I've made my choice and I know deep inside of myself that it's the right one – no matter the terrible cost to my own family.

Then in the evening, I asked Adam if we could eat dinner up on the terrace, pizza of course, with every topping we could think of. And as we demolished it with a small glass of chilled wine, I felt oddly content. Oddly full.

Yet not oddly at all.

Because as it turns out, I didn't really need all the big stuff, in the end – all the museums and the cathedrals, the skyscrapers and the lights, the mountains and the river rapids, as glorious as those things can be. All I really needed, all anyone really needs to live life, is right in front of them – every day is an adventure in itself, every moment an opportunity and a gift. Which is what the photography portfolio I got accepted into art school with was all about, I realised – the everyday, and the beautiful mundane. And that was what pulled it all together: you don't need a lot of time, you just need this day, this moment. And it's about living in that moment; even if it might seem small, even it might seem inconsequential.

It's about taking that dance class because you fancied it, it's about saying hello to that lonely neighbour and inviting in the stray cat; it's about trying new flavours and savouring an amazing coffee. It's about getting out there in the world and figuring out what you actually want from it. It's about making mistakes and learning from them, it's about living on your own terms and doing things that light you up inside, it's about loving fiercely and letting yourself be loved in return. It's about following your heart.

Even if you only have a year left.

Even if you have five minutes left.

And when you do that, you inspire other people to do the same – you lift them up just by being. Just as I did for William, I've realised. Just as he did for me.

Just as Emily has been doing for me this whole time.

I get up out of bed now, but not before gently kissing Adam on the forehead as I go, and as he murmurs a 'see you later, love you,' I know that's the last time I will ever hear his voice – he's heading off to the workshop early this morning after all. Then I slip back into my sweater and shorts, and head back quickly across the hall.

Because I have a plan for today – and the plan is this: stay in my flat and do not leave it for anything. Seal myself off from the world, and stop whatever accident happened to Emily the first time around from happening today.

Save her life and the baby's, and let mine go.

I know what being alive really means now. I've seen it with my own eyes, and tasted it with my own tongue. And I know that I would rather have one year of living fully like this, than twenty safe years of not really living at all. I have finally learned to follow my heart to the end, and maybe that has to be enough.

Now it's Emily's turn to go on and live with Adam and their baby.

And I'm going to make sure she gets to.

So I pull down all the blinds and bolt the door. I unplug all electricals and turn my phone off. Then I head into the bedroom and sit on the end of the bed. We got the call about the heart at twelve noon that day, which means I only have to get through another few hours before I'm out the other side. Before I go, and she comes back.

Then she'll wake up here, in her room, like nothing happened. And walk straight back into her life.

It has to work.

I can feel it inside of myself too, this build – this surge – like change is coming. Like all of Emily's memories and experiences are coming to a boiling point. My dreams have been filled with them this week, of images that are not mine, all jumbled together.

It is coming.

Minutes pass; hours. And I think about how this was essentially my life before, just staying in one room like this. Scared of the world and everything in it, and I count my lucky stars that this happened to me, even as my heart races in my chest as I try to imagine what it will feel like to finally go.

To finally disappear.

Will Cat be there to meet me?

I'd like to think so.

I think about my parents, Jess, Graham and the boys. Cat. I think of a memory of us as young girls, screeching through the forest in waterproofs, I think of my parents hugging me between them one Christmas, I think of Adam, kissing me good morning, every morning, and I try to draw them all close to me in these last moments – everything I hold dearest.

I cling on to that thought as I wait, that shred of comfort, as I place my hand across my belly and I stare out the window, concentrate on the leaves waving in the breeze. I focus on the green shape of them, the blue behind them, which seems to be getting hazy for some reason; blurry.

I feel a little nauseous suddenly, maybe one of those pregnancy symptoms again.

Then it hits like a sledgehammer: the most intense pain in my head.

Blinding agony.

CHAPTER THIRTY-SEVEN

'Maggie,' a voice says above me.

Then again, 'Maggie.'

Bright light, blurry faces above me. That chemical-human smell of hospital again. I'm lying down on a bed.

Where am I?

Who am I?

My eyes snap open now and I look around to see Mum – *my mum* – hovering above me. Jess, too. Dad. And even as I'm overjoyed to see them in front of me, a great crushing panic comes over me.

Emily.

This isn't what was supposed to happen.

It's not supposed to be me waking up.

It should be Emily.

'I need a mirror,' I say hoarsely, my old voice shocking and reassuring me in equal measures.

'Oh, Maggie,' Mum sobs, her face a mixture of joy and trauma, 'you're speaking. What did you say, dear?' She turns to Dad. 'What did she say?' But he looks just as lost and worried as her.

'I didn't quite catch it, dear.'

'She said she needed a mirror,' Jess says with some confusion, even as she starts rummaging in her handbag. Her face is tear-stained, and I realise in this moment how terrified they all must be. And I already know in my heart what I'm going to see in the reflection.

I just have to see it myself.

'Here you go,' Jess says, handing over her scruffy compact.

And as I hold up the little circle smeared with the boy's fingers I love so dearly, I see her.

Me.

Maggie.

I drop the compact, even as the tears start to run down my face, into my long red hair.

Doctor Peterson arrives in the room at that moment and everyone steps away from me, as the doctor steps forward.

'Good to see you awake again, Maggie,' he says, his pale-blue eyes tired but happy at the same time.

'What happened?' I say eventually. Because right now, I'm just as lost as anyone, in so many ways. Images of Adam come to me unbidden now too – his kind eyes and lopsided smile. And I wish more than anything that he was here with me right now, holding my hand, telling me it was all going to be OK.

Tears stream from my eyes again.

'We don't exactly know what happened,' Doctor Peterson says now, gently. 'As you know, everything was absolutely fine at your last check, there was nothing to . . . indicate that this would happen. Ultimately, we think perhaps your body temporarily and very inexplicably, rejected the heart. You were lucky your family was close by.'

It didn't work.

I try to think about that last moment before I blanked out in Emily's flat.

But nothing happened? Nothing fell on me or hurt me. I just . . . went away.

But oh god, Emily – the baby in her belly.

'Maggie,' Doctor Peterson says now, looks at me. 'Are you OK?'

'I . . . I don't know,' I say now.

But maybe there's a chance – she could still be alive too, right? Her and the baby growing inside her.

They can't just be gone.

Maybe in some way I've managed to change something, knock something off-course.

'When . . .' I say to Doctor Peterson, through my tears, 'when did I get my heart transplant?'

He looks at me oddly, but then he says, 'The twenty-fifth of July. One year ago today.'

But it could still be a coincidence, right? Lots of things probably happened on that day.

I know exactly what will confirm it.

'My phone,' I say, panic flooding me now. 'Where is it?'

'Maggie,' Mum says now, resting her hand on my arm, 'you really have to rest, try not to strain yourself.'

But I don't care about straining myself – this is too important.

'Please, Mum,' I say, looking at her. 'I can't explain it right now; I just really need to look at something.'

'OK,' she says eventually, reaches into her bag. A second later I have it in my hand, and then I'm stabbing in my pin code, searching the internet for her name. And then I see it – an obituary.

With the name Emily Perin at the top.

I open it.

And through my tears I see a picture of her smiling face flashing up on the screen, or should I say my face – it was only moments ago, after all. Then the article below about an Emily Perin, who died tragically on 25 July one year ago of a brain aneurism.

Brain aneurism.

Which means I couldn't have stopped it; could never have done anything at all.

And now I'm weeping as I read the rest, about how she was an only child, and leaves behind her devastated parents and partner.

Adam.

Except this time, I'm crying for the real Emily – not just one on paper, but for the girl who I know really lived her life, who, when faced with a life that made her sad, had the tenacity to go change it, not really knowing what would be there on the other side, or who she might meet along the way. The girl who found her passion in life and in the world around her. The girl who allowed herself to love again after the worst hurts and be loved back by the most amazing man. The girl who got pregnant and learned to live in the smaller moments, before realising those were the biggest of all; right up until her final second.

I know it because I saw it; all of it.

Call it a parting gift from her or a glitch in the universe, but I felt it with every fibre of my being, every high, every low, every wonderful moment this world has to offer.

And I know now that that was why I was there.

What the reason was all along.

'Maggie,' Jess is saying now, holding my shoulder as I sob; tears of grief, tears of absolute devastation, but at the same time, something I've never experienced in this body before.

'Maggie, are you OK?' she's saying through the fog of it all.

And then that feeling surges up through me – a mixture of vastness and newness and most importantly, hope.

And as Jess grips my shoulder, all I can do is smile up at her through my tears, and say a simple, 'Yes.'

* * *

CHAPTER THIRTY-EIGHT

AFTER

It takes a day or two to be released from the hospital, even though I keep reassuring the doctors over and over that I'm absolutely fine. I know I need to take it slow again, now that I'm in my old body, but at the same time, I don't. I've spent a whole year running around carefree, finally feeling intensely alive, and then being convinced that I'm about to die – that I have this endless feeling of wonder about the body I'm still in.

That I have more time – time to see the people I love, time to pursue my interests, time to enjoy pasta and cake and champagne, if it's called for.

Because in whatever long, stretching years (because they are long when I really think about it now) I have left, it would be an insult to Emily and her unborn child to waste one moment – one second.

The first thing I do – the first thing I have to do – as soon as I'm discharged from the hospital, is go see her. Because the obituary also mentioned a remembrance spot and as I read where it was, it all made total sense.

Mum started fretting, of course, when I headed out alone into the sunny afternoon, talking about coats and medications and being careful. But I simply turned to her and told her calmy, but firmly, that I would be absolutely fine. And even though she didn't look entirely convinced, I'm sure I saw a hint of smile when I walked away down the street.

I just hope she's ready for everything I'll do next.

Walking through the leafy Meadows as children play on the sun-soaked grass and runners pass me by, I can't help thinking that, just over a year ago now, it was Emily running through these pathways.

It was me too.

And I wonder who came here a few days ago, on the actual anniversary of her death. Probably not her mum, as the official grave was in London.

But Adam?

Adam. Even his name makes me ache all over. Because it feels like only five minutes ago that I was lying beside him in bed as the sun rose on his skin, those lips I kissed a hundred times. I miss him every second of the day.

But I realised in the end I could never keep him. Never find what we had as me, Maggie in my own body, because he won't remember a thing. And all those memories between us – as unique to us as they were – must surely all be gone, leaving nothing but his time with Emily.

The way it was always supposed to be.

I can't help being grateful, though, that he's still out there somewhere. I've looked up his upholstering website and it's active at least, though it says he's not taking orders over the summer. And I wonder what's he doing instead.

It doesn't take me long to find the bench, not too far from the children's play park and with a view of Arthur's Seat up to the side. Because it was here where I used to come running, where she must have run too.

I read the words on the inscription—

'*Every adventure requires a first step*'
    In Memory of Emily Isabella Perin, loving daughter, friend, and partner in life.

And I know, even if no one else does, that it all really did happen, some way, somehow. I lived that life, I was that daughter, that friend – that partner.

The happiest and most incredible year of my life.

'Hello,' a deep voice says beside me, and I turn sharply to see him – William, looking at me curiously. A year older perhaps, but no older-looking somehow. His eyes are still that pale-blue, his white hair tucked neatly back under a flat cap. He's wearing his chinos and trainers, a light-green jacket, and my heart floods with warmth at the sight of him.

My friend.

I want to hug him but I won't. I can't alarm him.

'Hello,' I say back instead, and smile.

'Did you know her?' he says, roughly, but with a strangely hopeful look in his eye. 'Emily.'

I swallow. 'I did . . . once. We were very close'

He nods at that. 'Well, then you're one of the lucky ones.'

'I know,' I say. 'She was inspirational.'

He lets out a small laugh. 'Yes, she was, wasn't she? We miss her terribly, but I still come here most days on my walk. Just to say hello to her, and we have a natter about what mischief her cat's been up to, or what adventure I've had that day.'

'That's lovely,' I say, trying to fight back the tears.

A beat.

'You're welcome to take a little memento from her flat if you like? Before the rest goes to charity, I mean.'

I turn to him sharply. 'What do you mean, her flat? How could it still—'

'Oh, it's silly, really,' William says, waving a hand at me. 'I couldn't bring myself to rent it again after it happened, and then I wanted to give her family the opportunity to come up and take a look around. They did eventually, after quite a few months, took a few personal items of course, but her mum was a bit of a state at the time. I'm not sure if she really knew what she was doing. We've cleared most of her things into boxes and a young couple is taking the keys next week, but I could take you in for a quick look around, if you'd like?'

My heart – her heart – skips with the idea. 'I'd love that.'

'Good, shall we walk?' he says, offering me his arm, and breathing in that peppermint scent of him, I take it.

Ten minutes later and we're back at the building I grew to love so very much and my heart thuds at the idea of going in again. As we go up each stone step slowly together, it all rushes up at me, a thousand moments and memories of happiness and sadness and everything in between.

'Are you all right?' William says, stopping briefly.

I nod silently. 'I'll be fine, thank you.'

At the top, I let William fiddle with his keys for a moment. Glancing around at Adam's door, my eyes searching frantically for signs of him. There are no boots outside his door and the paintwork is slightly chipped – something he'd have always fixed if he were here.

'Here we are,' William says and I turn back to see him walking into the place I called home for a whole year.

Stepping inside the now quiet space, I take in the scent of it; find it's still very faintly there, those roses and lemons, and shutting my eyes briefly, I drink it in.

William closes the door behind us now and walks into the living room. Following behind him, I scan over everything quickly – a wall of colour, which is sort of like mine, but also not; her photos of Edinburgh, which line the walls – but from slightly different angles to mine; her little diving figurines, which were exactly the same, of course.

It is my home, and hers, and ours.

And I can't help wondering what else was the same, or different? Did we really track the same course?

Perhaps I'll never know what really happened in her version.

'You can take a look around if you like,' William says, sitting himself down on the little dining room chair near the window, through which I first smelt those intoxicating scents.

'Thank you,' I say softly, and walk slowly back through to the hallway. A lot has clearly already been packed up and put away, her jackets and shoes for one, but the little mirror is still there and I look at myself in it now, half expecting to see the dark hair and kind eyes. It's just me and my red hair reflected back, of course, but for the briefest moment, I see her still, smiling out at me from somewhere.

In the bedroom, I stop, look around. There is the bed I first woke up in, the dreamcatcher against the window, the cupboard of colourful clothing, likely empty now, I assume. All the same, I walk up and open it again, remember how it was just a week ago – when I'd wake up every day with an adventure ahead and wonder what I should wear to do it in. It's all gone now as I suspected, but then I see something.

Up on top of the wardrobe, a black case of some sort. Is it . . . no, it can't be.

But as I reach up to take it down, I realise it really is – my camera.

Her camera.

Unzipping the case with trembling hands, a thousand thoughts flash through my head. How is it still here? Why didn't her mum take it away with her? Why didn't Adam take it?

And what's on it?

Pulling the camera out of the bag, I brace myself for it to have no battery left after all this time. But then, who was the last person to touch it? Pressing the 'on' button, I'm amazed to find it flashes to life, and what I see makes me stop and stare in amazement.

Even as the tears are falling from my eyes, I head back through to William. He'll be wondering what I'm doing.

When he sees me walk in with the camera, he gets up quickly.

'Are you all right?' he says, kindly. He looks down at the camera, 'is that . . . we always wondered where it was. I assumed it was lost.'

I shake my head, trying to compose myself. 'No,' I say, 'she just liked to keep it safe. It . . . meant a lot to her, these photos.'

'You really did know her well, didn't you?'

'If it's not too much trouble,' I say, 'would you mind if I showed this to someone who needs to see these?'

William pauses, then nods. 'Of course. Please look after it though, for everyone's sake.'

I smile. 'Always.'

* * *

I take the train down to London again this time, not because I have any fear of flying anymore, but more because I need to start the process of sorting insurance with my condition first. I'm not sure who's more shocked, Mum or Dad, and when they ask why I'm going, I simply tell them there's someone I have to see – right now.

And Mum doesn't fight it at all this time.

Walking along the pretty, pristine street later that day, I can't help thinking about Simon and Fran again, wondering how they're doing. I looked them up online, of course, and while Simon seemed to be doing broadly the same as before, at least Fran had moved on – alone. The latest picture was of her beside a blue-footed booby in the Galapagos Islands, a big smile on her face, and it made me smile too.

Eventually I come to Morton House again. I don't know if anyone will be in this time around – it's been almost two months since I received the letter but that's also two months of her mum receiving nothing in return.

Ringing the buzzer on the huge gates, I hear a voice eventually say, 'Can I help you?'

Jackie.

'Sorry to bother you,' I start, 'but I'm here with something of Emily's.'

Immediately, the gates open wide and I walk up to the grand entrance, and standing there waiting for me on the doorstep are both of them – Jackie, and Emily's mum.

I'm led into the posh lounge I saw when I was last here, and surrounding the room are all the photos of Emily – Emily as a little girl with Jackie in the kitchen drinking milk, Emily spinning in circles in the garden, arms outstretched, staring up with wonder, Emily standing outside her school at eight, twelve, fifteen; Emily in her graduation photo, Emily in a restaurant in London somewhere.

Then nothing.

'Coffee?' Jackie says, her anxious eyes on mine.

And I know that this is just as important a visit to Jackie as to Emily's mum.

'Yes, please,' I say reassuringly, 'that would be lovely.'

Should I really have just dropped in like this? With absolutely no warning? God, maybe I should have written back first – taken my time.

Then I recall the letter again – *I wish I could connect those final missing pieces of my only child's life. But more than anything, I wish I could hold my Stella one more time and tell her I love her – tell her how she was my whole world, and always will be.*

After we're all settled in the room, Emily's mum sits forwards.

'So, what is it you have of Emily's exactly?'

And in that moment, all I can do is tell the truth.

'I got your letter,' I say slowly, simply.

And I can see the dawning realisation on both their faces, the tears as they start to flood down their cheeks, and mine now, because I know in this moment that this was the right call, coming here like this. Doing things now, and not later.

Then suddenly we're embracing, first her mum, and then Jackie. Her dad appears with his rumple of grey hair, clearly disturbed from all the noise, and Emily's mum is saying, 'It's her, it's the one with Emily's heart.' And then he is embracing me too, and it's the worst, yet most lovely, moment of my life.

Then after everyone has settled down again, I show them the camera.

'But . . . how did you find us? How did you get this?' her mum is saying, her pale cheeks stained pink.

I don't reply immediately because what can I say really? How can any of it be explained?

I have to try though.

'I went to her flat,' I try finally, hoping they don't ask me how I knew where it was, or who she was, 'and I found it there – I just knew she'd want you to see it.'

The three of them crowd around it, the camera with the missing pieces of her life. Hurriedly I go to the latest pictures and immediately it's like I'm there again, all of it, except it's her unique version and not mine – that first selfie of her smiling on the grass with an ice cream, the first pictures she took around the city when she was just feeling her way, trying to find that slower pace she'd always wanted, those walks with Adam and evenings with friends where their love began to blossom; a date with Adam in Glasgow, one on the Isle of Arran, too, it seems. A lot of fun with Charlie as well – dancing, driving, playing instruments and things I'd not thought of, like disco bowling. Then Christmas at Adam's flat and a ski trip up north, in a different lodge, in a different place and likely with no Charlie accident, and no trip to the hospital. And then it merges again on the train to London, just like I felt on the train tracks that day, when she went down to Fran's wedding, when she found out the truth about her fiancé and her best friend.

She did some travelling too after that it appears, largely to New Zealand from what I've been able to tell. Then finally to Canada, where she went to meet him and take a chance on love again.

Adam and Emily are holding hands in the next photo, their matching grins infectious, then Hope's birth at the hospital, a party in the Purple Pineapple with everyone the week before Emily died.

It's all there, her life in a year, slightly different to mine, of course, but still with the same outcome. Because that was the point of it all. That was why I was there I realise now.

It was a gift to me.

And now it's my gift to them.

EPILOGUE

Ten months later

It's a beautiful day outside, so I throw open the living room window of the little flat I found near the Meadows. I take in that early summer scent, the blue in the sky, the way the light is glinting merrily against the sandstone tenements opposite.

They certainly picked a good day for it.

First things first, though, I go to stroke my dark-haired cat, Polly, who is basking on her sunspot on a zigzag rug. Then I head out for my morning run, just through the Meadows and the surrounding area today – I don't need to go crazy to get the blood pumping through me after all. On the way back, I stop off at the Purple Pineapple for a coffee and my weekend croissant, which I eat at the counter while I chat to Zoe, before heading home again. I still miss the old building along the road, of course, think about it every day, but I get some comfort from knowing it's not too far.

Next, I go shower, letting the water run all over my skin, my scar. I press my hand gently to it and feel Emily close to me; feel the glorious life coursing through me for yet another day, and hope I'll make it good, for her sake, for Cat's sake, and mine too.

Then when I get out and wrap myself in a towel, I stand in front of my now colourful wardrobe and consider what to wear. After a few seconds, I pick out an apple-green dress, which I team with my silver trainers. I'll need to be agile today, of course.

A little light make-up on the face and a brush of my red hair, which I let flow out around my shoulders, and I'm done. Picking up my camera bag at the door, I head back out again into the sunshine.

It doesn't take long to get there in my little second-hand car (I passed the test in no time, of course), but I savour the trip the whole way; that drive down The Bridges and across the Royal Mile, the swoop down the Mound with the old buildings and blue skies above, and then the busy hub of town ahead. I come into the centre quite a lot now, to have dinner with a friend or coffee with one of the folk on my photography course. Sometimes I go to a theatre production with Mum when we find something we like. I'm always busy, always out the house, and even though I might not be throwing myself off cliffs, I have a pretty full life.

Because it's my one and only. I wouldn't swap it for any other one either – healthy body or not, because I reckon I live more in a day now than a lot of people do in a lifetime. And I know that being able to do any normal things is a miracle – taking a walk, seeing a show, having dinner with my sister; helping other people for a change. It is all so very beautiful.

Eventually I reach my destination on the other side of town, and pull up next to the Botanics. To my left, the park opposite is already filling up with people running and playing tennis; doing some sort of outdoor dance class, where the male instructor dances like nobody is watching.

Smiling to myself, I get my kit out the car before heading into the Botanics itself. I haven't been here in a while, and as I gaze up at the ash and the sycamore trees, I think about how different everything was on my heart anniversary last year. We're changing up this year's location completely as it happens, and will go out to see Jess and the boys in Amsterdam – for the second time in twelve months.

I can't help feeling pretty nervous as I head towards the lawn at the heart of the Botanics, start seeing figures dotting around the place. After all, I have no idea if he'll be here at these birthday celebrations – Adam. We met briefly already about six months ago, after I eventually told William who I actually was and whose heart I now had. And though it shocked me to hear, Adam wanted to meet me. It was strange and just a little bit stilted in the Purple Pineapple with William a week later, but it almost felt like a relief too – to see him again, to let him know I really was keeping Emily's heart alive, in the right way. And I got a chance finally to tell him all about my actual life too, about my family and Cat, about being at home most of my life with a condition but being inspired by Emily to try something new – to try again. He seemed glad in a way, but looked as though he was digesting it all too, and then he went back to Canada again that summer – to our cabin on the lake. I think he might be back working in the UK now, though, from what I've seen on his website.

I suppose I'll find out soon.

When I'm only metres from the large mish mash of picnic blankets, which have been set out for the occasion, I clock William.

'Oh, you're here.' He smiles as I approach. And he just looks so smart today, in his blue shirt and freshly pressed trousers, I could cry.

'Thank you for doing this,' he says, gripping my hand. 'It's so decent of you.'

'It's absolutely my pleasure,' I say, thinking back to the conversation we had with Ruth months ago now, when I'd gone over to theirs for a tea, and Ruth had told me they were planning this. 'Such nonsense for an eightieth, but my wife was adamant,' he'd said, and I could see he was smiling too. So, I offered my photography services, and said that as

I was still training, I'd be happy to do it for free – for a friend. He told me he'd pay me in cake and liquor.

From the corner of my eye, someone else familiar approaches, a robust toddler on her hip.

'Maggie, good to see you again,' Charlie says with some surprise, leaning in to give me a big hug. Hope lets out a shout of delight, and I laugh.

'You two know each other?' William says with a slight frown.

I smile. 'Oh yes, I've been going to some of Charlie's Friday evening classes recently.'

'Fantastic,' William says softly, 'I knew someone else who liked to dance too, you know.'

I swallow. 'I know.'

A few other people I don't know appear now, and Charlie and William excuse themselves to go chat to them.

As I wander around the lawn, starting to capture the gorgeous skyline of Edinburgh to one side, friends hugging to the other, I can't help wondering again if it's too much, that I'm still doing some of the things that Emily did – photography, running and dancing. Is it unfair that I'm here while she isn't? Would she resent me, and the others, for doing what she no longer can? Because I wasn't the only life she saved, after being rushed into the hospital that fateful morning – her kidneys, liver, pancreas and corneas were given to others too.

And then, as usual these days, I simply tell myself that it would be more of a waste not to do all these brilliant things she inspired me to do.

It would, in fact, be a disservice to her to stop.

And I do a tonne of other stuff too, in fairness, things I never tried in my old life, or in hers – city wanders at dawn and life drawing with wine at a little studio in town; I even did a hot yoga class with Jess a few weeks ago when she was back briefly, and saw a theatre production of *The Lion King* in town by myself. Just because I could; just because I was curious.

Because I only get to see this world once, and I know now how quickly it could all be gone.

So why waste a minute of it?

I think less about the gloom of it all these days too – because what's the point? There is so much joy to be had, so many amazing experiences right on our doorstep. I'd be a fool to stop now. And just maybe, I can inspire someone else along the way. Maybe I can help them far more by living my life well.

By following my heart.

The other guests start to appear – some of whom I assume must be from Ruth's family, and another man with blond hair who I realise I recognise – and I feel warm inside when I see who it is. William's nephew and niece, who I saw once in a photograph, here to celebrate his big day.

He must have reached out to them, just as I'd suggested. Just as Emily must have done too.

I keep snapping away, heart thumping now, as Zoe walks in with her purple hair pulled up into a pretty bun, violets threaded through it, then someone else from dancing appears, and finally, I see a figure down my lens in a black shirt and jeans – a person I haven't seen in a while. Broad shoulders, dark hair, forest-green eyes I wouldn't be able to forget in a million lifetimes.

Adam.

And he is walking up to Charlie and William with that lopsided smile, then reaching in to give him a big hug.

My heart catches in my chest as my finger hovers on the button, and a second later, he turns towards my lens, and I lower it.

A strange moment passes between us, a look I can't quite read, and then he's saying something to William before walking slowly across to me.

'Hello again,' he says.

'Hello,' I smile, even though my insides are aching.

'So,' he says, 'thank you for doing this all for William.'

'It was no trouble; it's good experience for me. And I love this place,' I say, glancing about myself, at the trees, and the sky above.

I look back down to see him eyeing me quizzically.

'Everything OK?'

'I'm sorry,' he says, shaking his head, 'I had the oddest feeling the first time we met that I'd seen you before, and then I just got it again there. So, I thought I'd be that weirdo that actually tells you.'

I laugh, a bright feeling exploding inside.

'Perhaps we have, in another life.'

He looks at me curiously again.

Just at that moment, Dee appears with what must be the cake, and we both turn to see Ruth with her two daughters exclaiming over it.

'I suppose that's your cue,' Adam says, almost reluctantly.

'I suppose it is,' I say, lifting my camera up again. Then with a smile, I start to walk in Dee's direction, thinking to myself that that wasn't bad all considering, and perhaps I can finally go on my way now, knowing that someone like Adam is still out there in the world; someone as amazing as him. It is probably far too much to take on – her heart being in my body and everything. Far too many obstacles surely and there's no way it could possibly work out. As I pass by the radio Charlie turned on, though, a note hits my ear, a joyful sound, and I find myself turning to see him still standing where I left him. Watching me go.

And then I remember what William said; that just because Adam loved someone else before, doesn't mean he didn't love me just as much.

Without another thought in my head, I run quickly back across, camera in hand.

Standing in front of him, I'm sure I see him take a breath in.

'If you're not doing anything later,' I say, my voice slightly breathless, 'do you fancy maybe doing something, together I mean? We could grab a coffee, or a drink, or, I dunno, just take a walk somewhere?'

For a moment, I think he's going to say no. He just stands there like he's considering the question. And maybe there was a time where I would have felt embarrassed about this whole thing, regretted saying anything at all. But everything is different now. And just because something is scary, and may never work out, doesn't mean it's not worth a shot. Isn't it better to at least try?

While I'm here.

A second later, a smile starts on his face, a spark.

He takes a breath in; nods like he's landed on a decision.

'All right, Maggie the photographer,' he says. 'How about a coffee then, after all of this? We could take a walk somewhere. You game?'

And as my heart leaps from my chest – twice – I say,

'I'm game.'

ACKNOWLEDGEMENTS

If my first book was a team effort, then this book was a community one! To my lovely agent, Tanera Simons, thank you for holding my hand tightly as we navigated lots of publishing changes, thank you to Rosa Schierenberg who swooped in to whip this one into shape and thanks to Caroline Hogg for all your brilliant observations and suggestions. Thanks also to Julia Cremer for sharpening edges, to Mary Darby for adding that extra sparkle of joy at the twelfth hour, and last but not least to Bethany Wickington for coming in with all your energy and giving my books a brilliant new champion – see what I mean by community?

Additional thanks go to Donna Hillyer for your brilliant copy edits and astute medical observations, and also to Michaela Twite for your beady eye. Thank you to Jennifer Edgecombe, Isabelle Wilson and Marta Juncosa for all your endless hard work and enthusiasm.

To my first reader and lifelong friend, Jennifer Gibby, thanks for putting yourself through this a second time around – I really couldn't do it without you. To Toni Marshall and Angie Spoto, thanks once again for early reads and helpful comments. Thanks to Sophie Barbour for your London knowledge, to Andrea Riswick for the Canadian details and to Sara Bracceschi for the Italian ones. Thanks in particular goes also to Mr Stuart Grant for providing brilliant medical facts around heart transplants and to my brother Dr Mark Mitchelson for your layers of medical knowledge over the top.

The roots of this book grew largely from sister bonds, so thank you to Sarah for being the sort of sister who encourages me like Jess and Cat do, and for answering one thousand questions yet again. To my parents, given this is a book about living life, thank you for encouraging me to live the life I truly want to, and to my mother for all the reads again and for telling me to keep going. Thank you also to Paula and Rob for all the support and encouragement. Ben, thank you for supporting me 100% along on this crazy journey – you really do get the strangest questions thrown at you daily! And as ever, to Flora and Daisy - thank you for putting up with all my "tippy tappy writing". Thank you also Sunny for being the bestest canine writing companion. I love you all lots.

And to my readers – this book is for you really, so if it makes even one day feel more joyous, then that's my job done.

Thank you!

ABOUT THE AUTHOR

© Suzanne Black

Emma Steele is a solicitor and writer. Born on the
rain-swept west coast of Scotland, she studied law at
The University of Aberdeen before making her home in
beautiful Edinburgh. When Emma's not reading or
writing, she's spending time with her husband,
two daughters and excitable dog, Sunshine.

X @EmmaSteele85
@emmasteeleauthor